Don't Tempt the Phoenix

Look for these titles by
CJ England

Now Available:

The Mylari Chronicles
Eyes of Fire

The Don't Series
Don't Spank the Vamp (Book 1)
Don't Tempt the Phoenix (Book 2)

Loropon Lust Series
Bless the Beasts (Book 1)

Don't Tempt the Phoenix

CJ England

A Samhain Publishing, Ltd. publication.

Samhain Publishing, Ltd.
577 Mulberry Street, Suite 1520
Macon, GA 31201
www.samhainpublishing.com

Don't Tempt the Phoenix

Print ISBN: 978-1-60504-735-5
Digital ISBN: 978-1-60504-641-9

Editing by Jennifer Miller
Cover by Scott Carpenter

First Samhain Publishing, Ltd. electronic publication: August 2009
First Samhain Publishing, Ltd. print publication: June 2010

Dedication

I dedicate this book to Mr. Aaron Remple, my friend and science teacher who taught me there is more to science and the world than meets the eye. His love of God and legends helped spark my imagination. His mentorship changed my life.

Rest well, my brother.

STORE: 0167 REG: 03/71 TRAN#: 4417
SALE 09/18/2010 EMP: 00049

specified below. Returns accompanied by the original sales receipt must be made within 30 days of purchase and the purchase price will be refunded in the same form as the original purchase. Returns accompanied by the original Borders gift receipt must be made within 60 days of purchase and the purchase price will be refunded in the form of a return gift card.

Exchanges of opened audio books, music, videos, video games, software and electronics will be permitted subject to the same time periods and receipt requirements as above and can be made for the same item only.

Periodicals, newspapers, comic books, food and drink, eBooks and other digital downloads, gift cards, return gift cards, items marked "non-returnable," "final sale" or the like and out-of-print, collectible or pre-owned items cannot be returned or exchanged.

Returns and exchanges to a Borders, Borders Express or Waldenbooks retail store of merchandise purchased from Borders.com may be permitted in certain circumstances. See Borders.com for details.

Prologue

In the days of old, a legend is told of a most wondrous animal called the Phoenix. He lived in the Garden of Eden and was beloved by all for his wisdom, his compassion and his beauty. He had feathers that rivaled the sun and a voice as pure and lyrical as the angels themselves.

The garden was a very special place. Fashioned by Yahweh himself for his creations, it was filled with all species of animals and of course...humans. There was plenty of food and room enough for everyone. It was a good life and all were at peace.

Then, something very sad happened. Man and Woman, who were called also Adam and Eve, ate the fruit of The Tree of Knowledge, which was forbidden. Their eyes were opened, and they became aware. Because of this, Yahweh removed them from the garden so they wouldn't eat of The Tree of Life and become immortal.

But the legend states Eve became jealous of the immortality and the purity of the animals still living in the garden, so she persuaded them all to share in her fallen state by eating the forbidden fruit.

All but the Phoenix, who in Hebrew was called Milcham.

No matter how Eve coaxed and cajoled. No matter what she promised him, the Phoenix stood firm. His mate had already eaten of the fruit and was lost. The Phoenix must have been sorely tempted to be with her, but he would not betray his god by disobeying him.

And so later, when the Lord came walking in the Garden of Eden, there was no one left in the paradise he'd created.

Except the Phoenix.

Milcham explained to Yahweh what had happened, and the Lord was most pleased with his sacrifice and faithfulness.

Because of the Phoenix's great loyalty, Yahweh rewarded Milcham. He built him a beautiful walled city with large healthy trees and sparkling pools of the purest water in the world. He gave him special foods of nutmeg and other rare spices. He built him a tower on the edge of the city so he could sing his songs to the world. Yahweh promised the Phoenix if he stayed within the walls he could live in great peace for a thousand years.

Milcham agreed. He went and lived in the beautiful city, and it was good. A thousand years passed in this manner, but in the last months of the last year, the Phoenix got very old and very tired. His feathers lost their radiant glow, and his song became hoarse and raspy. He had trouble chewing the delicious foods and had difficulty getting water from his special pool. Yahweh was forced to gather other birds from outside the walls to care for him.

Finally, the Phoenix cried out to the Lord for help, and God heard his prayer. He told Milcham to build a nest of the spices and herbs that grew in his forest city. Once the nest was built, the Phoenix was to climb into it and face the sun at the dawn of a new day. Yahweh told him to lift his wings and sing to the sun.

The Phoenix obeyed and built his nest. On the dawn of the last day of the thousandth year in his walled city, he climbed shakily into the nest, and lifting his tattered and dull wings to the sun...he began to sing.

He sang of hope and of love, of faith and eternity. He sang and sang until his voice was broken and rough. His wings shook with fatigue, but the Phoenix sang on unflinchingly.

Suddenly, there was a blinding flash of light. Flames burst out of the nest and consumed the Phoenix. He became a burning figure of red-gold fire.

After a while, the flames died down. Amazingly, the nest and the tree it was in *were not* burned. But the Phoenix?

He was gone. All that remained was a pile of golden-gray ash.

Then, the ash moved. It trembled and slowly began to heave upwards. From under the ash, there rose up a young Phoenix. Featherless and bald, it was small and scrawny, but it stretched out its naked neck and lifted its tiny plucked wings to the sun.

In a voice that could barely be heard, it sang. This time it sang of rebirth and life, of immortality and Yahweh's constancy. As it sang, it grew, growing stronger and stronger with every melodious note. Beautiful feathers of gold and red, purple and yellow sprouted and covered his nakedness. Eyes that were blind opened, to reveal orbs of glowing gold.

The Phoenix had risen from the ashes and been reborn.

Yahweh appeared to the Phoenix, and Milcham bowed before him. Yahweh told the Phoenix he would taste immortality as long as at the end of every thousand-year period, he would build this nest and allow the fire to consume him. In this way he would be reborn, and the Angel of Death could never touch him.

Milcham agreed. He thanked Yahweh by gathering a selection of the finest food in the city. Using his newly acquired power, the Phoenix sent forth flames from his wingtips and set it on fire, thus giving Yahweh a burnt offering. The odor of the sacrifice pleased Yahweh.

And it was good.

Many years went by. Milcham lived happily in his walled city. He sang his sweet songs and taught the birds of the air how to carry the melodies across the world so all could enjoy them. He found his tears had healing powers, so he used them as he could to ease the suffering he sensed all around him.

Every thousand years, the Phoenix built his nest and sang to the sun and was reborn.

Five millennia passed and Yahweh came to visit Milcham. He saw immediately the Phoenix was not happy and asked why.

The Phoenix was ashamed. He was the most envied animal in the world, but he wasn't happy. He was lonely. Since his female had fallen to Eve's temptation, five thousand years ago, he had no one. All around him, he could see other creatures with their mates, but he was always alone. He'd been in solitude for most of his existence.

Now, he bowed down before the Lord, his beautiful feathers trailing in the dirt. He admitted his loneliness and asked Yahweh to help him. He wanted permission to go out into the world and find his twin-flame, the other half of himself...his mate.

Yahweh agreed it was not good for Milcham to be alone, so he gave his consent for the Phoenix to walk the earth to find his mate. He gave him the power to shapeshift into other creatures so he could blend in with those around him. Allowing the Phoenix to keep all his powers, he told Milcham there was one thing he must do. He must still come back to the walled city and be consumed by flame at the end of the millennium if he wanted to keep his immortality.

Milcham agreed. He'd heard many stories from the other birds and was curious to go see this new world. He still had many years before he would need to come back and go through the refiner's fire. Surely he would find his mate by then.

That night, while Milcham slept, the Ancient One, who is also called Satan, visited Yahweh. Angered that one of such beauty and pure heart would be allowed to roam *his* earth, he asked Yahweh how he knew the Phoenix was still loyal.

The Lord answered that of all the creatures, both animal and human, the Phoenix was the only one who truly honored him.

Satan shook his head. How did Yahweh know? For the last five thousand years, the Phoenix had been given all he needed. He lived in safety in his city and had no worries about food or water. Satan told the Lord if he were to remove his protection from Milcham, the Phoenix would surely curse him.

But Yahweh had heard this argument before when Satan tried to destroy his servant, Job. He knew the Ancient One wished the same ruin on the Phoenix. But the Lord believed, like faithful Job, the Phoenix would stay true.

He told Satan he would remove his protection over Milcham, but the Phoenix would *not* be given over to the Ancient One as had happened before. Satan was commanded to leave Milcham alone and let the creature discover his own destiny.

Satan was not pleased. He argued that tempting the Phoenix would be the only way to see if he was still faithful. He said if Milcham found his twin-flame too easily, he would not be truly thankful. As with most creatures, love must be a challenge to be justly appreciated.

Yahweh considered Satan's words and found they held truth. So he told the Ancient One the Phoenix could be tempted, but within reason. And the Lord would be the judge.

Satan was still not pleased, but he knew Yahweh had made his decision. Instead of arguing further, he requested specific rules be laid out.

All through the night, as Milcham slept the contented sleep of the blameless, Yahweh and Satan argued over his fate. When the sun arose the next morning, everything had been decided.

The Phoenix was brought before them and he was told of what had been determined. He listened with surprise and confusion as the Ancient One smilingly told him what he must do to complete his quest.

He must keep his identity a secret until he found the creature he would choose to be his mate. Only then could he tell her who and what he was.

If Milcham found his twin-flame, in order to keep her forever, she must prove her love for him by joining the Phoenix in the refiner's fire. If she was worthy, she would perish with him in the flames and be reborn as a new creation...immortal. But if she wasn't, she would be consumed in the inferno.

Once told of this, his mate-to-be would have to make the decision to leap into the fire herself. The Phoenix would not be allowed to coerce her in any way. It would have to be her choice.

Milcham bowed his head in submission. He would never trust the Ancient One. His temptations had caused many a soul to fall into a burning hell. But, as always, he would obey his Lord. And he wondered when Yahweh told him not to worry about being faultless, but to use his loving heart to find his soulmate. He was to search for a female he could love, not for a mortal moment, but for an immortal's eternity.

As Milcham left his walled city, his feathers glowed one last time, turning him scarlet-orange with fire. Then he shifted and walked down the path to his destiny—an immortal Phoenix...in the form of a man.

Chapter One

The air was filled with the sounds of laughter and the wheezing music of the calliope as it played mechanically above the noise of the crowd. "Talkers" on game row hawked their games of chance to the "Towners", who meandered up and down the midway. The screams of those riding the Zipper battled with those who had braved the Octopus. In the background, the loud whirring of machinery could be heard as the Ferris wheel turned lazily in the late afternoon sun.

The warm September breeze sent the sweet smell of cotton candy wafting through the fairgrounds. Along with the slightly burnt smell of popcorn, it was an odor that spelled out *CARNIVAL* in big bold letters.

The whole town had waited for this one special day. The last *hurrah* before school started and the weather changed. People had come out to play and eat and take their chances on one of the games. Coins disappeared as young men sought to win that oversized teddy bear their girlfriends *just had to have.*

Aithne walked slowly through the crowd, enjoying the afternoon and the freedom she would never again take for granted. Inhaling deeply, she knew her senses were still highly attuned, even though she'd been freed as her brother's familiar three months earlier. She suspected that allowing her brother to feed from her for over a century had given her not only temporary immortality, but it had done something permanent to her perceptions. She could still feel and do things a normal human couldn't.

Smiling, she thought about her brother. She'd just gotten off the phone with Aidan. He called her several times a week, his protective instincts still strong. Even though he was madly in love with Dawn, the woman who had taken Aithne's place, they were family and had been together a very long time. That type of bond never went away.

He hadn't wanted her to go on this adventure, but he wouldn't stand in her way. Aithne had given up so much for him, his conscience wouldn't allow it. But he fretted, thus the phone calls.

She'd been pleased to hear her brother was going on a journey, too. Dawn had a showing of her sculptures in New York at the end of the month, and she'd finally convinced Aidan to come along with her. With proper precautions, no one would ever know he was a vampire.

Tears threatened as memories surfaced of her brother and his mate. They were so happy together. They had almost lost each other when Dawn found out the truth about Aidan, but the fates were not to be denied. She very quickly realized he was her soulmate...her *twin-flame*, as she'd been told in a tarot card reading. Dawn had come back to him just in time to prevent the vampire from wasting away from grief and hunger.

Their love was so strong, so beautiful, Aithne knew she too must find her twin-flame. She'd been so lonely for such a long time the thought of finally discovering the man who would truly complete her made her shiver in anticipation.

That shiver became a reality, and her neck prickled. Turning, Aithne found herself staring into a pair of brooding amber eyes. She stiffened. He was doing it again.

Ever since Milcham Phoenix, the owner of Flight of the Phoenix Carnivals, had returned from his trip, she'd caught him gazing intently at her more times than she could count. She'd been hired by his assistant while he was gone, and she had the feeling Mr. Phoenix wasn't too happy about having a gypsy fortune teller on the payroll.

The fact she never told anyone anything but the truth didn't seem to matter. He watched her as if he was waiting for her to make a mistake, and then he'd pounce. It was creepy. And the fact he was one of the handsomest men she had ever seen just made it more frustrating.

Tall, at least six-foot-four, he was long and lean and hard. He always wore tight-fitting jeans, and some sort of muscle shirt that left very little to the imagination. Broad shoulders, muscled chest and arms, and a trim waist made her want to drool every time she looked at him. His legs were as muscled as the rest of him and when he walked away...poetry in motion. His butt was the finest she'd come across in her long lifetime.

Even better was his face. He was gorgeous. There was no other word for him. He had longish blond hair that was always in need of a brushing. It framed a tanned face with high, sculpted cheekbones and a square, masculine jaw. His strong nose pointed to sensuous lips and a chin that looked as if it lived with a five o'clock shadow all day long.

Then there were his eyes. Aithne shivered again. They were large and slightly tilted, giving him an exotic look. The color of newly minted coins in the sunlight and surrounded by long eyelashes, he was a dream to gaze upon.

Until he looked at her. Then it was all she could do not to turn tail and make a run for the nearby hills.

But she refused to do that. She loved it here, enjoying the excitement of the traveling carnival. Her life with Aidan had been for the most part sedentary. The only time they moved was when the neighbors became suspicious they didn't age. She'd be damned if she'd let this man chase her away without good reason.

He'd been back with the carnival for over a week and still hadn't said a word to her. All he'd done was stare. It was frustrating. She laughed to herself. If she *had* been a real gypsy, she'd curse him or something. That would show him.

Glaring back at him, she lifted her chin in defiance, turned and continued down the midway. If he didn't want to talk to her...fine. But she wasn't going to stick around so he could stare holes in her, either.

Milcham Phoenix cursed under his breath. *She* would dare stare at him with such arrogance? She was nothing but a charlatan. A witch, who pretended to know the future. He'd been furious when Rufus, his assistant, called and said he'd hired her. This type of act wasn't allowed in any of his carnivals. But one look at the woman who called herself simply *Aithne*, and he knew why his man had done it. She was stunning.

Tall and slender, she was the very picture of feminine beauty. Milcham figured she would fit perfectly under his chin, and her ripe body begged to be touched. Her ebony hair flowed over her shoulders and down her back to below her waist. Its silky curls danced in the breeze, tempting him to take one and wrap it around his finger.

She had the face of an angel. He'd seen the like of it carved on cameos, delicate and fine. Her tiny nose and full, rose-colored lips, sat in a heart-shaped face with soft, creamy skin. Eyes the color of emeralds surrounded by lashes dipped in ink completed the masterpiece.

He gritted his teeth as she walked away. He could hear the tinkling of the tiny silver bells she always wore at her wrists and around the crown of her head. His gaze went to her swaying figure. She dressed in long, colorful silk skirts that molded against her body in the wind.

Milcham's cock hardened and he swore again. The last thing he needed was to be tempted by a witch. He had just less than a month before he had to leave this place for good and head back to his walled city.

And he would be doing so alone.

He turned away from the luscious figure in silk, grief again filling his soul. He'd been so sure he'd find her. The one female to complete him. Milcham had hunted for hundreds of years, in all the countries of the world. In the last four centuries, he narrowed the search down to the human species, but even that hadn't helped. She was still nowhere to be found.

Granted, his time in the world hadn't been completely lonely. He'd found and wooed many women, learning the human art of lovemaking easily. But none of them carried the spark. The telltale knowledge *she* was the other half of his soul. He'd loved them and then left them, always moving on to search for the one woman he needed to make his life complete.

Unable to help himself, he glanced over his shoulder at Aithne. She was talking to one of the clowns, laughing gaily at something he'd said. She put her hand on the clown's striped shirt and leaned up to whisper in his ear.

Milcham clenched his fists as the unfamiliar emotion of jealousy ran through him. He didn't understand it, but he didn't want her touching anyone.

Anyone...but him.

Cursing again, he whirled around and stomped off towards his office. He'd stood by long enough. Tonight he would talk to the witch and get her out of his life, once and for all.

High above the carnival, crouched down on top of the now still Ferris wheel, the Ancient One frowned. He stared down at the retreating figure of the Phoenix, and then at the sweet-voiced woman who stood laughing in the light of the sun.

A wildcard, she was. This woman with her strange powers and wise eyes tempted the Phoenix, but since he hadn't sent her, Satan was wary. She seemed familiar to him in some way, but who and what was she? Her thoughts were unknown to him, hidden by a pure and innocent heart. It was for that reason, she troubled him.

For close to a thousand years he'd succeeded in keeping Milcham distracted by women from all over the world. Satan had tossed dozens, hundreds, maybe even thousands his way, but though the Phoenix had enjoyed them and even loved a few, he'd never made the ultimate commitment and told them who he was.

Satan gnashed his teeth. His plan from the beginning was to tempt the Phoenix with women who were *not* his twin-flame...*not* his soulmate. He *wanted* him to tell these women about himself and maybe even take one of the false soulmates with him to try the renewing fire. He'd used every trick and lure he could, always careful to abide by the agreement he'd made with Yahweh. But nothing had worked. Milcham always stopped short of admitting who he was.

But time was running out. In a month, whether the Phoenix found his soulmate or not, the thousand years would be up and he would return to his nest and gain another millennium of immortality. Satan was determined that wouldn't happen. He wanted this favorite of Yahweh to do one simple thing.

Die.

Closing his eyes and snarling words that were black and corrupt, he called on the very powers of hell to help him. The agreement between Yahweh and himself be damned. He would see to it the Phoenix would fail to find his true love. And, he would do everything possible to destroy him, as well.

And woe to the woman who truly was his soulmate. If she ever darkened the Phoenix's door, the Ancient One would do what he tried to do when he first knew of her existence.

He would destroy her.

Later that night, Aithne stretched tiredly. Even though she usually didn't open her tent until dusk, the midway didn't close until midnight, and six hours in a chair made her stiff.

She'd made good money that day. The price of the readings plus quite a few tips. Aithne's soft lips quirked. She knew it wasn't the card sessions that earned her the extra money. The tips came from young men who wanted her to take notice of them. But she ignored them. She read their cards and took their money, but they were like children to her. After a hundred years all men seemed too young.

She smiled again, this time sadly. Or was it because she was too old? Not in years, but in experience. Would she ever find a man who was wise beyond his age?

Milcham stood in the doorway watching her. His eyes burned when she put her arms over her head and stretched. He fought down the desire to rush over and pull her to the ground. When her mouth tipped in a sad smile, he fought emotion again, but this time he wanted to pull her into his arms to comfort her. What was she doing to him? Was she bewitching him without a single word?

Ignoring the rising heat in his body, he stepped forward into the light. She froze and looked up at him. He felt the same jolt he always did when their eyes met, and he gritted his teeth at the unwelcome sensation.

"Mr. Phoenix," she said after a moment, her husky voice curling around him like a siren's song. "What can I do for you?"

He cleared his throat, forcing back his desire. "I thought it was time we talked."

She inclined her head, never taking her eyes from his. "Please, sit and be comfortable."

Milcham crossed his arms over his chest. He couldn't afford to get comfortable around her. "Thank you, no. This won't take long."

A perfect ebony eyebrow arched. "Indeed? That sounds most...serious." She folded her hands in her lap. "What have you to say to me?"

He laughed to himself. Damned if she didn't make him feel like a peasant standing before a queen. Was she trying to intimidate him? He who had lived for millennia? "I want you to leave."

"Why?"

She answered so quickly, he knew she wasn't surprised at his request. "I don't want your kind here. Rufus overstepped himself by hiring you." His eyes raked over her curvaceous form. "Though I can understand why."

Stiffening, she raised her chin. "And why do you think that is, Mr. Phoenix? Perhaps, because he believed my readings would benefit this carnival?"

Milcham laughed sourly. "More like he thought it would benefit him. You are a beautiful woman as you well know."

A blush stained her cheeks. "Whether I am beautiful or not makes no difference to how I do my readings. I promised Rufus nothing. I am an honest woman trying to make a living."

"You're a witch."

Aithne's mouth dropped open, and she was shaken out of her calm demeanor. "I beg your pardon?"

His eyes glowed in the darkness of the tent. "You are a witch."

"I heard you the first time," she said irritably. "I'd like to know what you mean by that."

His broad shoulders moved in a shrug. "You tell fortunes, you read cards, you predict the future. You are a witch."

All she could do was stare at him in astonishment. She'd been called a witch before, but not with such a tone of utter disgust.

"I will not have your type of...game in my carnival. I will buy out your contract, but I want you to leave immediately."

Fury raced through her, pushing out the shock. "You dare walk in here and say such a thing? I have a gift I use to help people. What's wrong with that?"

Phoenix's eyes flashed. "Thou shalt not suffer a witch to live," he said sternly. "But I will make do with tossing you out. People frown on murder."

Aithne came to her feet, filled with so many emotions she couldn't name them. He'd threatened her. Actually threatened her. "You...you," she sputtered. "How dare you!"

His eyes narrowed. "You said that before."

She took a deep breath, reining in her temper. She didn't lose it often, but when she did, even her brother ran for cover. She stared at the handsome man before her. Too bad he was a prejudiced, arrogant, self-righteous bastard. She put her hands on her hips and prepared to do battle. "How do you know my gift isn't from God himself? That it isn't in my very blood? There are all kinds of...what you would call 'witches' in this world."

He growled and stepped towards her. "Do not mock me."

She stood her ground. She looked into his eyes and was taken aback by what she saw...what she sensed there. They were full of mystery and anger and sadness. But she saw longing, too. Her whole being softened. Suddenly, she knew it was very important to make him understand.

She placed a gentle hand on his arm and almost smiled when he flinched. "I am no evil witch, Mr. Phoenix. I am a simple woman who has been given a gift. How can I prove myself to you?"

Milcham had to stop himself from jerking away from her. "Do not try to tempt me! I know what you are, and I will not allow you to corrupt my people."

Her eyes narrowed again, all gentleness gone. She looked like an angry goddess ready to destroy him. "Test me."

He blinked. "Test you?"

She stepped back and waved at the table. "Test me. Allow me to do a reading for you. If I am accurate, then you know I am truly gifted. If I miss things, you will know I am a charlatan."

He thought for a moment and then shook his head. "The evil one could give you the true information to deceive me."

She rolled her green eyes. "Please. If you are as righteous as you think you are, pray with me for protection. You will see I am telling the truth."

His curiosity was piqued, and truth be told, he was enjoying sparring with her. He almost hoped she would put on a good enough show he might pretend to be convinced. Then he shook his head, knowing he could not allow her to tempt him into wrongdoing.

"Please."

Her voice was again soft and husky, and before he could stop himself, he nodded. Immediately, he wanted to kick himself.

"Then sit," Aithne said, smiling in obvious relief. She walked back to her place and seated herself. When he stood unmoving, she rolled her eyes. "I can't do a reading for you if you don't sit."

Reluctantly, he sat gingerly on the folded metal chair. His big form dwarfed the small table, making everything look smaller.

"I do not like this," he grunted.

Aithne shuffled the cream-colored tarot cards, her lips moving as if in silent prayer. When she was done, she smiled mockingly. "I'll be gentle with you." She set the cards in front of him. "Cut them, please."

Milcham sent his own prayers to heaven as he picked up the cards. A bolt of heat shot through him, and he shuddered, his body tightening dramatically. Quickly, he cut the cards and pushed them back at her. When she reached to pick them up, she gasped and fumbled them, her eyes lifting to meet his. Could she have felt the same thrill of warmth he did?

"Do you have a question to ask?"

He frowned. “I don’t understand.”

“You may ask a question of the cards and they will answer. Or, you may just allow the cards to speak to you. Either way will work fine.”

His brow furrowed in thought. “I will ask a question.”

She nodded and fanned the cards out on the table. “Speak it out loud.”

Milcham stared at her. It couldn’t be just anything. It had to be something he alone would know the answer to. After a moment of thought, he smiled. “I wish you to tell me where I came from.”

Aithne tipped her head in thought. “You mean where you were born?”

He folded his arms across his muscular chest and grinned. “Exactly what I said. Where did I come from?”

There was a trick to it somewhere. Aithne knew it immediately. He was trying to trip her up. She took a slow breath to calm her nerves and steady her thrumming heart. She held her hands out over the cards and prayed for guidance. Then, lifting the cards, she began to deal.

“Since you don’t know anything about tarot cards...” She glanced up at the silent man. “You don’t, do you?”

“No,” he grunted.

“Then I will make it easy. First off, the cards can’t tell you the exact place you came from. They aren’t created to do that. What they will do is tell you about where and how you came. Do you understand?”

“I thought you could tell me my past and future.”

Aithne shook her head, and the tent filled with the sound of jingling bells. “I can tell you only what the cards tell me. But they will answer your question and speak about your past, this I promise.”

She cut the cards into three piles. “With your left hand, choose a single card and lay it before you.”

"Just one?"

She nodded. "We will start with a simple single-card spread. If you want to continue after that, we can do another."

He smirked and leaning forward, picked up a card. "There will be no need." Tossing it down in front of him, he frowned. "So...what is it?"

Chapter Two

Aithne stared at the card lying on the table. A tiny shiver went up her back, and she took a deep breath. Closing her eyes, she tried to listen to the voice inside her that helped her read the cards. "It is The Judgment card. It symbolizes many things."

"Like what?"

Her eyes opened, and they were very green in the low candlelight. "You have placed the card in an upright position so it represents awakening, renewal, a well-lived life, better health, or a quickened mind."

She touched the card gently. "In your case I see long life and renewal. A rebirth if you like."

Milcham was shaken by her words. To cover, he cleared his throat. "What does that have to do with where I came from?"

She licked her lips, causing his body to go tense again. "I believe...where you came from has to do with the journey you are on. You look for renewal...for your body and your...heart. Where you came from is tied up in this." Her eyes met his. "I am correct, am I not?"

"I don't believe any single card," he bluffed, uncomfortable with how accurate she was. "Do another."

He could tell she was suppressing a smile, but he was very curious now. He leaned forward and waited while she shuffled the deck. At her nod he reached out and picked another card, setting it gingerly in front of him. His neck prickled as he looked at the picture. "What's this one?"

Looking up at him, her face was a study in amazement. "It is The Six of Swords. It represents a journey, a passage away from sorrow where harmony will prevail." She caressed the card with one long fingertip. "Basically, it is saying the same thing to me. You are on a journey to find yourself. Where there once was sadness, soon you will find joy."

Milcham's throat closed. Could this be true? Was this witch speaking the truth? How else could she know this?

Aithne gathered up the cards quietly. "I will do one more reading for you. Then you will tell me if you think I'm still evil." Without waiting for his answer, she shuffled the cards again, and with her left hand, she laid them out in the same three piles.

"Use your left hand and choose three cards, from any pile. Lay them in front of you left to right, one at a time."

Silently, he obeyed, until three cards stared up at him. "Tell me what they mean."

"This spread represents your past, your present and your future," Aithne said tightly. Looking at the cards made her somehow frightened. "I can tell you the meaning of each card, or I can tell you what I see in them."

"Both."

She sighed. Her heart was beating very fast. She tapped the first one with her finger. "This is your past. You have chosen The Sun card, but it is upside down. It can mean loneliness and unhappiness, lack of friends or loved ones. What I see is you...on your own. Not just once..." She frowned at the card. "But over and over again. As if you lived many lifetimes, yet always alone."

"The next one?" His voice was hoarse.

Aithne swallowed. She smoothed her thumb over the next card. "This next card is your present. This is The Eight of Cups, and it is also reversed. It is another card that signifies journeys.

More specifically, it speaks of a search for pleasure, seeking joy or success, a new love interest."

She glanced up at the big man and blushed. "You seek a woman. But not just any woman. She is special. And you will search until you find her."

Milcham's body was so tight, it hurt. He stared at the small woman before him, not knowing whether he should curse her or kiss her. He stared at the last card and a tingle went up his spine. "And this card?"

She bit her lip again, but this time he was concentrating on the cards too much to notice. "This is your future, and this card is The World. It is a good card to get, Mr. Phoenix."

"It is?"

She nodded, pleasure in her voice. "It means completion, perfection, recognition, success, fulfillment, triumph, and eternal life." She closed her eyes and sighed. "I see..." Her voice became very low, yet it kept its husky, musical tone. "I see you are from a faraway place. I don't understand why, but this place is your home and you love it, yet you feel trapped. I see you there again and again. It's like looking at the same picture superimposed on top of itself."

She tipped her head, as if waiting for something. "You are sad and alone, and then you are allowed to leave to travel the world on a quest for...for love." Her eyes popped open and met his. "You seek your soulmate," she said in an amazed whisper. "Your twin-flame."

Milcham jumped to his feet. "How do you know this?" He leaned over and grabbed her by the arms, jostling the table as he did so.

She stood very still, her eyes wide in her delicate face. "You're hurting me!"

Immediately, he let go of her. In all his life, he'd never used force with a woman. "I'm sorry, I..." He trailed off when he saw her look down at the table and the color in her face drain away. Without thinking, he grabbed her again, this time to steady her.

"Aithne," he urged, his hands running up and down in an unconscious effort to steady her. "What is wrong?"

Freeing herself, she pointed to his cards. The jostling of the table revealed a second card beneath the card marking his future. Milcham frowned. "They must have stuck together. So what?"

Aithne sat down hard in her chair. Shakily, she touched the card. "A second card means your future is unsure. Your destiny is still to be written. The first card in this pile speaks of success, of triumph and eternal life." She hesitated.

Another shiver went up his back. "And the second?"

She didn't speak for several long moments. Then she sighed. "The second card…is The Death card."

That chill went straight up his back and shot deep into his chest. "The Death card? What does it mean?"

She lifted worried eyes to him. "Just what you think. In the way it is positioned and partnered with this other card, it means loss, failure, illness, bad luck or even…death. You have two possible futures, Mr. Phoenix. You will either succeed in what you have been doing and find the soulmate you seek, or…you will die."

For a long time he didn't move, his mind and body stilled by her words. Then his temper rolled up and out of him.

"*You think you can frighten me into allowing you to stay!*" he roared, his voice making the crystals that hung from the ceiling shiver at his wrath. "You dare such a thing? Is this the type of *help* you plan on giving the locals? This witch's carnival trick?"

Aithne gaped at him, totally shocked at his twisted reasoning. "I gave you a reading. One you know very well was accurate!" she shouted back, her own temper flaring. "I've been doing this long enough to see the truth on someone's face."

"You know nothing," he snarled.

"I know you're a coward. You know I spoke the truth to you, and you're afraid to admit it. I honored our agreement! Will you?"

He swore aloud. "We made no agreement! You wanted to do a reading, and I said yes. That was all."

She thought her head would blow off in her fury. Never had she been so angry before. "You...you bastard! You liar! You have no honor!"

Milcham swept the cards off the table. "You challenge my integrity? How dare you?"

Flinging her long hair back, Aithne stood her ground. "I dare because it's the truth!"

"I want you gone by sun-up!"

"I have a contract," she spat at him. "And I'm not going anywhere!"

He took a step forward, his jaw clenching and unclenching, but still for some reason, she wasn't afraid. Instead, there was an excitement in her that wasn't logical. She watched with luminous eyes as he brought himself under control, and then turning on his heel, marched out of her tent.

Suddenly, all the fight went out of Aithne, and she sank to the ground. She stared after the man who had sent her senses racing. Part of her still seethed at his attitude towards her, hating him, yet another part...a gentler one, knew there was something more.

Slowly, she gathered the cards that had fallen around the table. She methodically shuffled them and held them to her breast as she prayed. Then, setting the stack of precious cards on her flowing skirt, she blew out her breath in a sigh.

"Who..." she whispered, "who will this man be to me?"

Taking a deep breath, she reached out and turned over the top card. The breath rushed out of her in one long *whoosh*.

The card was The Lovers.

After Milcham stomped out of the tent, he headed for the nearby woods, intent on walking off some of his anger. Unfortunately, he was stopped by two of the roustabouts who were having trouble with a Towner who had groped one of the ladies selling cotton candy. It felt good to blow off steam while he gave the drunken local a taste of his mind. When he saw his people looking at him with raised eyebrows, he knew he was acting out of the norm.

As soon as he was able, he left the crowd and headed deep into the forest. It was a cool September night. The mountains of Tennessee loomed above him, and the tall trees made him feel like he was home again.

A pang of dark homesickness went through him. In that, Aithne had been correct. While he enjoyed his time out in the world, he missed his home with a fervor that at times threatened to strangle him.

He could tell his time of renewal was getting closer. He tired easier and his strength, usually as great as ten men, was much diminished. He slept more and ate less. Soon, he would have to leave this place and head for his walled city. Soon, it would be time to step into the fire once more.

Milcham's mind went again to the words Aithne had spoken. They had been too close for comfort. He shook his head. How could she know about his quest for a twin-flame? He spoke of it to no one.

She'd also been correct about his searching. He'd never stopped, never given up, never forgot the reason he was out in this human world. No matter where he went or what he did, his goal was always to find her. He thought back over all the women he'd met. Had he ever even been close?

Memory stirred. There had been that one time. When was it...a century ago? He'd been passing though a small town in California. He thought for a moment as he passed below a low branch in the path. That's right...Sonora. It was a place with a history, and he'd enjoyed his time there.

He'd been walking down the street one night when he'd sensed a tingle in his inner being. He'd stopped, barely breathing as he tried to capture the elusive summons again.

Milcham's heart had leaped when he felt it close by. But before he could track it down, it was gone. Snuffed out like a candle, as if it had never been at all. After several hours of fruitless searching, he'd all but convinced himself he'd been dreaming.

He'd moved on, but the memory lingered. And now...with Aithne's words of prophecy ringing in his ears, he couldn't help but think of it. Could he have missed the woman he was seeking way back then? Or was she still out there, somewhere...waiting for him?

Aithne walked slowly through the meadow, enjoying the soft breeze teasing her hair. She had been walking for some time, allowing the night air to soothe her frazzled nerves. Now, she turned back towards the carnival, yet she still was uneasy. Her altercation with Milcham Phoenix had bothered her more than she realized. And then to draw *that* card? She wrapped her arms around herself and shivered.

There was no way she was going to get any closer to that arrogant, opinionated, judgmental bigot, even if he was gorgeous and—she sighed—had such sad longing in his eyes. The cards weren't infallible, and she would make her own destiny. The man she would take as her lover wouldn't be so hard and angry, but caring and genuine. She would find her own twin-flame, and like the man who refused to leave her thoughts, she would search until she found him.

She was so lost in contemplation, she didn't notice she had company until they were upon her. Her senses prickled, and the hair on the back of her neck stood on end. She looked up just in time to see three young men blocking her way. Her pulse raced in sudden fear.

Looking over their shoulders, she saw she'd wandered too far from the carnival grounds to be heard. A man laughed, and her eyes snapped back to him. Immediately, she became even more cautious. One of the guys standing in front of her had been in her tent earlier in the evening.

She cursed her own stupidity. It was late at night, she was in a strange town and completely isolated from anyone who could help her. When she'd been Aidan's familiar, no one would have dared touch her. He would have protected her. Now she had no one but herself.

"Excuse me," she said, pleased her voice didn't tremble too much. "I'd like to get by."

The three men laughed. One, the same redheaded guy who'd made a pass at her in her tent, spit on the ground. "If it isn't the gypsy. It must be my lucky night, no matter what your fuckin' cards said."

Aithne remembered the cards had warned this man would be hurt. The Ten of Swords warned of sudden misfortune, ruin of plans, defeat and pain, while The Knight of Swords told of a brave man being involved. She had told him to be careful, that someone whom he'd wronged would take vengeance on him. Could she have made a mistake?

Her heart pounded. "I need to be getting back."

"You're not going anywhere." The three men fanned out around her, and Aithne swallowed hard. She may still be stronger than a normal woman, but she didn't think she could beat three young men in their prime. And since all of them stank of drink, she was pretty sure she wouldn't be able to talk them out of whatever they were planning to do.

She hated the helplessness that came over her as she watched them. Every woman in the world would know exactly how she felt right now. But she wouldn't make it easy. She'd fight them tooth and nail.

"I'm warning you," she said angrily. "I'm stronger than you think. You won't get away with this."

"We'll get exactly what we want," one of the others said with a sneer. "You...flat on your back...*bitch.*"

The redhead moved suddenly and grabbed at Aithne's arm. She spun away and slapped him, connecting hard with the side of his face. He swore and recoiled, but the third man grabbed her from behind. She struggled, and when the second man lunged at her, she kicked out, connecting solidly with his balls. The man gave a high-pitched shriek and grabbing his injured crotch, fell to the ground.

The first man recovered and slammed his fist into the side of Aithne's mouth. She saw stars and tasted blood, but still managed to elbow man number three in the stomach. Breaking free, she ran.

She didn't get far before she was jumped from behind. She let out a piercing scream and then fell to the ground, rocks and stones stabbing into her outflung hands. Her stomach rolled as a man's sour alcoholic breath rasped in her ear.

"Where do you think you're going, cunt? We caught you fair and square."

Aithne struggled, using her supernatural strength to toss him off of her. Rising to her hands and knees, she tried to scramble to her feet, but her long, flowing skirt hampered her efforts. She got one knee up off the ground, but then he was on her again, this time with help, as another man grabbed at her arms.

She screamed again as they turned her to her back. The three men loomed over her, all grinning evilly. The redhead stepped between her legs. "I'm going to do you hard." He unzipped his pants. "And because you hit me, I'm going to hurt you."

With his friends cheering him on, he came down on top of her. His friends still held her arms, but her legs were free, and she used those to kick at him. His slobbering mouth brushed against her breast and she almost gagged, but it pushed her harder to fight. Calling on what was left of her strength, she pulled her arm away from one of the men and used it to rip out the man's hair.

When he shouted in pain, she lifted her knee. She connected, but because he felt her coming, he was able to move enough so it had only partial impact. She fought harder as his hand crept up her naked thigh.

Suddenly, there was a rush of wind and an almost blinding glow of light. An unearthly scream rent the air, almost melodic in its song. The man on top of her was lifted and tossed away as if he were no heavier than a feather. Using the distraction, Aithne raked her long nails down the side of the face of the man who still held her. He screamed and let her go, and she scooted away, turning back when she heard a grunt and a loud cry. In the darkness, all she could see were two men fighting.

She could hear the impact of fists on flesh, and the sound made her sick to her stomach. She watched breathlessly as the larger man pummeled the other into submission. When he fell to the ground, she couldn't help but give a sigh of relief.

But it didn't last. "Look out!" she screamed. The big man turned just in time to see the redheaded guy swing at him with a broken branch. It hit him in the side of the head and both men fell to the ground.

All she could hear were more grunts and the sounds of fists flying. They rolled, battering at each other, the fight seemingly lasting forever. Then, there was a sharp crack and they both went still. Aithne tried to scramble to her feet to see what happened, but her leg was jerked and she fell back.

Looking at her feet, she saw the third man. His face was feral in the moonlight, and she knew a spasm of fear. But when he leaped at her, she reacted, using the skills learned over a century of living. Her leg whipped out and she caught him under the chin. His head snapped back, and he crumpled to the ground. She crawled quickly away from the still body in case he was playing possum.

Glancing back over her shoulder, she saw a large form walking her way. The moon had slipped behind the cloud and she couldn't see who it was. She whimpered under her breath.

Shock was setting in and her strength was failing. With the last of it, she lurched to her feet and tried to run.

The arm that caught her was so hot, she cried out, thinking she was being burned. She pushed away...terrified one of the men was after her again. But instead of hurting her, the man folded her against his chest in such a gentle, protective way; it brought tears to her eyes.

"Hush, *assai*," the man whispered. "You are safe now."

Aithne froze at the sound of the deep, melodic voice. Carefully, she lifted her head and looked incredulously into glowing amber eyes.

"You?"

Chapter Three

Milcham held her tightly against him. His heart pounded in a mixture of anger and relief. He smoothed his hand over her hair. "It is all right," he reiterated. "They cannot hurt you anymore."

He thought of the moments in the forest when he'd heard her scream. He'd known instantly it was Aithne, and she was in trouble. His head had shot up, and without even thinking, he'd shifted into his bird form, his whole being intent on getting to her.

Launching himself above the trees, he'd headed in the direction of her cry. When she screamed again, fury such as he'd never known filled him, and he'd arrowed down in all his fiery glory, right into the middle of the group.

When he saw what was happening, he let out his battle cry, and morphing back into a man, he pulled the would-be rapist off her body and flung him away.

Then, he'd grabbed another man and set to tearing him apart for daring to touch her. It was primitive, instinctual, but he knew deep inside him he wasn't protecting just any woman.

He was protecting a mate.

But he pushed that knowledge away, refusing to admit it, even to his deepest self. Instead, he fought, enjoying the sensation of the human male's flesh tearing beneath his fists.

He watched Aithne, impressed she didn't cringe against the ground, mewling for help. She shook off the last man, clawing at his face with her sharp nails. She wasn't totally helpless, that was certain. There had been marks on the rapist's face as well.

He took the man out with a last blow to the jaw, and when he fell, he turned and met Aithne's gaze. He didn't think she could see him clearly, yet her eyes were still filled with admiration. Before his chest could swell with pride, the look changed to one of horror, and she'd screamed for him to be careful.

A well-placed branch to the side of the head made him see stars. It would have killed a normal man, but it just angered Milcham. He grabbed the redheaded man who'd swung it, and they both toppled to the ground.

He was even angrier when he saw the third man, whom Aithne had scratched, get to his knees and go after her. Afraid she'd be hurt, he made short work of the man he was fighting. A blow to the stomach made the drunken man gag, and then a crack to the side of the jaw put him down for the count.

Milcham jumped to his feet just in time to see Aithne take out the last guy with a dance-like kick to the chin. He shook his head in astonishment as the man crumpled like a wet napkin and fell to the ground.

Striding to her, he didn't see the fear in her face until it was too late. Then, all he could do was wrap her in his arms and try to soothe her. Her cry of pain alerted him to the fact he was still hot and burning from his anger. Immediately, he doused his inner flame and held her tightly.

"How..." she whispered, "how did you get here?"

His arms tightened. "I was taking a walk. I heard you scream."

She shuddered and buried her head in his chest as her knees gave out. They sank to the ground, and he pulled her into his lap. "I wasn't paying attention. I wandered too far away from the carnival. It was stupid."

Privately, he thought so too, but since she'd learned her lesson, he didn't think he needed to rub it in. "It's over now."

She gave a watery laugh. “You frightened me to death. Where’s your flashlight?”

Milcham blinked. “Flashlight?”

“The one you shined in our faces when you first got here. It was so bright, I couldn’t see anything.” She lifted her head and looked up at him. “And the way you howled. Now that was scary!”

Milcham realized his bright light had prevented her and the others from seeing his true form. He’d never before been so careless. Breathing a sigh of relief, he only shrugged. “The flashlight was destroyed in the fight. And I’m sorry my shout frightened you. It was only my...family’s battle cry.”

“And I’m sorry you had to be involved in this. I should have known better. My brother would kill me if he knew I’d been so stupid.”

So she had a protective brother. “Older than you? He must be. You can’t be...what? Eighteen? Twenty?”

Aithne laughed and he saw her cringe as the movement made her bruised lip split and bleed. She wiped carefully at the blood. “Thank you, but I’m twenty-four. I’m...much older than I look.”

“You’re bleeding.” He took her gently by the chin and lifted it up to the moonlight. His voice reverberated with rage. “One of those bastards hit you?”

“To be fair, I hit him first.”

Milcham swore a pithy and concise oath. “There were three of them and only one of you. Nothing about this was fair.” He stroked his index finger over the swollen lip and his eyes glowed briefly. “This is going to bruise.” He wished he could chance healing her, but it would cause too many questions.

Aithne held her breath at his touch. Her heart suddenly beat very fast. “I’m afraid that...that won’t be the only one.”

His hands moved gently over her. “You are hurt elsewhere?”

She wanted to moan aloud as his palm brushed the side of her breast and trailed down her side. Moisture gathered between her legs, and she wanted to wriggle in his lap. "I'll…I'll be…fine."

"Perhaps I should check closer." Milcham's voice had deepened, and when she looked up at him, her breath caught at the hungry look in his eyes.

"Maybe…you should," she heard herself say.

Milcham fought with himself. He knew he shouldn't touch her, but the scent of her soft body in his arms tempted him beyond caring. With a little growl, he bent his head and covered her lips with his own.

Heat. Fiery, soul-searing heat was the first thing his mind screamed before it blanked out completely. He forgot to think…he could only feel. His lips burned as they caressed hers. When her mouth opened, he groaned and his tongue licked in between her soft lips, touching the bruise soothingly, before moving away. He tasted her, his body tightening even more at her flavor. All woman, dark and wonderful, yet with a taste of innocence that made her even more desirable to him.

He pulled her against him, molding her soft body to his. He felt her breasts through her thin silk blouse, their pointed tips erect and hard. Smoothing his hand down her back, he pressed his throbbing cock against her hip, wishing he could slide it deep into her warmth.

Aithne was tossed into a fiery storm of desire. A simple kiss had turned incendiary, making her whole body seem like it was licked in flame. No virgin she, but her times with men were few and far between, and it had been several years since she'd even made the effort. The toys in *Don't Spank the Vamp* had been her only lovers.

But this…this sensation of total heat and passion roaring through her like a river of fire? This, she had never before experienced. He parted her mouth and dove in, careful of her injury, yet still forceful and possessive. Milcham kissed her as if he knew exactly how and what she liked, and she had to admit...he was right.

He tasted like candy...caramel apples and peanut brittle. Sweet and slightly smoky—she knew she would never forget his taste. When he murmured her name, she reached up and clutched his messy hair, tangling her fingers in it and pressing even closer.

His arms pulled her hard against him, and his heated erection pulsed against her thigh. Her whole body melted, surrendering against him like a moth drawn to a hot flame.

He felt her yield. Felt the softness of her body, and his eyes flared with the need to mate with her. To thrust inside her until they were both flying into the sun. He started to lay her down in the soft grass when a loud groan made them both freeze.

Instantly, they broke apart, both remembering at the same time the three men who lay close by.

Milcham stared at her. Her beautiful face was flushed, and her lips were wet from his kisses. His body ached to touch her again, but the thought he'd nearly taken her while others were near cooled his ardor dramatically.

"We should go back to the carnival," he snarled. Anger at himself and embarrassment at what he'd done made his voice sharper than intended. As passion died away, his memory of who this woman was returned. He had been tempted, and it infuriated him.

Aithne heard the emotion in his voice and her cheeks reddened. He regretted. It was plain on his face. Her anger rose as well. He wasn't the only one who was embarrassed. Right now she could almost kiss the guy who'd cried out and prevented her from making a huge mistake. She didn't even like Milcham Phoenix. It must have been his gentleness that threw her. God knew he wasn't really like that all the time. The memory of the tarot card she'd chosen flitted through her mind, but she ignored it.

She lifted her chin and looked down her nose at him. A great feat since she was still sitting in his lap. "I think we should both forget this ever happened!" she said freezingly, pleased to see his eyes narrow in anger. "A heat-of-the-moment thing neither of us really wanted. You stay away from me, Mr. Phoenix, and I'll stay away from you!"

"Gladly," he bit out, angered at her dismissal. "But since I've had my tongue down your throat, I think you might as well call me Milcham."

Her faced flamed, but when she spoke her words were frosty. "Since I hope never to speak to you again, I don't see the need to call you anything!" With that, she rose to her feet in a swift, graceful motion and stepping over the nearest body, walked away from him.

Milcham swore. She was so fucking stubborn. So completely irritating. He raced after her to walk by her side. He may not like her, but he'd be damned if he'd let anyone hurt her again.

Above them in the trees, a shadowy figure moved. It spread black leathery wings and flew high away into the air, chortling evilly. The human woman and the Phoenix had almost copulated in the grass. It rubbed gnarled hands together. Soon, they would fall to the temptation and the Phoenix would be completely distracted by this woman. Then, not only would he stop looking for his twin-flame, if all went correctly, this woman could be used to deceive the Phoenix into thinking she was the one he could take into the fire of renewal. The plan was going splendidly. The Master would be very pleased.

Aithne tossed and turned on her narrow bed. Damn the man for making her feel so...needy. She plumped the pillow and lay down again. Ever since she'd stomped back into her tent, she'd been unable to settle down. Her body still throbbed from his touch, and just the thought of how he tasted made her go immediately wet. With a curse, she sat up in bed and wrapped her arms around her legs.

"This is insane," she said aloud. "I don't even like the guy!"

Her mind went to when he'd pressed against her, his large cock throbbing at her thigh, and she moaned. "Not helping."

Restlessly, she tossed back the covers and got out of bed. Her tent was divided in half: the main larger part in front where she did readings and the back part set up as a simple living space, with a narrow cot and a small area to cook in. She usually didn't use the hotplate. She had her reasons for being nervous about fire. Aidan had been vulnerable to it, and she...she'd gotten into the habit of avoiding it due to her own past. The thought of setting her tent on fire made her shiver.

She walked over to the shelf and poured herself a glass of water from the pitcher she left there at night. She drank it down thirstily, but it didn't help put out the fire that burned inside of her. Sighing, she turned to the cheap, full-length mirror that was set against the side of the tent.

Gazing at her silk-covered form, Aithne wondered briefly what Phoenix...Milcham saw when he looked at her. Her hands lifted of their own accord and smoothed over her breasts. They were plump and high, and—she shivered as her thumb grazed a pointed nipple—very sensitive.

Her lips parted as she did it again. Fire shot through her stomach, and she closed her eyes, imagining it was her amber-eyed savior who was touching her. Slowly, she caressed herself, gently squeezing and rubbing until her distended nipples could easily be seen through the pale silk of her nightgown.

Biting her lip at the pleasure that coursed through her, Aithne pinched and plucked at them until her breasts were aching for more.

Suddenly, the scratchiness of her gown was intolerable. With a quick tug, she had it over her head, tossing it to the ground uncaringly. Now, completely naked, she watched herself in the mirror, pretending again it was Milcham who touched her. The very thought made her whole body shake.

Milcham paced around outside his small trailer. He was restless and still angry with himself about what had happened earlier. His cock gave a quick throb in memory, and gritting his teeth, he adjusted himself.

During the walk back from the meadow, they'd both ignored each other completely. He'd left Aithne at her tent then headed to his own trailer to do paperwork. But that didn't last long, since he was too unsettled to do any real thinking. He couldn't get her out of his mind, and it was driving him crazy.

Reaching into his pocket, he pulled out the single strand of bells he'd found in the meadow grass. Their sweet music filled the night air. Aithne must have lost them in the struggle, but for some reason, he kept them, needing to have a piece of her with him.

Rubbing them between his fingers, he thought of her and how she'd made him feel. His cock jumped again, and he gave a little growl of irritation. Enough was enough! He turned to go inside, but at that moment a cry rent the night air, and he whirled around, recognizing immediately it was Aithne. But she was nowhere to be seen.

Staring into the darkness, he clutched tightly to the tinkling bracelet he held, not understanding what was happening. Suddenly, a picture formed in his mind, so fast...so vivid, it made him stumble and grab onto the side of the trailer. Milcham blinked, but the image didn't go away. He realized he was having a vision, brought on by the simple touching of her jewelry.

Another moan sounded and his body went hard. It wasn't a sound of pain or fear...but one of desire. His focus sharpened and then his mouth gaped open. In total shock, he realized he was watching Aithne as she stood naked in front of a mirror…touching herself.

She kept her eyes half closed as her fingers gently caressed her breast. Her hardened nipples begged to be touched, and she whimpered again as she took them between two fingers and squeezed. Electricity shot through her, making goosebumps appear on her body. Again, she thought of Milcham touching her this way, and her breath quickened.

She remembered the taste of his kiss and sighed. One of her hands moved slowly down her body, covering her silky mound. Gently, Aithne separated the tender folds and touched the swollen bud that was already pulsing with desire.

Her knees almost buckled at the sensation that shot through her. Heat filled her with just a single touch of her hand. She continued to squeeze her nipples as her other hand massaged her clit with sensitive fingers.

Milcham's face filled her mind. She bit her lip as she pictured his strong fingers teasing her folds. When she thought of his callused finger pushing into her heated quim, her head fell back and she shuddered.

Milcham groaned. His body heated in a second at the delicious picture he saw before him. Aithne was the most beautiful woman he'd ever seen. Her long, shapely legs smoothed up into slender, yet womanly hips, a tiny waist and breasts that would fit perfectly into a man's hands.

He'd felt her against him in the forest, but now he saw reality right in front of him. She was perfect in his eyes. His cock stiffened until it hurt, and he had to adjust himself again. The touch of his own hand almost put him over the top, right then and there.

He almost went to his knees when he saw her hand move down to between her legs. Her passion-filled cry filled his mind as she began stimulating herself by rubbing her clit. Milcham wasn't even aware he'd undone his jeans until the cool air washed over his naked cock. His teeth clenched as he tried to control himself. What was he doing? What was *she* making him do?

Her fingers moved faster and faster over her slippery folds. Her passion rose until she could barely breathe. She pictured Milcham standing naked behind her, sucking and kissing her neck, his big cock throbbing against her. One large hand plucked at her nipples while the other massaged between her legs. His big finger slowly penetrated and she cried out at the sensation. Slowly, he moved in and out of her heated quim, and she leaned back and rocked her pelvis against him.

Aithne's eyes opened and she stared at herself in the mirror. Her breath came quickly and she shuddered again. Suddenly, she wanted more than her finger inside her. When Milcham had pressed against her in the field, she knew how big he was. If she was going to imagine him making love to her, she was going to do it the right way.

She stumbled back to her narrow bed, fumbling in the small side table nearby, and smiled as she pulled out a small black case. In it was one of *Don't Spank the Vamp's* most popular toys.

Aithne let out another soft sigh as she lifted her favorite dildo out of the box. *Silicone Dreams* was the only thing that had been between her legs in a very long time. She leaned back on the bed and began stroking it over her stomach and thighs, pretending it was Milcham's cock. Closing her eyes, she covered her breast with one hand and started again to tease and tickle her swollen nipples.

Her desire grew again as she plucked at her hardened tips. Gently, she slipped the dildo between her legs and carefully parted her nether lips. Her stomach clenched in need as the soft silicone flesh rubbed against her sensitive clitoris. In and out she went, her hips rocking against the dildo as her desire crested higher and higher.

When she couldn't bear waiting anymore, she slowly eased the flesh-colored cock into her tight channel. She moaned and flicked on the vibrator.

He was dying. In all his long, immortal life, he'd never been closer to death then he was right now. Watching Aithne pleasure herself was so painfully erotic, he didn't know how much more he could take before he just keeled over in satisfaction.

Milcham watched as she twisted and tweaked her nipples, panting from her own pleasure. He groaned again when her finger disappeared from view, deep within her own body. Unconsciously, he started moving his hand up and down his own swollen cock in the same rhythm Aithne was using. His hips began to pump slowly.

When she suddenly stopped and opened her eyes, all his breath left his body. Her gaze was dark and dreamy, her face flushed. But when she turned and walked to the bed, he wanted to shout at her. Surely, she couldn't be done.

His mouth dried up when she removed the fake cock from the nightstand. As she touched herself with the flesh-colored dildo, his whole body tightened again.

He knew the second she slid it inside of her needy body. Her head tipped back and she bit her lip against screaming. When she jumped, he knew it was vibrating.

Milcham clenched his teeth. It took everything he had not to race to her tent and pull that vibrator from her body. He wanted to be the one inside of her, squeezed by her sweet flesh as she exploded around him. The thought almost sent him over the edge.

Her legs drew up, giving him a clear view of her glistening flesh. The dildo moved in and out, her hips moving along with the vibrating toy. Again, he pumped his own cock along with her. Her body took on a sheen of perspiration, and her cries became louder. Hearing her was just as much a turn on as seeing her was. Milcham knew he should stop. He should try to end the vision, but he was frozen, tied to the picture she made as she brought herself to fulfillment.

She gasped with pleasure. Her heart was racing, and her fingers moved frantically over her nipples, plucking and rolling them until they were swollen with need. Her body rocked against the vibrator, bringing her closer and closer. She pictured Milcham, his hard body above hers as he plunged deep inside. His cock thrust in and out, their flesh slapping together in rhythm with her own movements.

Suddenly, it was too much. Her fantasy took her to the edge, and when she pushed the dildo against her pulsating clit, she came apart, crying out her climax as she plunged the machine deep inside her quim.

Milcham stroked himself as he watched Aithne. He was so close to coming himself, his balls were drawn tight against his body and were burning with heat. He was panting as if he had run for miles. When her eyes flew open and she cried out, he lost control, pumping his throbbing cock until his own orgasm raced through him and he exploded. He bit back his own shout of release as jets of silvery semen dotted the side of the trailer and the ground. He came with such force he became lightheaded.

Leaning his head back, he drew in great breaths of air. When he had more control, he refocused on the vision. Aithne lay sprawled on her bed, the dildo lying beside her. She was still breathing heavily, but she had a look of relief and contentment on her face.

Milcham stuffed his wet cock back in his jeans, completely confused and suddenly embarrassed. Never before had he behaved in such a manner, and he didn't know why this woman affected him so. He was attracted to her—yes, he understood that part—but to stand in the dark and do what he just did? That was beyond his ken.

Was Aithne a witch come to tempt and destroy him? Or could she be something much, much more? Unable to find an answer that made sense, he stood in the dark until the vision faded away. Then he turned and made his way back inside his lonely trailer.

Chapter Four

Aithne pushed back her tangled hair and put the last of her things in her suitcase. Closing it, she looked around the now empty tent. Her bed, tiny kitchen and table were already in the small trailer she shared with several other carny folk. Once she stowed this away, she could begin to take down her tent.

Hefting the suitcase, she walked outside to the six-by-eight wooden trailer. She stowed her suitcase in the appropriate place and then looked around her.

The carnival was gone. In its place were skeletons of the games and rides that just yesterday were bustling with life and activity. The tear-down was almost complete. A couple more hours and they would be on their way to the next town, and it would start all over again.

She sighed, not minding the traveling they did, but she didn't like having to set up and tear down her tent each time. She gazed over at the large trailer that belonged to Milcham. One of these days, she was going to get one just like that. She had the money. Aidan and she had plenty in the bank. She'd just been putting it off because at first she wasn't sure she was going to stay, and then she'd gotten too busy. But now, after a month, she was tired of the constant upheaval. The next big city they got to she'd see about purchasing a little home on wheels of her own.

She frowned as she stared at the curtains of his trailer. She hadn't spoken a word to Milcham since their time in the woods, three days ago. After their passionate kiss, the ensuing argument and her heated fantasy about him, she'd taken to turning around and walking the other way whenever she saw him. There was no way she wanted to be anywhere close to him if a simple kiss could turn her on so much she dreamed of him every night.

She chewed her lip as she began removing the outside signs and other small decorative items. At least he hadn't tried to force her to leave again. She hated his judgmental attitude about witches. Aithne knew there was a huge difference between a hereditary witch and one who'd sold her soul to the Devil for her powers. She wondered if Milcham did. Heredity witches meant no evil. In fact their motto was, *And it harm none.* If he did know...he was definitely grouping her in with the evil ones. That made her even angrier—and hurt, too, that he would think of her that way. Shaking her head, she put her *Gypsy Fortune Teller* sign in the trailer.

A few minutes later, she was joined by Jarrod, one of the roustabouts and Alexander, who was billed as Chortles the Clown. Both men were her closest friends in the carnival, probably because their backgrounds were as strange as hers.

She watched Jarrod pull the tent stakes from the ground with one easy tug. His muscles rippled in the sun, and she had to admire his masculine form. Big and blond, with a rough-hewn face and feral eyes, the two of them had been drawn together immediately.

Alexander was the opposite of Jarrod. When you met him out of costume, it was hard to believe this was the same man who could make you roll with laughter at his silly antics. In reality, he was quiet spoken and studious. He was a whiz with numbers and often helped Milcham out with the accounting.

But both men had secrets. Aithne had figured them out almost immediately. Perhaps it was because she herself had spent so much time in the paranormal world that two other supernaturals were easy to spot. She wondered if Milcham knew his carnival was a haven to these two...true *freaks.*

Jarrod was a werewolf, and Alexander could speak to ghosts.

She'd known from the beginning there was something different about them. Jarrod, with his rough-and-tumble ways, and Alexander, so quiet unless he was performing. They were the unlikeliest of friends.

The first week she was with the carnival, she had discovered their secret. Walking back to her tent, she stumbled across them standing near the fence behind the arcades. She watched in amazement as Jarrod suddenly shifted into a dark-colored wolf and sped into the trees.

She thought she was quiet, but suddenly Alexander turned his head as if he was listening to someone, and then he'd spoken.

"I know you're there."

Aithne wasn't afraid, just curious. She'd met others like them in her long life with Aidan. Supernaturals seemed to attract each other. As she walked forward, Alexander thanked someone before turning to her.

"Who are you talking to?" she'd asked curiously.

He'd told her then she'd been seen by one of the spirits—Ethereals, they called themselves—who haunted the fairgrounds. And the Ethereal had told him.

Eventually, Jarrod returned from his run and the three had talked long into the night. Aithne told them about her time as her brother's familiar, and the men told her about themselves as well.

Jarrod was a rogue. Without a pack to call home, he'd wandered around the country until he'd found the carnival. For the first time he belonged somewhere. Aithne knew there was more to the story. No werewolf went rogue without cause, but since he didn't share more, she didn't push. There was a stoic sadness and deep anger swirling in his dark brown eyes.

Alexander had joined the carnival to get away from his family. They were the type that either believed because he saw "ghosts" he should be put away in a mental hospital, *or* if they were feeling generous, he only needed to be prayed over so the demons would leave him alone. Eventually, he had enough. Alexander packed a bag and disappeared after one too many attempts to "help" him. Dark-haired and blue-eyed, he was very striking, but he rarely dated. He found having ghosts as chaperons rarely made an evening go well.

Aithne had the sneaking suspicion both men were attracted to her. But each of them knew it, so neither would do anything about it. That was okay with her. Having them around made it seem like she had a brother again. Or rather—this time—two.

Now, they argued companionably as they helped her take down her tent. Since they shared a trailer, they had little to do before rolling out. She was grateful for their help.

She sensed him before she saw him. The back of her neck prickled again, and she swung around to see him standing right behind her.

Milcham stared at the men who were making short work of Aithne's tent. A wave of jealousy raced through him. He wanted to order them away from her, but he knew that was ridiculous. He shouldn't be surprised they were helping her, she was—as he'd said—a beautiful woman. But his anger wasn't reasonable. Alexander was a close friend, and Jarrod, for all his moodiness, was a good worker and a man he could count on.

He knew about them both...of course. For a creature as intelligent as he, it was easy to recognize their unique characteristics. Now, he didn't know whether to caution Aithne she was messing with monsters out of a faerie tale or warn the men she was a witch.

Since he'd had that erotic vision, he'd dreamed about her every night. He was sure she'd given it to him, just to drive him crazy. Afterwards, he'd jerk awake, his cock standing straight up, as hard as a spike. The only way he'd get any relief was to finish himself off, while he pictured her sexy body naked beneath his.

His thoughts were broken by her husky voice. "Is there something you wanted, Mr. Phoenix?"

Anger flared again as he met her green eyes. Every time they'd met in the last few days, she'd turned on her heel and walked away from him. Now she wouldn't call him by name? It was suddenly too much.

"I told you to call me Milcham."

She raised a dark eyebrow. "And I told you, I wouldn't need to."

"You are so damn stubb—" He stopped himself and took a deep breath, refusing to let her get to him. No matter how much he wanted to drag her into his trailer and fuck her senseless. Changing the subject, he motioned behind her. "Will you be done in time? I need you out of the way."

Aithne narrowed her eyes. Nasty, arrogant, opinionated man. She'd like to— Stopping herself before she blew up at him, she said instead, icily, "Alexander and Jarrod are a great help. We will be finished long before *you* are."

His own eyes flared. "Just be sure that work comes first."

"I beg your pardon?"

He gave her a smirk. "I know how you pay the men who help you, remember?"

Her mouth fell open, and hurt filled her eyes. She didn't say anything for a long moment. Then, her chin lifted and she tapped the faint bruise that still graced her pink mouth. "And the men who did this. What was I paying them for?"

His own lips firmed, but he said nothing. Aithne shook her head. She opened her mouth and then shut it again, turning away as if there were nothing more to say.

Guilt rolled greasily in Milcham's stomach. He'd been out of line and he knew it. She didn't deserve his words. He'd just been reacting to the thought of her with either of his friends. He started to apologize, but then saw both Alexander and Jarrod staring at him thoughtfully. Embarrassed at his own actions, he thrust his hands in his pockets and stomped away.

Tossing his pen across the room, Milcham swore angrily. No matter what he did, he couldn't stop thinking about Aithne and the cruel words he'd spoken to her. He'd started to go back once, but she'd climbed into the truck with Alexander and Jarrod, and they'd driven off.

Guilt again warred with fury that his two good friends were with the woman who was becoming a constant distraction to him.

He rubbed his eyes. It was quiet. The last townie had left the carnival, and he was counting up gate receipts. It was another small town in Tennessee, but the money was good...considering. There had been no gate crashers, no breakdowns and no fights with the locals.

Giving up, Milcham gathered up the paperwork and cash and put it into the safe. He had to apologize. He'd been wrong, and it was time he admitted it.

Stepping out of his trailer, he walked swiftly towards her tent. Remembering his vision made his penis twitch, and he groaned. He'd had a hard-on since he'd first seen her standing outside her tent smiling at some mark. Immediately, he'd gone painfully stiff. Now he wondered if part of his anger with her might be fueled by unexpressed lust.

When he got to her tent, he cleared his throat, suddenly nervous. He didn't often make mistakes. He wasn't used to apologizing. "Aithne?" he said loudly as he pushed his way into the outer tent. "Are you here?"

The tent was dark and silent, and he frowned. Where the hell was she? The least she could do was be where she should be when he wanted to apologize. He moved to the back of the tent, struck anew by how small it was.

It was exactly like he'd seen in his mind, and again the memory made him throb. Swearing under his breath, he left the tent quickly, taking a deep breath of the fragrant night air.

His peripheral vision caught the sight of Jarrod padding silently towards a wooded area off to the left of the carnival. Milcham knew he was going out for a run, but as always, pretended not to know.

"Jarrod!" he called. "Do you know where Aithne is?"

The big blond nodded. "She is at the funhouse. She goes there sometimes to think."

"To think?"

"Yes." Jarrod glanced longingly at the woods, and his nostrils flared in his eagerness to go. "She had a phone call from her brother that seemed to upset her. So she went to sit and think."

Milcham thought of all the nooks and crannies in the funhouse. It was a good place to hide away. "Thanks. Where you off to?"

Jarrod glanced sharply at him. "For a walk."

He nodded. "Be careful...townies."

The werewolf grinned with real humor. "They're the ones who should be careful."

Milcham chuckled. He was right. No human in his right mind would ever try to fight a full grown male werewolf. Watching Jarrod lope off into the forest, he made his way across the carnival grounds to the dark house at the back of the midway. A garish-looking clown made of red and white light bulbs laughed down at him. It looked dingy in the darkness, unlike the brilliant welcoming sign that shone brightly when it was open.

Knowing the most likely place for her to hide, he made his way past the moving staircase and the cargo nets to the center of the building. There, in the middle of the maze of mirrors, he saw her.

She was dressed in another long flowing skirt with matching off-the-shoulder sweater, and his pulse raced when he saw the top of her left breast was showing. She was leaning back against one of the mirrors with her eyes closed. A single tear traced down her porcelain cheek.

Something sweet and painful moved through him, and without thinking he rubbed at his chest. Any anger he had disappeared. "Are you all right?"

Her eyes flew open. When her head whipped around and she saw him, he watched the emotions fly across her face. Fear, anger, embarrassment and yes...even desire, before she hid them.

She climbed to her feet. "What are you doing here?"

"I could ask the same thing," he said as he moved closer. "Jarrod said you were here...thinking. Is everything okay with your brother?"

Her eyes flew to his. "How do you know about Aidan?" Then understanding lit her face. "Jarrod's *real* chatty this evening."

"You haven't answered me." He used his thumb to wipe away the tear, marveling at the softness of her cheek. "Your brother?"

She swallowed hard, and her breath wavered at his touch. "My...brother is fine. He and his mate...I mean wife...they are going to New York for a showing." Her eyes filled. "I just miss them, that's all."

Milcham started at the term *mate*, but her tear-filled eyes pushed it out of his mind. Without thinking, he gathered her to him, wanting to soothe. "Hush, *assai*...don't cry. What is this showing you speak of?"

Aithne cuddled against him, needing to be held even if it were by him. "Dawn is a sculptor. She's having her first show in a few weeks. They wanted me to come see them, but it's their first time away together. They don't need a third wheel."

He smoothed a large hand up her back. "Perhaps she would like to have her family with her during this important time."

She sniffed inelegantly. "It's best I don't go. It's hard to explain."

"Family issues are not easy for outsiders to understand."

Putting her head back, she looked up at him. "Sounds like you've been down this road before with your family."

Before her eyes, his face saddened. "I have no family, Aithne. I am alone in this world and always have been."

A piece of the puzzle clicked. "Is that why you search for your twin-flame?"

He stiffened slightly. "Yes...I have searched and will continue to do so until I find her. In that, you were correct."

"I'm sorry."

"Don't be. My life has been good without her. When I find her, I will be complete."

Aithne's throat tightened. The thought of Milcham with another woman made her heart hurt for some inexplicable reason. Why did she care so much? They didn't even like each other...did they?

"I must apologize to you."

She blinked up at him. "Apologize?"

Milcham sighed. "What I said yesterday. It was cruel and ugly and completely wrong. I am sorry."

"You really hurt my feelings."

He swallowed hard, and his face reddened in embarrassment. "I...was angry with you. For avoiding me, for refusing to use my name. Hell...I was even angry because Jarrod and Alex were helping you."

He put his finger under her chin and lifted it. "I know you aren't the type of woman who uses her body in such a way. I ask your forgiveness."

Aithne stared into his golden eyes. He did care, even if he didn't want to admit it. They were more alike than they knew. Her heart warmed and she reached up to kiss his cheek. "It's all right, Milcham. I think we both have been behaving foolishly lately."

He stiffened under her kiss. Feeling it, she tried to move away from him, but he held her tightly, his eyes still on hers. His heart beat very fast against her, and suddenly the atmosphere around them thickened with heated desire.

With a groan, his mouth swooped down on hers.

Instant conflagration. Both their bodies, so starved for the other's touch, burst into needy flame. Their moans filled the small room. Milcham pushed her back against the mirrored wall, while she reached up and filled her hands with his hair.

Their tongues dueled together as they tried to get closer. Aithne cried out when he pulled the sweater off her shoulder, revealing her naked breast. When his mouth swooped down and sucked the rosy crown into his mouth, her knees went weak. He held her. One hand on her ass, while the other reached up under her sweater to touch her other breast.

It was just like in her fantasy. He sucked on one breast while he rolled the nipple of her other breast between his fingers. Whimpering, she held his head as she arched up to him, her panties going damp with need.

"Milcham," she whispered as he switched breasts, pulling the sweater off her head completely so he could feast on her nakedness.

Any control he might have had disappeared in a fiery ball of lust when she said his name in that sexy voice of hers. Bracing her against the wall, he reached under her skirt and pulled her drenched panties off with a sharp tug that separated them at the seams. He fumbled with his belt, swearing as his own top jeans button tore off and pinged against the mirror.

Seconds later, he was between her spread legs, her skirt pushed up and his strong arm still holding her against the mirror. They stared at each other for one long moment, then unable to wait any longer, he guided the broad head of his penis to her waiting nether lips. With one strong thrust, he buried himself deep inside.

Chapter Five

They both cried out and then stilled at the wonder of their bodies finally being connected. For a long time, they continued to stare deep into each other's eyes, unable to move or breathe. Then Aithne shuddered…just once, and the spell was broken.

Tucking his head into her shoulder, Milcham pounded into her. His lust spiraling out of control, he had little grace or finesse. Just the primitive need to imprint himself so deep in this female's flesh, she would never forget him.

He held her flush against him so he could feel the damp softness of her clit against his cock as he penetrated her. Her soft moans and cries poured fuel on the heat of his passion. He was so hard, so swollen, every stroke was a painful pleasure.

Aithne cried out with the joy of finally having him deep inside her. He was big and hot and so hard, she wanted to weep from pleasure. Her fantasy had been wonderful, but the reality was more than she could have imagined. Now, she could see their reflections in a hundred different mirrors, and it made her desire rise even higher. Digging her hands into his shoulders, she leaned her head back against the mirror and enjoyed.

They were both so needy for each other it was no surprise their climaxes came so quickly. Even though in her mind she wished it could last forever, her need for release was too overwhelming. When the passion that was coiling in her belly suddenly exploded, she screamed, convulsing in his arms like a wild thing. Heated emotions rolled through her with such strength she thought she might go mad. When he groaned and plunged into her one last time, his cock swelling almost painfully, she climaxed again, clenching down around him as he came apart inside of her.

Milcham had never felt anything like it before. She was so hot, so silky and wet. But there was something else. Something he couldn't put a finger on. Something that made him wish never to stop touching her.

His balls were drawn up so tightly, he could barely stand it. He couldn't stop his thrusts...didn't want to. When Aithne clutched at his shoulders and then screamed, he too cried out as her burning quim milked his cock. His release poured through him, his orgasm so strong and so pleasurable, it made any other thought in his head disappear.

He buried himself as deep inside of her as he could, pumping his life's seed within her body. When she pulsed around him a second time, he almost wept with the beauty of their mating.

She shuddered as he slumped against her. Their hearts raced together. He was still burning hot, a fine mist of perspiration on him. She laid her forehead against his messy hair and they both tried to breathe. Neither of them moved for a long time, each lost in their own thoughts. As they both came floating down back to earth, reality intruded with a crash. What had they done?

Carefully, she dropped her legs down from their uncomfortable position. He lifted himself and pulled out of her body. Now...they couldn't even look at each other. Embarrassment ruled.

Pushing back her hair, she slipped her sweater back on and slowly adjusted her clothing. Tears threatened, but she refused to give in to them. She had been a willing participant. He hadn't forced her.

"Are you all right?" His voice was deep and gravely. "I was...rough with you."

Aithne swallowed. "You didn't hurt me, Milcham. Not at all."

He pulled away and straightened his own clothing. Combing his hands through his unruly hair, he looked as uncomfortable as she was.

"Milcham."

"Aithne."

They spoke at the same time. Their eyes met, and they both looked away. He sighed. "I'm sorry. I didn't mean for that to happen. I just can't stop thinking about being with you."

Her heart stuttered. "I..."

"But we know it was wrong." He laughed bitterly. "We don't even like each other. And I am too old to be led around by my cock."

Her heart hardened at his words. "We are both old enough to know the difference between right and wrong. And we're wrong for each other."

Milcham's chest squeezed painfully. "As you say," he choked out. "We won't let it happen again."

"No...we won't." She gazed at him with steady green eyes, but her lips trembled, making him long to hold her again. She lifted her chin.

"We are also old enough to deal with any...repercussions of...a mistake."

He reddened when he got her meaning. "I...I am disease free, Aithne. You have my word. And you needn't worry about a child. I am sterile."

That surprised her, he could tell, but she didn't ask any questions. After a second she nodded. "All right, I believe you."

He couldn't help himself. He caught her cheek in his hand. "I wouldn't lie to you, Aithne. Especially not about something like that."

She shivered at his touch. "I'm clean, too. It...it has been a long time for me."

Again, something dark and primitive moved in Milcham's chest. The thought of her being with another man after what they had just shared made him tighten his hand. "I know we can't do this again, but...I have to be honest. It was the best...sex I have ever had."

Instead of making her happy, his words seemed to wound her. Her eyes overflowed, and she bit back a sob as she jerked away from him. "But that's just it," she whispered brokenly. "It doesn't matter how wonderful it was. It was just sex."

Turning, she ran out of the maze, her many mirrored reflections mocking him as he stood staring after her. As she disappeared, he knew that something very important had been snatched from his reach.

Aithne poked disinterestedly at the food on her plate. She sat with Alexander and Jarrod near the midway, sampling one of the concessionaire's new sandwiches. She barely listened as the two men argued over types of cheese to use.

"Girl—" Jarrod bumped her with his massive shoulder, "—what is going on with you? You've been as quiet as a ghost." He smirked at Alexander. "Sorry."

His friend narrowed his eyes. "Don't tell me." He motioned to Jarrod's left. "Tell Mitzi."

Aithne frowned. "I thought she stayed behind. Wasn't she haunting the last fairground?"

"She liked the carnival better." Alexander shrugged. "She and Boris have a thing going." Boris was a *blade glommer*, a sword swallower from the nineteenth century who'd died in an accident when a tent collapsed around him. He'd been haunting the carnival ever since. Since Mitzi went for the dark, dangerous type when she was alive, now that she was dead, he fit the bill just fine.

Jarrod rolled his eyes. “Sorry, Mitzi.”

“He’s right, you know,” Alexander said quietly.

“About what?” Aithne nibbled on an overcooked fry and wrinkled her nose.

“You’re acting weird.” The clown took a bite of his hoagie and chewed thoughtfully. “Ever since the other night.”

Aithne turned red. “I don’t know what you’re talking about.”

Snorting, Jarrod stuffed the rest of his sandwich in his mouth. “That’s lame.”

She stuck her tongue out at him. “Lame or not, it’s the truth.”

Alexander suddenly choked on his food. He turned and stared at Aithne. “You had sex with Milcham?”

Her mouth dropped open and her face turned beet red. “How did you...?” Her eyes narrowed and she glared at the empty space on Jarrod’s other side. “Damn it, Mitzi. You aren’t supposed to watch. That was private.” Then she looked at the two men. “And it was a mistake!”

Jarrod was having trouble breathing. “You...and Phoenix?”

Aithne put her face in her hands. “I don’t want to talk about it.”

“No wonder Milcham has been acting like a wolf with a sore paw lately.” It was Alexander’s turn to smirk at Jarrod.

Jarrod growled lightly at his friend before turning back to Aithne. “I can’t believe you slept with him. Jesus...you hate each other.”

Sighing, she pushed her plate away, her hunger disappearing. Irritated at herself and the nosy ghost, she snapped, “We didn’t sleep together! What we did had nothing to do with sleeping.”

Both men stared at her, and she rolled her eyes. “I’m not going to go into specifics, guys! Unlike Mitzi, I don’t kiss and tell!”

There was silence at the table for all of ten seconds. "But why?" Jarrod asked. "Why Phoenix?"

Aithne slammed her hands down on the table. "I don't know why! It just happened. We couldn't help ourselves. One minute we were talking and the next, we were all over each other. When we were done, we realized what a colossal mistake it was, and we walked away...okay?"

"If you say so," Alexander answered in his quiet voice. "But I don't think either of you has forgotten it." He gestured down the midway where you could see a group of men working on the broken Tilt-A-Whirl. "He's been breaking his and everyone else's back. Seems to me, he's burying himself in work like he's trying to forget something."

Jarrod cracked his knuckles. "I'd be down there helping right now, but he's pushing so hard I figured I better get something to eat first. I may never see daylight again." The side of his mouth went up, and he grinned crookedly at Aithne. "And we have you to thank for it, huh?"

"It has nothing to do with me," she spat as she jumped up from the table. "It was a one-time thing, and it's over. Understand?" Turning on her heel, she stomped away from them.

They both stared after her.

"Methinks, she protests too much," Alexander said thoughtfully.

Jarrod grunted and started in on Aithne's abandoned plate. "I can't believe it. Aithne and Phoenix."

"The air is on fire whenever they are close to each other," Alexander argued. "Some werewolf senses you have."

The big man shrugged. "I guess I didn't want to see it." The two men shared a look of understanding. "But I tell you, Alex, if he hurts her, I don't give a damn if he's the boss or not." Jarrod flexed his hands. "I'll break his neck."

Alexander smiled. "I'll hold him down for you."

Again, there was a companionable silence at the table. Then Jarrod turned to his friend. “Your ghosts haven’t said anything about me, have they?”

Alexander’s blue eyes lit with humor. “You? Of course not.” They both rose and cleared the plates from the table. As they were dumping them, Alexander spoke again. “Unless, you mean that time you did the nasty under the Carousel with Sasha, the Bearded Lady.”

“*God damn it,*” Jarrod thundered. “I knew we were being watched.”

Alexander chuckled. “The bearded lady?”

Jarrod punched his best friend in the shoulder. “Hey! Can I help it if I like ’em hairy?”

Sweat rolled off Milcham’s broad torso. He swung the heavy hammer hard, pounding the stake deep into the ground. It would be a pain in the ass to get it back out, but at least he wouldn’t have to worry about the Jumping Castle pulling free again.

Standing upright, he tossed the sledge down on the ground and made his way back to the generator. Picking up a wrench, he knelt and tightened the loose bolt. A woman’s laugh floated over the crowd, making him fumble. He flinched as bright red blood bloomed on his scraped knuckles.

Sucking on the offending digits, he cursed to himself. He heard her voice all around him, even in some woman on the Scrambler. Aithne was in his mind morning, noon and night, and it was driving him crazy. He’d thought by having sex with her she’d be out of his system, but he’d learned very quickly their time in the funhouse had made him want her even more.

Looking at his torn hand, he swore again. He glanced around, and seeing the others were on the far side of the ride, he squeezed his eyes shut so a tiny tear formed in the corner. Gently gathering it on his index finger, he smeared the moisture over the cuts.

Immediately, the cuts healed. The sides pulled together, and the flesh knitted so you couldn't even tell there had ever been an injury. Perfect healing, courtesy of a Phoenix's tears. Flexing his hand, he stared through the crowd. He could see Aithne sitting with Alexander and Jarrod, and his mouth tightened.

He pushed the anger away. He had no right to be jealous. She could be with anyone she wanted. They'd both agreed their lovemaking had been a mistake. So why did he keep thinking about it all the time?

Because, he argued to himself as he turned the last bolt, it had been good sex. No...he had to admit it. It had been *great* sex! His cock stirred hungrily as he remembered her wet, hot welcoming body. He could have stayed inside her forever.

The memory of her made him so horny, he'd actually tried to go out with another woman, but the thought of touching anyone else after Aithne almost made him ill. All he had to do was recall her coming apart in his arms and no one else could stir him.

With a muffled curse, he shot upright. It was over. There could be nothing between them. He damn well better recognize it. She was a temptation, but one he would fight against. She would not distract him from his real goal...finding his twin-flame.

Sitting above the crowd on the corner of the Tunnel of Love, the leather-winged demon narrowed its eyes. The Master had been furious when he'd discovered the Phoenix and the woman had been intimate. But the servant was confused. Just a few days before, it had been told to bring them together and now it was commanded to keep them apart. In fact...while the servant couldn't touch the Phoenix, the Master told it the woman was fair game.

It watched Milcham turn his back on Aithne and begin working again. "I will keep the two of you from getting close again," the creature snarled. "I am smarter than you, Phoenix, and I will do what my Master orders. The woman is not for you."

Aithne yawned as she made her way back from the community showers. It had been a long day, and she was exhausted. Ever since yesterday, when Mitzi had dropped her bombshell, she'd been on edge. She was tired and a bit sad, and she had to admit, she was horny, too.

After being with Milcham even her special toys didn't sound good. Though it had been a quickie, the sex they'd had was outstanding. Settling for a silicone cock just didn't seem as appealing.

As she passed the security guard watching the "back yard", which was where all the personal and storage trailers were placed, Aithne saw Milcham leaning tiredly against a ticket booth. Without thinking, she changed directions.

When she saw the look on his face, she wished she hadn't. "I'm sorry," she stuttered. "I...I just..." She gazed up at him, noting the tiredness of his face, and she swore there was new gray in his hair. "Are you okay? You look...beat."

He watched her so hungrily, she wanted to step closer and wrap her arms around him but she was stopped dead at his cool response.

"Thank you, but I'm fine. Just a little tired."

Aithne felt like a fool. It was obvious he didn't want to have anything more to do with her. Nodding, she turned to go.

They were both surprised when his hand shot out to stop her.

"I..." he muttered hoarsely. "How are you?"

She gave him a trembling smile. "All right."

"I didn't damage you."

Her face went pink. "No...of course not."

His hand dropped. "I was worried."

"There is no need," she said softly. "I'm a big girl."

"I can't seem to help myself."

He sounded so disgruntled, Aithne had to laugh. "You don't need to be annoyed about it."

"I am not annoyed. I just don't enjoy being distracted."

A smile curved her lips. "I'm a distraction? Me and about a thousand other things."

A grin touched his sensuous mouth. "You seem to have top billing right now."

"Milcham?" she said suddenly. "Can we be friends?" She searched his face anxiously. "I hate fighting with you."

His face went still. "Friends?"

"Yes...friends. We are going to see each other every day. We shouldn't be at each other's throats."

"You can forget the desire we have for each other?"

She blushed. "We decided we had to. Neither of us wanted that...distraction."

"I find it doesn't matter what was decided. I can't stop thinking about the sex we had together."

The air grew very warm around them. She swallowed...hard. "We're grown-ups, Milcham. We can be friends anyway."

He shook his head slowly as if finally realizing something. "I don't believe that's true, Aithne. I'm sorry. I can't be your friend. I can barely manage to be around you."

She gasped and her emerald eyes filled with pain. "That's a cruel thing to say."

Milcham looked away. His chest ached with suppressed emotion, but he would not give in to temptation. "I don't mean to be cruel, but I'm trying to be honest. I can't be friends with you without wanting a repeat of the funhouse. We don't belong together, so let's just leave it as is."

She said nothing, and when he finally looked back at her, Aithne's face was carefully blank. He touched her arm. "If you want to go, I won't hold you to your contract, you know that."

Her head shot back up. "Is that what this is about? Are you trying to hurt me enough so I'll leave?"

He growled angrily. "No, of course not. I just wanted you to know it is an option."

"Not for me," she said angrily. "I have people I care about here. And I'm staying. So you can take your *offer* and shove it!"

"Aithne!"

She tossed her head and turned away. "I don't know why I even bothered. But don't worry. I won't try to be nice to you...ever again." Without another word, she hurried away. He watched, his emotions in a tangle, as she disappeared into her tent.

"I told Alex if you hurt her, I'd break you in two."

Milcham jumped and cursed aloud as the big man slipped from the shadows. "Damn it, Jarrod, you scared the hell out of me."

"Why are you so tough on her? She's just about the sweetest gal I've ever known."

"Let it go."

"The hell with that. You've had sex with her, and now you won't even talk to her. That's cold, man! How do you think that makes her feel?"

"How do you know we had sex?" Milcham sputtered. "She told you? I can't believe—"

"She didn't say anything," Jarrod cut him off. "We found out through a third party. Weren't as quiet as you thought, were you?"

"God!" Milcham scrubbed at his face with both hands before looking at Jarrod. "It's complicated, okay? But trust me...I don't want to hurt her."

The wolfman stared into his eyes for so long, Milcham became nervous. The last thing he wanted was a fight with a supernatural. That would ruin everything. Finally, the man nodded. "Okay, Phoenix...but I'll be watching. If I even see you blink wrong, I'm going to—" Jarrod stopped suddenly and sniffed the air. "Do you smell smoke?"

Milcham froze. He trusted the man's greater olfactory skills. "Can you tell where?"

Jarrod shook his head. "No...but it's strong...and it's close."

He'd just finished speaking when a man's shout shattered the night air. Whirling, Milcham saw one of the hawkers. His heart stopped beating when he saw the man point straight at Aithne's tent.

"*FIRE!*"

Chapter Six

Aithne tossed her towel over the single chair and sat down hard on the bed. She sniffed inelegantly. He'd hurt her again. He seemed to make a habit of it. All she'd tried to do was smooth the waters, but apparently he really didn't want anything more to do with her. So much for great sex being the beginning of a relationship.

Frowning, she reached over and picked up the picture of Aidan and Dawn she had sitting on her table. "He's as much a pain as you were," she informed her brother. "Stubborn, arrogant, know-it-all."

Staring off across the tent, she battled tears. "I guess I have only me to blame," she said miserably to herself. "I did try not to, but..." She sighed as she admitted the truth. "I fell for him. As obstinate an alpha male as he is, I still care. You'd think in a hundred and twenty-four years, I'd have learned something about the opposite sex!"

Putting the picture next to her on the bed, she picked up her tarot cards and glared at them. "It's your fault, too," she muttered. "You and that stupid Lovers card." She opened the pack. "So maybe you can tell me what to do now."

Suddenly, she smelled smoke and she stilled. A lifetime of fear rose up and almost strangled her. Leaping to her feet, she glanced around but could see nothing. Where was it coming from?

Without warning, a billowing wall of fire leapt up between her and the front of the tent. It consumed the wall dividing the front and the back in seconds. Aithne screamed and stumbled back, falling against her cot.

All of her nightmares were coming true.

Her foot kicked something, and glancing down, she saw the oversized bag that held her wallet and other miscellaneous necessities. Instinctively, she snatched it up, dropping the cards and the picture of Aidan and Dawn inside. Slinging it around her neck, she looked around frantically for a way to escape.

The fire was monstrous. It seared her face and filled the small tent with choking clouds of smoke. She cried out again, terrified she wouldn't be able to get through. One of the side walls went up and the heat increased, filling the air with the pungent odor of burning canvas. Turning, she ran to the back, hoping she could slip out under the wall.

The second side wall flared up in an instant curtain of fire. The heat was so bad Aithne felt her eyelashes curl from it. Smoke filled her nostrils and she coughed, her throat burning from the acrid taste. Scrabbling at the back wall, she screamed for the one man she wanted to see more than anyone else.

"Milcham!"

Then a searing pain overwhelmed her and everything went black.

Outside, Milcham and Jarrod stared in horror as a curling tendril of flame wicked up over the top of Aithne's tent.

"*No*!" shouted Milcham hoarsely. He knew instantly it was a death trap for anyone inside. A second later, he heard Aithne scream and he forgot everything except the singular need to protect her. He ran for the door as a second wall of fire licked up the side of the tent with long, greedy bites. He could smell the burnt odor of canvas and the stronger scent of ozone.

A second scream rent the air and he swore out loud, heading for the still unburned front door of the tent. He was about ten feet away, could already feel the heat on his face, when he was hit from behind. Slamming into the ground, he swore and spit out dirt before leaping to his feet and glaring at the man who'd stopped him.

"What are you doing!" he shouted. "I've got to get to her!" He tried to continue, but Jarrod grabbed his arm.

The big man shook his head. "You can't do her any good getting yourself killed. You can't go in there half-cocked." His gaze slid to Alexander, who had arrived at the scene. "You go in like that, and we'll lose both of you."

Milcham pulled away. "I'll be fine. I can get to her." He stared at the two men. "Trust me. I don't have time to argue."

"Milcham—" Alexander began.

"What I need from you is to keep all these people back."

Jarrod snorted. "Don't be a fool. Let us help you."

"No," Milcham said sharply. "I have to do this alone. I need you to keep everyone...say...a hundred feet back. I don't want them to see anything." He stared at the two men. "You both have special abilities to do it. Make it happen."

The two men gaped at him. There was a tense, silent moment. Then, they nodded in sudden capitulation. "Go," Alexander said. "We'll do what we can."

"Milcham!" Her scream rose over the howling sound of the fire.

At the sound of his name, he turned and ran into the now blazing tent. He heard shouts from the other people outside, but his whole being was focused on finding Aithne. Terror rose inside him when he saw the whole inside of the tent was in flame. Was he too late?

His own inner flame burst into life, and he was enveloped in a white ball of protective fire. As he moved through the burning room, he instinctively dodged fiery pieces of canvas that rained down from the top of the tent.

His heart almost stopped when he saw Aithne lying behind her now burning cot. Flames licked at her feet and the wall behind her was starting to smoke. He rushed to her, and then hesitated. Would his fire do any less damage than this one?

She coughed, and he shrugged. What choice did he have really? He either flamed her with his own unique fire, or she would be burned alive in this one. Bending down, he lifted her into his protective arms.

Her eyes fluttered open, and she whimpered.

"It is all right, *assai*," he murmured. "I have you."

She blinked slowly at him. "You...you're on fire."

"You're hallucinating, Aithne," he answered soothingly. Standing upright, he stared around him at the walls of flame between him and freedom. "Go back to sleep. All will be well."

Obediently, she closed her eyes, going limp in his arms. Milcham prayed Jarrod and Alexander had taken care of the crowd. It was bad enough he would reveal himself to those two. He didn't want the entire carnival to know what he was.

He looked down at the unconscious Aithne, and a certainty filled his soul. He would have told the world if that was the only way to save the woman in his arms. She may not be his twin-flame, but he knew without a doubt that somehow...without even trying, she'd become the most important person in his life.

Outside the tent, Alexander's Ethereal friends and Jarrod's fierce demeanor were successful in keeping the carnival crowd far away from the burning tent. The two men stood and watched as Aithne's tent was consumed in red-orange crackling flames.

"There's no way they're going to make it out of there," Alexander said rawly. "No way in hell."

Jarrod's jaw clenched. "He said he could do it. We gotta believe him."

Alexander's sapphire eyes misted with tears. "But look at that place. He's not God, you know. He's just a simple man."

Just then a figure appeared in the fire. The crowd was too far away to see it, but the two men had a clear vision of what it was.

Alexander's mouth dropped open. "Okay…maybe *not* such a simple man."

Tall and strong, its wings wrapped around the small woman in his arms, the glowing figure of a large bird stepped forth. Its feathers shone with all the colors of the rainbow and light played eerily around its head. It was surrounded by fire, but this was different from the fire consuming the tent behind it. His flames glowed with light and music and beauty.

As it stepped out of the fire, it morphed into the smaller figure of a man. Still tall…still strong…still glowing from the backlight of the tent fire.

Milcham.

Pulled from their frozen trance, both men ran forward and grabbed him by the elbows, supporting him and the weight he carried out away from the fire. Behind them, they could see the other carny folk run forward with hoses and buckets, now free to keep the fire from spreading.

Dropping to his knees, Milcham laid his precious burden on the grass. Bending, he put his ear to her mouth.

"Damn it," he rasped. "She's not breathing."

Alexander quickly checked her pulse. "I don't feel anything."

Milcham cleared her airway and tilted her head back. "Do you know CPR?" At Alexander's nod, he put his mouth over Aithne's and gave her his life's breath.

"One, two, three," chanted Alexander along with the chest compressions he used. "One, two, three."

In between, Milcham breathed for Aithne. "Come on, *assai*," he murmured. "Don't leave me now."

Over the top of them, Jarrod clenched his fists impotently. "Come on, Aithne. *Breathe, damn it*! *Breathe*!"

As if she heard him, Aithne made a choking sound. Milcham rolled her onto her side where she coughed and gagged. Then he laid her back on the ground, stroking the hair away from her face. Her eyes opened slowly and seeing him, they filled with tears.

"Am I dead?" she rasped out. "Are we both dead?"

"No," he answered soothingly. "We are very much alive. You are safe now."

"I...thought I was dead," she murmured. "I saw an angel in the flames. I thought he was coming to take me to heaven."

The three men exchanged glances. Then Milcham smiled. "You must have seen me, *assai*. I rescued you before the fire got too bad." When Jarrod snorted, he narrowed his eyes at the big man. "You are sick from the smoke and you have a cut on your head, but other than that, you seem fine."

"You...you...okay?"

His chest tightened and bending, he kissed her dirty cheek. "I am well."

"Good," Aithne whispered. She reached out a hand, holding tight to his shirt. "I don't want...to lose you." She seemed to fall back into unconsciousness as she spoke, but they all breathed a sigh of relief. At least she was alive.

Jarrod fell to his knees. "Shit! That was too close."

Milcham watched her still face. "It was indeed."

"You saved her life." Alexander's quiet voice brought his head up. "And you were right. You *were* the only one who could do it."

There was quiet for a moment and then Milcham shrugged. "So now you know. As I know about you."

"How long?" Jarrod questioned roughly. "How long did you know I was a werewolf?"

"From the beginning."

"How?" Now it was Alexander who asked. "And why didn't you say anything about either of us?"

"I can see things most humans cannot. I respect your privacy. I know what it is like to be...different. You are both excellent workers and men I call friends. I would never betray that."

"What are you, exactly?" questioned Jarrod.

"I can answer that," responded Alexander. "You're a Phoenix, right? Your nature as well as your name."

"I am *the* Phoenix," Milcham corrected. "The only one in existence." He looked down at the sleeping Aithne. "I left my home centuries ago to look for a mate."

Jarrod grinned. "Looks like you found one."

"No!" Milcham shook his head. "She must not know what I am. I cannot tell her. There are...complications." He gazed at his friends. "I am not allowed to tell anyone who I am. I had no choice but to show you tonight—I had to save her—and there may be repercussions for me. But now I would ask you keep my nature a secret from everyone. Even Aithne."

There was a short silence, and then Alexander nodded. "We'll keep your secret, but I do think you should tell her. She knows about us."

"She does?" That was news to Milcham. He pondered a moment then spoke. "Still...she wouldn't understand. She is a normal human woman."

The two other men exchanged a look. "You'd be surprised, Boss," Jarrod snickered. "But it's up to you. We won't say anything."

"We can do no less," Alexander remarked. His azure eyes darkened with emotion. "You saved her life."

Milcham sighed and bending, gathered Aithne back into his arms. "I don't know why yet, but I have this sneaking suspicion by bringing her out of the flames it was my own life that was saved." He glanced over at the stinking, smoldering tent. "I'm going to take her back to my trailer and care for her. Will you make sure everything is all right out here?"

"Sure, Boss," Jarrod agreed with a nod. "I doubt anything can be saved. Where will she stay now?"

"With me." There was no doubt in his mind. He had made his decision when he saw her lying lifeless in the flames. She would belong to him for the time he had left. Thinking of how he almost lost her before he even really had her, Milcham suppressed a shudder. "I want to know how it started. Did she leave something on or..."

"We'll check," Alexander assured him. "I'll even ask around. There are several Ethereals watching."

Milcham nodded absently as Aithne shivered in his arms. "I will be in my trailer if you need me."

The two men watched as he walked away. "He may not think he's found his mate, but I'll bet differently," Alexander muttered.

"I ain't taking that bet," laughed Jarrod. "We both knew she wasn't for us. Now we know why."

"Still..."

Jarrod nodded. "I'm way ahead of you. If he hurts her, he's a dead man. Immortal Phoenix or not!"

Neither of the men saw the black figure slip away from the burning tent and fly into the darkness of the night sky.

Once in his trailer, Milcham wasted no time in setting Aithne down on his bed. He had to heal her before she woke up. He refused to let her be in pain, but he wasn't going to give away his secret.

It didn't take long to manufacture tears. One thought of losing her to the fire and his eyes misted immediately. Using his finger, he smeared the wetness over her filthy forehead and into the wound.

It was a deep cut, possibly made by something falling from above and hitting her on the head. Gradually it healed until the only sign was a thin, white line that over time would also eventually disappear. Once she was healed, he got a warm, wet cloth and ran it over her smoky face and neck.

Aithne climbed up through the smoke and haze, knowing twin emotions of fear and comfort. When her eyes opened she found herself looking at the grim, dirty face of Milcham. She sighed as he gently washed her face with a wet cloth. The anger on his face was in such contrast to his careful ministrations, she didn't know what to do, so she said the first thing that came to her mind.

"Are you...angry with me?"

He stilled. "Angry? No, I'm not angry. I was too scared to be angry."

"You look angry."

"Do I?" He smiled and it chased away the annoyance. "I'm sorry. I was thinking about how close I came to losing you."

Her heart skipped a beat. "I would think...having me gone would please you."

His eyes darkened. "Don't be an idiot."

She tried to lift her chin stubbornly, but coughed instead. "You were the one who tried to buy me off just before the fire started."

He stopped wiping her face and stared at her incredulously. "You think I did this? I tried to burn you out?"

Her mouth dropped open. "No! I didn't mean it that way. You'd never do something so despicable. I just meant you don't want me around."

Relaxing at her words, he nodded. "In that you are…were correct. But things have changed."

Her heart beat faster. "What do you mean? What's changed?"

Without hesitation, Milcham bent and pulled her carefully into his arms. "*I* have changed, *assai.* I have stopped fighting what I feel for you. Seeing you lying there, surrounded by fire made me realize how foolish I was being. I will not pretend you aren't important to me. I don't know what the future holds for us, but I will not waste any more time pushing you away."

Aithne listened, her eyes filling with tears. When he bent and brushed his mouth over her forehead, she pressed closer to him, her soul expanding with happiness. "You are special to me too, Milcham. I wanted to be friends with you. I still do."

Pulling back, he lifted her chin with an index finger. "I do not want to be friends, Aithne."

Her heart fell. "You don't?"

He smiled and her heart picked itself up and started racing again. "What I want is for us to be whatever we are destined to be." He leaned down and kissed her gently. "What you would like us to be."

The thought of The Lovers card flashed through Aithne's mind. "I want us to get to know each other. Without all the anger and ugliness between us."

"That, we can do," he agreed. "We will discover each other…in all ways."

The way he said it made her shiver in anticipation. She looked up at his smoky amber eyes. "In all ways."

Aithne stepped out of the shower, finally feeling clean. It was wonderful not to have to go use the public ones. Now she *knew* she would be getting her own trailer. This was the life.

Drying her hair slowly, she looked at herself in the small fogged-up mirror.

She'd been lucky. Other than being pale, and her eyelashes a little singed, she was no worse for wear. She'd thought she'd been dreaming when she saw her angel standing over her, but it had been no dream—it was Milcham who had saved her.

Frowning, she ran his brush through her long hair. She had seen him with flames all around him. It had been bad...that she knew. How had he managed to get to her without being burned?

Shrugging off the thought, she pulled on one of his white dress shirts. He'd handed it to her with a sexy smile saying he'd dreamed of her wearing it. She wasn't sure she believed him, but it made her body tingle at the thought.

Pulling it up around her face, she inhaled deeply. It smelled of him. Dark, sexy and all male. With shaking fingers, she buttoned it, smoothing it down over a body that was suddenly all too aware of the man in the other room.

After she found a new toothbrush and was able to brush the smoky taste out of her mouth, she felt a hundred percent better. At least when she faced him this time, she'd be clean.

When she opened the bathroom door, her mouth fell open. Milcham was standing in front of his stove in nothing but a pair of sweatpants. His messy hair was wet, and for the first time since she'd met him, he looked as if he'd shaved. His chest was bare, and she could see a dark tattoo of a phoenix in flight on his chest. The creature's wings were open, and its head was thrown back as it cried out to the heavens. It was beautiful and proud, yet in some way...so very lonely.

Just like the man who wore it.

The thought made her want to wrap her arms around him, but embarrassed at the idea of doing so, she blurted out instead, "You took a shower?"

He turned and saw her, and thanked God he'd put briefs on underneath his sweats. She was so sexy standing there in his oversized shirt with the arms hanging down over her hands, tails trailing to mid-thigh. Never had any woman looked so good. She filled out his shirt just fine, and she'd forgotten to close the top button, so he could see the shadow of her cleavage and the droplets her shower had left behind. Her long hair fell over her shoulders to her waist in an ebony waterfall.

"I didn't take all the hot water, did I?" she asked.

He took a deep breath, hoping the bulge at his groin wouldn't embarrass him. "No, I needed to check on things at your tent anyway, so I jumped over to the public house and took one at the same time."

She nodded and absently pushed back the sleeves of the shirt she was wearing.

"Here, allow me." Milcham walked over and carefully rolled back each sleeve. Inhaling the fragrance of his own soap on her sweet body made his cock twitch and he wanted to groan. "This way you won't be constantly pushing it up."

"Thanks," she murmured shyly. "I...I like your tattoo." She brushed her fingers over it. "A phoenix...right?"

He nodded, covering her hand with his own. "It is appropriate. It helps me remember what is really important."

She frowned at that cryptic comment, then bit her lip and looked up from under her lashes at him. "I used your extra toothbrush."

He nodded. "Good. That's what it's there for."

Stiffening, she pulled away. "Yes. You probably have a drawer full of them."

Milcham couldn't help but grin. Pulling her back into his arms he lifted her chin with his finger. "I will not insult your intelligence by telling you no other woman has been with me in this trailer." When she huffed, he wrapped his arms tighter. "But I *can* say no other woman has ever spent the night with me. Ever."

Chapter Seven

She went very still. "Really?"

"Really."

"And is that what I'm doing?"

Milcham cradled her face in his two strong hands. "Yes. Not only because you have no place to go." He kissed her again. "But, because I want you here...with me."

She chewed her lip, and he squelched another sigh. "I will not ask you to do anything you aren't ready for. This has been a long night for you."

Aithne cocked her head. "You'd sleep on the couch?"

He grinned sexily and ran a thumb over her full bottom lip. "No. I have a perfectly fine bed, and I'll sleep great holding you in my arms." He gave her a squeeze. "Only holding you...if that's what you want."

She grinned back up at him. "I'll think about it."

Laughing, he bent to brush her lips with his. "You do that, *assai.*"

Distracted, she pulled back. "What is that you keep calling me?"

"*Assai...* It means precious." He bent and kissed her again more lingeringly. "And you are...precious to me."

Reaching up, she grasped both his wrists. "I am?"

"I walked through fire for you, Aithne. Do you still doubt that I care?"

His words made her heart melt. “I know you care. It’s just...we didn’t start out so well, and I’ve never really been in a relationship before.”

Now it was his turn to pull away. “Never? A woman who looks as you do?”

Sighing, she relaxed into his arms. “I had a protective older brother and a set of extenuating circumstances. Maybe I’ll tell you about them someday.”

The feel of her body molded against his made him forget what they were talking about. He didn’t care about the past. All he was concerned about was the present. Spearing his fingers through her still damp hair, he slanted his lips over hers and kissed her. All the fear and need and emotion inside welled up out of him and into her.

Fireworks. Heat and light and color again filled both their minds. The kiss was a thing of beauty and they had only barely begun. Milcham speared his tongue into her mouth, forgetting his promise he wouldn’t push her. He needed her. Needed to know what they had shared before was no fluke. It had been an indescribable pleasure. Would tonight be the same?

Before he could take the next step to find out, there was a loud knock at the door. They sprang apart and then grinned at each other. Threading his fingers through hers, Milcham walked to the door.

“I’m not dressed,” she protested.

“You are as dressed as you need to be,” he argued. He wanted whoever was at the door to see her. It was primitive, but he wanted all to see her in his shirt. He would make his claim clear.

She huffed again but followed him. He opened the door to Alexander and Jarrod both. Their eyes swept past him and straight to her.

“You okay, Aithne?” Jarrod asked roughly.

She smiled. “Fine, thanks to you all.”

Alexander stared at her temple. “Your wound...it’s gone.”

"My…wound?"

Milcham glared at Alexander over her head. "I thought your forehead was cut, but it looked much worse than it was. You weren't really injured."

Too late, Alexander remembered about the healing properties of a Phoenix's tears. Now he understood what Milcham meant when he said he would take care of her. "Ummm, must have been all that soot."

"Did you have something to tell me?"

Jarrod was staring at Aithne's naked legs, so Alexander answered Milcham. "Wanted you to know what we found at the tent." His gaze flicked to Aithne. "Sorry, sweetie. It's a total loss."

Aithne's eyes filled with tears. "Oh my God."

Milcham put his arm around her and held her close. "You're alive. That's what counts."

"I know," she sniffed. "But there were things that couldn't be replaced. A portrait of my brother and his wife and my tarot cards. I put them in my purse when the fire broke out, but I must have lost it."

"Purse?" Jarrod snapped to attention. "You mean this?" He pulled Aithne's oversized bag from behind his back.

She gave a squeal of gladness. "You found it!" She gave him a hug and a kiss on the cheek. "Thank you!"

Jarrod shrugged. "It was around your neck when the boss carried you out. It must have come off when we were working on you."

"I have to see if everything is there." She flashed a smile at them. "Excuse me." Whirling around, she carried the bag to the bed to examine it.

The three men watched her indulgently. Then Milcham turned around. "What else did you find out? Did she leave her hotplate on?"

Jarrod swore under his breath as Alexander shook his head and answered. "No. It wasn't Aithne's fault, Milcham." He looked at the taller man, fury building in his usually quiet eyes. "It was arson. Someone doused the side of her tent in gasoline."

After Jarrod and Alexander left, Milcham sat beside Aithne. She was packing up her purse and smiling broadly. One look at her told him he wouldn't be telling her about the arson. She'd already been through too much that night.

She glanced up at him. "All my things are here. The miniature of Aidan and Dawn, my cards...even my wallet." She sighed. "Now I can get money to replace my clothes."

Milcham grinned. "Don't do it on my account." He flicked a long finger at her lapel. "I like you in my shirts!"

When she blushed, he laughed and pulled her against him. "'Course, I like you out of them, too. Remember, I've seen you naked."

Her emerald eyes widened. "I beg your pardon."

He nodded. "That night after those thugs attacked you in the woods? I got the vision you sent me."

She pulled slowly away. "Vision?"

Reaching out, he wrapped a strand of hair around his finger. "If you wanted to punish me for what I said in the field...you succeeded."

"Milcham. I don't know what you're talking about." She stared up at him. "I can't give anyone visions. My gifting is in reading the cards, that's all."

He started to laugh, but then stopped. She was serious. "You didn't send me a vision?"

"No."

Frowning, he thought of the overwhelming lust that had overtaken him. "I don't understand. It seemed so real."

"Tell me about it."

Slowly, he smiled. "You sure you want to know?"

The look on his face made Aithne's insides go warm. "I think I do."

"All right then." He leaned back and played with the top button on her shirt. "It was of you...and you were naked."

Her heart beat faster. "I was?"

"Not at first. You started out with a nightgown on."

"And then what?"

"Then you took it off."

"Were you with me?" Aithne thought of all the dreams she'd had of Milcham.

"No," he replied, surprising her. He flicked open the top button of the dress shirt so he had full view of the swell of her breasts. "You were alone. You were touching yourself."

"*What?*"

Milcham laughed and ran a long finger down the shadow of her breasts. "Yep. You were all alone and standing in front of a mirror." He opened the next button. "You were playing with your breasts, rolling your nipples between your fingers." Gently, he put his own action to the words, and she gasped. His hot hands covered the soft globes, making her nipples peak into his palms. They both groaned at the feeling.

"In...front of...a mirror?" That seemed familiar, but she had trouble thinking through the pleasure of what Milcham was doing.

"Umm hmm," he murmured as he undid the rest of the buttons, spreading the shirt open. "Yes...this is exactly what I saw." He cupped her breasts in his hands. "I wanted to be the one touching you." He licked his lips. "Tasting you."

Aithne's head fell back as he bent and sucked the crown of her breast into his warm mouth. Moisture pooled between her legs. When he bit down gently, she cried out and grasped his long hair.

He gave a hoarse snarl. "That's what you did then, too. You cried out as you pleasured yourself. I was so jealous. I wanted it to be me."

She arched against his seeking mouth. "You're touching me now," she gasped. "Please...don't stop."

"I don't plan to." His head moved down again, and he licked at the other nipple. Fire shot right to its tip. His swirling tongue never stopped. It sucked and teased and caressed until she was crying out his name.

Suddenly, he released her throbbing breasts. He kissed down the valley between them to her flat stomach. His tongue swirled around the small indentation in her belly and then moved lower.

"Milcham," she gasped as his mouth traced down over one thigh and up the other. His amber eyes glowed as he moved down over her curly mound. Without warning, he separated the soft folds and circled her clit with his tongue.

She almost came up off the bed in her surprise, but his hands held both her hips so she couldn't move. He stopped for a moment, pulling her forward to the edge of the mattress. Then he knelt between her legs. Gazing into her shocked eyes, he spread her folds with his thumbs, exposing her to the air. "My God," he muttered hoarsely. "You are so beautiful."

Her hands went to his head as he bent and licked at her wet opening. He ran his tongue up one side of her clit and down the other, making her whole body catch fire. He did that over and over again until she was writhing against him. Then suddenly, he blew on the throbbing flesh he'd teased.

She cried out his name. Desire curled in her stomach as her nipples went hard and pointed with need. She let go of his hair and covered her own breasts, rolling the aching nipples between her fingers.

Milcham growled aloud when he saw it. His body went from aroused to painful in a matter of seconds. It was just like the vision, but this time, he was with her. She was so sexy it hurt.

Ignoring the clamoring of his own body, he bent back to feast on her heated mound and pulsating clit. He licked and sucked, leaving the needy flesh to stab his tongue deep into her quim. She was dripping wet, and Milcham almost exploded just by tasting her. Sweet and spicy and delicious.

Her movements became wilder as she shifted back and forth against his seeking tongue. Wanting her to explode around him, he used his finger to squeeze and tickle her clit, while he buried his tongue inside of her, swirling and sucking.

She screamed as her climax hit her, pushing against him and almost falling off the side of the bed. He held her firmly with one hand as she clenched down on his tongue, filling his mouth with her juices.

He muttered against her, but refused to stop even as his cock burned with need. He continued to suck on her extended clit until she screamed a second time and convulsed, falling backwards onto the bed.

Stripping out of his sweats and underwear, he kissed his way up her panting body. "I have wanted this for so long," he muttered in her ear as he lay down on top of her. "You alone can make me burn."

Slowly, he slid inside her. His thought was to make this time slow and gentle, but once he was within, all his plans went out the window. She was wet silk and heat, and it had been too long since they'd made love. Gathering her tightly against him, he thrust hard and deep, already sensing his release was imminent.

Aithne moaned at his first driving stab. Her legs wrapped around his narrow waist, and her hands grasped at his shoulders. The movement brought him even closer to her.

God! He felt so good. He was big and hard and so hot, she wondered if he had a fever. He knew just how to move to stroke her nerve endings and it wasn't long before that same rapturous pleasure coiled up in her again. Reaching down, she gave his sculptured butt a squeeze.

He shuddered beneath her hands and his thrusts became wilder. He ground himself against her, bringing her aching clit flush against his driving cock.

That was all it took. She unraveled. The desire coiled within her released with a shower of heat and light. Her climax triggered his, and with a shout he pounded into her hard for several more seconds, then he went still, shuddering and throbbing inside her. Her hot channel milked him, pulling every bit of life from his body, before finally they both relaxed, collapsing into each other's arms.

His heart pounded against hers as it slowed, and smiling, she wrapped her arms around him. They were sprawled half on and half off the bed, their need for each other too great to move into proper position.

He rose up on his elbows and looked down at her. His face was possessive, with masculine satisfaction easily seen all over it. Bending, he kissed her, so gently, so tenderly, it brought tears to her eyes.

"I was going to take it slow. Finesse you with my wonderful lovemaking skills," he murmured. "But again...you destroyed me."

Aithne planted a kiss on his smooth chin. "You don't make it easy for a girl to go slow. I wanted you just as much."

"Impossible," he said as he pushed back her tangled hair. "I know how you make me feel."

She giggled. "Are we going to argue about who wants the other the most?"

Milcham gave her a crooked grin. "I know of much better ways to spend our time rather than arguing. If I hadn't been so stupid, we could have been together that first night. Instead I had to watch you pleasure yourself with a toy."

She froze in his arms. "You saw a *toy* in your vision?"

"Yes." Grinning, he nibbled the side of her jaw. "It looked just like a cock, very well endowed, I might add."

"You're bigger," she said absently, her eyebrows drawn together in a frown.

He blinked. "I am?"

Aithne touched his face. "In this vision, I was first in front of the mirror and then I...ummm...finished up in the bed?"

He nodded.

"I didn't send you a vision, Milcham, but what you're describing to me did happen that night."

"What?"

"I couldn't sleep because I kept dreaming about...your kiss." She blushed. "I was all hot and bothered, so I got up for a drink and...things just went on from there."

"Are you saying what I saw...actually happened?"

"Yes. Somehow you were allowed to see it. Don't you think that's weird?"

He nodded again. "Very. I found your string of bells in the meadow after the fight and was holding them in my hand. That's when I saw everything. But I don't know why it would happen. I'd thought you put a spell on it just to make me go crazy."

"As angry as I was with you, I don't have that ability." She chewed her lips in concern. "But where did it come from? And how?"

Milcham snorted. "I don't know. The vision made me so hot, I couldn't control myself. I couldn't stop." His cheeks reddened. "I took care of myself, standing outside my trailer. Thank God it was late, and there was no one around."

Her body warmed at the thought of him pleasuring himself as he watched her do the same. His cock swelling inside of her told her it was having the same effect on him.

"Hold on," he grunted. "I'm not going to be hanging off the bed when I make love to you a second time." Wrapping a strong arm around her lower back, he eased them both up the bed, then laid her down gently on a fluffy pillow. "There. Now we can at least be comfortable."

Aithne giggled, forgetting her worry about the vision. "I was comfortable before."

"Try being on top next time."

She smiled seductively at him. "Okay...is that an order?" She trailed her hand down his side to his hip, and his flesh stirred again. "It feels like you might be up for it."

His eyes flared, and with a strong move of his body, he rolled so that she lay over him. "I think I'll be up for anything you want to toss at me."

She sat up, slowly straddling him as he hardened within her body. "Be careful what you wish for. I never did tell you what job I had before I came here."

He could imagine her as a dozen things. Model, singer, actress. It would be something to show off her beauty, he was sure. "What did you do?"

Taking her long-nailed finger, she traced the intricate phoenix tattoo on his bare chest. He was completely hairless except for a fine line that went from his navel down to his groin. Milcham swallowed. If he was lucky, she'd follow that line with her tongue someday soon.

"My brother and I ran a toy shop."

"A toy shop?" The picture of the classic toy store FAO Schwarz came into his mind.

"Very special toys," she grinned. She ran her nail over his flat nipple and a shiver ran through him. "Kind of like what you said you saw in your vision."

Suddenly, it clicked and his mouth dropped open. "You and your brother ran a *sex* toy shop?"

She bent over him, her long hair tickling his chest as she nibbled on his neck. "Not just sex toys. I read the tarot cards, and we had an apothecary—an herb shop as well."

His mind went fuzzy with the way she was touching him. Already he was hard again and ready for action. He moved underneath her. "*Assai*... The only toy I am concerned about right now is you."

Her mouth moved to his chest and he grabbed at her hips as she licked at his nipples. "Aithne!"

"Do you want me to stop?" she murmured against him. Her teeth nibbled delicately, and he couldn't prevent a groan.

"God, no," he choked out. "But I want to last this time. And that doesn't make it easy."

"We have all night," she whispered seductively. "You can love me slow later. This time, I want to make you explode!"

And she did. Over and over again. For the first time in months, he seemed to have renewed strength and the virility he did when he was first reborn. When he thought back about it later, he knew it was the best night of his long life.

Aithne touched him as if he were the only man in the world. Her kisses made his heart race. And when she finally began moving up and down, riding his cock like she was an expert, his heart almost stopped, the pleasure was so great.

She took her time, bringing him close to the edge before backing off and kissing him until his heart evened out. Then she would do it again, lifting herself almost completely off of him and then easing down, inch by inch with excruciating slowness.

Milcham found himself arching up to meet her, his heels and elbows dug into the mattress while the rest of his body bowed up with the need to be closer.

When he heard himself begging for her to take him deeper...to finish him off, his own words shattered his self-control. Grabbing her hips, he slammed her down on top of him, making her cry out with pleasure. He didn't last long after that. With one push of his whole length into her, he came, his orgasm so powerful, he saw stars. He convulsed beneath her, barely aware she, too, was crying out in her own sweet release.

He felt like he would never move again. She felt like she was completely boneless, lying over the top of him. Neither had the energy or the inclination to separate their bodies. It went on that way the rest of the night. Sometimes, they would snatch a little sleep, but then one would reach for the other, and it would start all over again.

When she finally fell asleep in his arms, her soft cheek pressed against his beating heart, Milcham knew that soulmate or not, he was falling in love with this ebony-haired witch. And he had no idea what to do about it.

Chapter Eight

When Aithne awoke the next morning, she was alone. Rolling over on her side, she smoothed her hand across the pillow to touch the indent Milcham's head had made and grinned. It was the first time she'd ever spent the night with a man, though she hadn't told Milcham that. A girl had to keep her secrets.

She sat up, hugging her knees to her chest. What a wild night. She knew women were multi-orgasmic, but she'd had no idea a man could make love so many times. She'd lost count of the amount of times he'd been inside her.

Her tummy warmed. Milcham was an incredible lover. Even though they really never did the whole slow thing like he wanted. Every time they touched, it was like a fire exploded between them. Amazing.

She swung her legs off the bed and stood. When she took her first step, she gasped. "Okay," she muttered to herself. "I played, now I'm paying!" She gingerly made her way to the bathroom. If being sore was the cost for such a great night of sex, she'd pay it...gladly.

After a quick shower, Aithne wrapped a towel around herself. She still hadn't any clothes and she had no idea where Milcham had gotten to. Some carnival business, she hoped. She worried her lip. Or had her presence driven him from his own trailer? Maybe he was regretting his invitation she stay the night.

She glanced out the small window, and her eyes widened. It looked like most of the carny folk were gathered around what was left of her tent, working, sifting through the rubble and cleaning it up. Her heart expanded when she saw a shirtless Milcham in the middle, handing debris to Jarrod. Maybe he'd left her to go take care of that.

"I should be out there," she fretted out loud. "Not in here pretending to be sick." She went over to Milcham's closet and pulled the door open. There wasn't a lot there, mostly jeans and his ever-present muscle shirts. Then she noticed the sweats he'd been wearing last night, kicked carelessly into a corner.

She pulled them on, giggling at how they dwarfed her small body. Even though she was tall for a woman, in Milcham's clothes she looked as tiny as a doll. She cinched up the sweats as tight as she could, but they still sat low on her hips.

Shrugging, she wriggled into one of his muscle shirts and smiled. It covered her...barely. The sides dipped so low they showed the curves of her breasts, but she really didn't have much of a choice. She couldn't stay here naked while everyone else worked on her tent, and she wasn't about to wear one of his expensive dress shirts to get dirty.

She quickly braided her long hair, using a popped balloon from the dart toss game to tie the end. But she was stuck when it came to shoes. She'd lost all of hers and Milcham's shoes were definitely too big for her.

Digging through the bottom of his closet, she found a pair of cheap rubber flip-flops. They were about four sizes too large, but at least they'd protect her. She grinned, thinking she would rival Chuckles for clown feet.

She almost tripped climbing out of the trailer, but giggling, she continued on. As she got closer she could smell the choking scent of burned material, and she couldn't help but shudder. And when she saw what was left of her home, she gasped. How had Milcham saved her from that?

Carefully, she walked closer and bent to lift the remains of her sign out of the wet mess.

"What the hell are you doing?"

She jumped, tripping on the oversized shoes and falling back on her butt on the ground. Lifting her head, she glared up at Milcham. "What does it look like I'm doing? Knitting?"

There was a ripple of laughter as Milcham hauled her up off the ground. His eyes widened when he saw what she was wearing. The shirt was as tight on her as it was on him, her nipples showing plainly through the thin material. He growled, torn between appreciation and the knowledge he didn't want anyone else seeing her.

"You should be resting."

She rolled her eyes. "I'm not tired, even if I didn't get much sleep last night."

He ignored the stirring in his body. "You were almost killed yesterday, Aithne. I don't want you doing too much."

"It's my home you're sifting through," she returned quietly. "I need to be here." She bent and picked up what was left of the burned sign, making him curse under his breath at the display of her breasts against the shirt.

"You need to find some other clothes."

Her lips quirked. "I don't have a big selection. It was either this or go naked."

"Naked is good," tossed in Jarrod with a teasing look. He grinned at Milcham's glare.

"Everyone can see your…" Milcham gestured futilely at her chest. "You know!"

She wanted to laugh, but the expression on his face forbad it. "I don't have a choice. I refuse to wear one of your nice shirts."

"I will take you shopping, then."

Aithne looked at him in horror. "You will not! I can tell by the way you're acting, if it was up to you, I'd dress like a nun!"

"At least it would cover you," he grumbled.

She patted his arm. "I'll be fine."

He groaned when she lifted her arm and the side of her breast showed. "I don't know if I'll be."

"Then don't look!" she retorted tartly.

Narrowing his eyes, he caught her to him and pressed his mouth against hers. After a moment of shocked struggle, she surrendered, fitting herself against him to take what he was offering. The hoots and catcalls from their friends finally made them separate.

Aithne tossed her head at him, her cheeks stained with embarrassment. "I don't know what you want from me. You weren't there when I woke up."

He pulled her back to him. "I was trying to be a gentleman," he gritted out quietly. "You must be sore, and all I wanted was to fuck you again."

The rude word made her go moist between the legs. How could she want him again so soon after all they'd done last night? "I didn't know if you'd want me around so I got dressed and got out. These were the only clothes I could find. I'll replace them, so don't worry."

"Want you around? Of course I want you around. And I don't care about the damn clothes. I care about you!"

She bent her head, still unsure of her ground. "I told you I don't know how to do this."

He touched her face gently and grinned. "I'll tell you what. You just listen to me, and everything will be fine."

"You aren't the boss of me," she said with a shy smile.

He gave her a mock glare at her humor. "What I am is still to be decided."

Not sure how to answer that one, she just raised an eyebrow and turned away. She shuffled over to where Alexander stood.

"Are you all right?" he asked quietly.

"I'm fine." She held out her arms. "See...not a bruise on me."

"I mean...you and Milcham. He didn't hurt you?"

She stared at him in amazement. "He would never hurt me, Alexander. Why would you even ask that?"

Her friend shifted uncomfortably. "He is...a different type of man, Aithne. Intense. I'm just worried about you."

Aithne thought about the glorious lovemaking of the night before. If that was the intensity Alexander was talking about, she'd take it in a heartbeat. Her face went pink at the memory, and involuntarily she looked at Milcham. He met her stare, his eyes a dark amber, and then he smiled...very slowly. And that smile of his shot straight between her legs. Tearing her eyes away, she bent and began to help clean up what was left of her home, wondering if last night would be the only one they would have together.

They got the mess cleaned up just in time to open. Aithne wiped a sooty hand across her brow and sighed. "I'll have to go get another tent when I buy some clothes."

"No," Milcham responded, shaking his head. "I have one you can use. See? Jarrod's putting it up now. It's fireproof."

"But—"

"No buts," he interrupted. "It's a special circus-made tent so it's well crafted and flame retardant. If you use it, I won't have to worry about you anymore."

Her heart fluttered. "Are you sure?"

"I wouldn't say it if I wasn't."

She frowned as she watched it go up. "But it's so small. I won't have room to move in there."

"It's big enough. Plenty of room for your table and a couple of chairs."

"But I can't sleep on my table."

"No, you are going to sleep with me."

Everyone stopped what they were doing and stared. Aithne's face reddened. "Excuse me?"

He stood over her, his hands on his hips. "You don't need a bigger tent. All you need is a place for your game. You are going to stay with me."

Aithne's temper rose at his high-handedness. "Is that an order?"

"Do you want me to make it one?"

"Who do you think you are?" she sputtered indignantly. "You have no right to order me around."

"You gave me that right last night!"

Her mouth dropped open and her cheeks went even more crimson. "Do you mind?" she hissed. "That's private."

"*Assai,*" he growled. "You are the one who came out here wearing my shirt. You are the one who responded to my kiss. Do you really think they don't know we spent the night together?"

She stomped her foot, making his eyes go to her bouncing breasts. "I don't need you planning my life. If I want to tell people about us, I will. If I don't want to stay with you, I won't. I won't be ordered around by any man!"

Milcham swore out loud, raking his fingers through his dirty hair. "You think you can dictate to me?"

Aithne tossed her head. "I will be in control of my own destiny...thank you very much."

"I can't believe this," he shouted. "I am a very mild-mannered man, but with you...I am constantly angry!"

"You? Mild-mannered?" she shouted back at him. "You have the worst temper I've ever seen. All you do is yell. And I'm tired of it. You can take your tent and your orders, and go to hell." Turning on her heel, she stalked away, tripping again on the oversized flip-flops.

Milcham thought his head would blow off, he was so angry. Stomping after her, he grabbed her arm and swung her around to face him. “Don’t walk away from me!”

Her eyes spit green fire as she balled up her fist and took a swing at him. He ducked it easily, then pulled her hard against him. “Stop it!” he ordered.

“I said. Go. To. Hell!”

“Why are you doing this?” he snarled at her. “We shared something special last night, yet today you deny me. Why?”

She struggled in his arms. “Let me go!”

“No…*assai*…please! Explain your anger to me.”

“You have no right to ask me anything!”

His eyes narrowed, and he let her go so abruptly, she staggered. “True.” He lifted his hands in a placating motion. “You’re right. I don’t. But I do care. I thought you understood that.”

Aithne stared at him, taken aback by his reversal. “I don’t know what you feel. Not really. Things have changed so fast, I’m confused.”

“Didn’t my body tell you last night?”

She snorted and crossed her arms in front of her. “One thing I learned at the toy shop is a man can get it up for many reasons.”

“I am not just any man,” he returned angrily. “I am the man who cares for you. I cared enough to save you from the fire last night. I cared enough to keep you with me all night long—something I have never done with any woman before. And I care enough to let you make the decision to walk away. But I do want to know *why* you are doing it.”

Her eyes filled. He stood in front of her so arrogantly implacable, she wanted to scream. He reminded her of Aidan when he’d lay down the law and make decisions without asking her opinion. He also reminded her of her brother who’d risked his life for her more times than she could count. Her anger fell away, and looking up at him, she could do nothing but tell him the truth.

"I'm afraid."

Milcham's arms dropped. "Afraid? Afraid of what?" He hadn't expected those words.

She looked at her oversized shoes. "I've spent a very long time doing what someone else needed me to do. I don't regret my choices. They were done for love. But now...now I want to be able to make my own decisions. I want to live for me...first." Her emerald eyes stared up at him as she whispered, "I have to."

The emotion in her face made his throat ache. His chest pained him in a way he'd never experienced before. He wondered just what it was she'd had to do before she'd come here...to him. Without any more thought, he held out his arms to her. "Then I'm asking you, Aithne. Not telling. I care. Very much. Stay with me, please. I want you with me."

When she stumbled into his arms, he held her tightly, closing his eyes against the sting of his own tears. It would not be easy to go against his own demanding nature, but he would try. He would give her the choices she asked for. For he had *no* choice. Not anymore. The thought of being without her was fast becoming unbearable.

Milcham rubbed his eyes as he stared blearily at the accounting sheets in front of him. He was tired of doing numbers. What he wanted was to be in bed with Aithne, her sweet lips tracing their way over his body.

Groaning, he stared at a nearby mirror, noting the new age lines appearing on his face. He could tell he was getting close to the end of his millennium. Another reason he wanted her with him. He was running out of time. If she was here, he wouldn't be doing these stupid books, he would be loving her. But she was out, doing who knew what with Jarrod and Alexander, while he was stuck working.

He shook his head at himself, knowing he sounded like a pouting child. But ever since Aithne had come to live with him three days ago, he wanted to spend every minute with her. In bed, out of bed, it didn't matter.

When she was working or out with friends, he was restless and impatient wanting to be with her. Plus, he was still worried they hadn't found the arsonist yet. He didn't like knowing Aithne was in danger, although he was careful to give her the space she'd asked for. It was too easy to remember her tears of before.

But he couldn't change his nature completely. And he refused to do so. When he wanted her, he took her, no matter what the circumstances. Once, he'd even bulled his way into her new tent between readings. He'd put the closed sign on her door, swept the cards off the table and tossed her on it.

It had been hard, fast and carnal. And...very satisfying. He'd left her with a smile on her face, even as she fussed at him for making a mess.

He grinned. For all her bragging about owning a sex toy shop, Aithne was actually very shy and careful with him in public. In private she was incredibly sensual, but when they were out and about, he could barely get her to hold his hand. It bothered him. A lot. He'd never thought he would be as demonstrative or possessive about a woman, but with her he was, and there was a part of him that wanted her to be the same.

They'd actually argued about it the night before. She'd stiffened when he'd touched her while she was reading the tarot for Alexander, and it pissed him off. They'd gone to bed angry at each other, but after a few minutes, he couldn't stand it anymore. He'd pulled her to him and while murmuring sweet words, he'd shown her just how much he wanted her...in bed or out. When her loving arms wrapped around him, he knew he was forgiven.

She was going to drive him insane.

A knock at the door startled him.

"Come in!"

The grinning face of one of the jugglers poked in the door. He bobbed his head in greeting. "Hey, Boss."

"Joe." Milcham nodded back. "What can I do for you?"

The man snickered. "Got this for you." He handed Milcham an envelope, and with another bob of his head, he was gone.

Milcham frowned, turning the note over in his hands. There was no name, just a blank envelope. Tearing it open, he took a deep breath as the scent of flowers tickled his nostrils.

It was Aithne's perfume.

Carefully he pulled out the missive. There, in Aithne's beautiful writing was a note...

My Dearest Milcham,

You have given me so much and expected so little. Now it is time for me to do something special for you. So put away your little scribbles and come to me. The rest of the evening is ours.

Meet me at the Ferris wheel. You won't be disappointed.

Aithne

PS... Don't wear underwear.

Chapter Nine

Milcham had never moved so fast before. He got his books put away and his clothes changed in record time. Now he was standing in front of the Ferris wheel...but Aithne was nowhere to be seen.

He glanced over at Jarrod who was the ride jock that night for the big wheel. He sat in the ride's doghouse with a sly look on his face as he watched Milcham.

"Lookin' for someone, Boss?"

"Aithne," he answered, knowing good and well the big man knew exactly what was going on. "Know where she is?"

Jarrod chewed on a straw. "Might."

"You want to tell me?"

The werewolf grinned. "Nope." He nodded to behind Milcham. "Don't need to."

"I'm here, Milcham."

Turning, he saw her. She was in the gondola that had just come to a stop. She smiled at him, and when Jarrod undid the safety bar, she patted the seat beside her, her sultry green eyes teasing. "Want to take a ride?"

"On the Ferris wheel?"

Her dimples flashed. "For a start."

Frowning, he climbed in beside her.

Jarrod snickered as he put the bar down. "Have fun, you two." He glanced at Aithne. "You remember what I told you."

She nodded and blushed. “Thank you.”

Stepping back, Jarrod saluted them both, and then turned back to restart the wheel.

Milcham raised a blond eyebrow. “What was that about?”

Aithne giggled. “You'll see.”

Sitting back, Milcham put his arm around her. He loved the view of his carnival from the top of the wheel. This late at night, all you could see were the lights of the nearby rides. It gave the car a feeling of being completely alone in the world. He pulled Aithne closer and dropped a kiss on her upturned nose. “I haven't done this in a long time.”

“Really?” Her voice was full of laughter, and when they passed by Jarrod on the ground, Milcham saw he was grinning like crazy. The ride stopped to let off and take on passengers, but it was several times around before Milcham realized they were the only ones on their part of the wheel.

“What's going on?” he questioned out loud, when the ride went to full circling speed. “We're only half full. Everyone's on the other side from us.” When the lights dimmed, he frowned. “We lost the lights, too! What's he doing?”

“I'd say he's doing me a favor. You, too.”

He turned back to her just in time to see her slip out from under the safety bar. “Aithne! What in God's name are *you* doing?”

“Okay, folks,” she whispered nervously. “Don't try this at home.” Quickly, she knelt between his legs and looked up at him with a shy smile. “So how 'bout it, mister? Wanna have some fun?”

He stared down at her, his cock going instantly hard. She couldn't mean what he thought she did...could she? “I—” The sound was too hoarse, so he cleared his throat and tried again. “I don't know if I understand.”

She smiled and reaching up, gently undid his belt. “I think you do.”

His hand covered hers as he thought about their angry words of the night before. “Aithne. You don’t have to do this. I didn’t mean—”

“I know,” she interrupted as she carefully undid the top button of his jeans. “But you were right. I was letting my worry about relationships get in the way. I’m not going to any longer.”

He groaned when she stroked him gently before carefully unzipping his pants. “Still...all I was talking about was letting me kiss you.”

She giggled. “You can kiss me later. Right now, all I want is a taste of you.”

Milcham swore as the car went by the ground. Luckily, his Ferris wheel had a gondola car-type of seat, so no one could really see what Aithne was doing. It was just the knowledge she was going to give him a blowjob in public made him completely aroused and achingly hard in seconds. When her hand pulled his already engorged cock from his jeans, he moaned.

Aithne smiled at the sound. Her cheeks were flushed with a mixture of embarrassment and arousal, but she didn’t stop. She wanted to touch him. To taste him. To prove to him she wasn’t ashamed of how they felt about each other. She was making this choice.

“You’re so hard,” she whispered as she stroked his naked penis. “Like steel wrapped in silk.” She closed her hand around him and pumped gently. “Do you like this?”

“*Assai*, I like it too much.”

She laughed softly. “Never too much, Milcham.” She continued pumping until a tiny bead of pre-come appeared on the head. She bent and licked it off, causing him to groan even louder. “I do like your taste.”

Bending lower, she tugged his pants down slightly so she could get to his balls. They were tight and drawn up hard against his body, but she pulled them free and carefully rolled them in her hands.

"*Christos*!" Milcham exclaimed as he grabbed onto the side of the car. He closed his eyes, his face tight with pleasure.

"I think you're ready," Aithne murmured. Gently, she tasted him. Starting at his balls she licked slowly up the underside of his shaft until she got to the small ridge of flesh just below the base of the head. There, she rapidly flicked her tongue back and forth. She heard him swear, and his hips thrust forward involuntarily.

Again, she started at the bottom and made her way up, but this time after the teasing flick of her tongue, she licked the weeping head, swirling her tongue into the slit where even more pre-come oozed.

"Aithne," Milcham gritted out, his voice tight with need. "Don't tease me."

She was heady with the power she held over him at this moment. So often when they made love, he was in charge, but this time she was, and she intended to savor it. "Am I teasing?"

"You know you are!" He growled out the words.

"But Milcham," she whispered, giving his cock a quick swipe with her tongue. "I haven't even started yet."

Without another word, she took him into her mouth. He tasted dark and hot and smoky, and her panties went wet at his flavor. Refusing to hurry, she moved her mouth along his hard length, taking a little more of him in with each stroke.

Milcham's eyes rolled back in his head. Her mouth was so warm, he almost exploded immediately. Each suck, each sweet flick of her tongue brought him closer to ecstasy. His hips began to move with her, and he muttered again as she took him deep into her mouth.

Up and down she went, flicking her tongue at the head with each stroke. Heat shot through him with the strength of a firestorm, and without thinking, he grabbed the back of her head to pull her closer.

She whimpered, and the sound was like touching a match to already hot tinder. Her mouth moved quicker now and he found himself matching her rhythm as he thrust against her sweet lips with his hips. His balls ached, and his release started low, down deep in his stomach. He swore again.

"*Assai*," he said through gritted teeth. "I am too close. Pull away or it will be too late."

She shook her head, her hand wrapping around his lower shaft and squeezing as she continued her sucking motions. When he tried to push her away, she glared at him with hot emerald eyes.

His eyes glowed with his own golden fire. So she would take all of him? Without any further fight, he kept their gazes locked as he allowed her to finish him.

Her strokes grew harder as his hips plunged wildly against her. Her mouth pulled at him greedily, and when he cried out her name, she reached up and gently squeezed his balls.

Lights danced behind his eyes as he exploded into her mouth. Holding her head against him, he cried out and convulsed, unable to control himself. She swallowed frantically, trying to take it all in, and those motions set off other tremors, making his release even stronger. He'd had blowjobs in the past, but nothing could prepare him for how this woman made him feel.

He shuddered against her until he finally was able to let go of her head and she released him. The cool air touched his wet cock, and he sighed at that erotic sensation. Leaning his head back, he sprawled over the seat, completely undone.

Aithne wiped her mouth on his pant leg, and then carefully put him back inside of his jeans. As sensitive as he was, he shuddered at her touch, so she decided to leave the zipping up to him. The last thing she wanted to do was ruin a good high by getting some short and curlies caught in the zipper.

Slipping back under the safety bar, she cuddled next to him, stroking his still heaving chest. "Should I tell Jarrod to go again?" she murmured after several long moments.

Milcham chuckled and pulled her close. He framed her face in his hands and kissed her deeply, tasting himself on her. "*Assai*...that was..." He broke off and shook his head, searching for words. "Indescribable. Thank you."

She giggled and nipped at his lower lip. "I hope I've shown you just how much you mean to me."

He groaned again. "If you show me any more, I will die a happy man."

"Don't die yet," she said mischievously. "The evening's just beginning."

He sat up and stared at her. "You mean there is more?"

She nodded and then pointed at his pants. "You better put that away. The lights are going on."

Red touched his cheeks as he gingerly zipped up. "Was he watching us the whole time?"

Aithne grinned. "Jarrod? No. He was very careful to give us our privacy. No lights, no riders close to us. The guests won't complain. They got a nice long ride out of it."

"Now that it is over, I can't believe you did it."

She touched his cheek. "I wanted to, Milcham. I promise. I didn't do anything I didn't choose to do."

He pulled her close and held her tightly against him. Her body was very warm, and she moved against him restlessly. "What about you?" he murmured. "Am I being selfish?"

She kissed the side of his neck as the car came to a stop. "Don't worry about me. I have something fun planned that we both will enjoy."

Even though he'd just finished coming, his cock stirred at her words. But before he could answer, he saw Jarrod's amused face.

"Have a good ride there, Boss?"

Milcham's neck went red. Then he laughed and pounded his friend on the back. "It was the best ride I have ever had on that wheel," he pronounced, ignoring the giggling Aithne. "You are a hell of a ride monkey."

Jarrod gave a crooked grin. "My pleasure." Then he chuckled slyly. "Or should I say...yours!"

"Jarrod!" Aithne huffed as she grabbed Milcham's hand and pulled him away. "Enough...ride talk."

The men both burst into laughter and she blushed prettily.

"Come on, *assai.*" Milcham tried to control himself. "Lead on to your next enjoyable...activity."

"Have fun, you two," Jarrod called before he loaded up the next set of riders. He watched enviously as the two lovers disappeared into the crowd. It took a special type of woman to handle a *were* like him, and he'd yet to find her.

"Well," Milcham demanded as he steered Aithne out of the way of a drunk carrying a huge stuffed elephant, "where to now?"

"Where else?" She smiled up at him. "The Tunnel of Love."

He pulled her closer to him. "You know that's a special place. Full of nooks and crannies, where who knows what could happen."

She smacked him smartly on the butt. "I'm counting on it."

A few minutes later, they stood in front of the attraction. One of the two dark rides in the carnival, The Tunnel of Love was a crowd favorite. When the ride jock saw who was standing there, he grinned and motioned them forward.

"Hey, Boss...Aithne. Was expecting you."

"Does everyone know what you're up to?" Milcham murmured in her ear.

She giggled again. "No...just a few."

Once they were seated and on their way, he pulled her close to him. The Tunnel was set up with soft lights and dark passages so you had the sense of a slow gondola ride down the canals of Italy. Soft music played and the scent of roses filled the air. Italy was one of Milcham's favorite places in the world, so when he'd designed The Tunnel of Love, he'd thought of that most special lover's outing. "You know these rides all have cameras, right?"

She nodded. "Yes, which is why Alexander is in the control room tonight." She waved at the overhead camera. "He's the only one I'd trust to make sure they got turned off at the right times."

"I thought he had a show tonight."

Aithne shrugged. "He got someone else to do it."

Milcham shook his head, incredulous she had made so many changes to his show. For a moment he couldn't decide whether to be annoyed she'd done it, or impressed she cared enough to go to all that work. What he was thinking must have showed on his face because she said worriedly, "I overstepped, didn't I? I'm sorry. I was trying—"

He silenced her with a long deep kiss. He didn't stop until she moaned and relaxed against him. "I'm not upset, *assai*. It just shows me how important this night was to you. How can I be angry over that?"

"We did make sure everything was covered...I promise."

He stroked the hair back from her face. "I'm not worried. Alexander knows almost as much as I do about running this place. With him in your corner, I know all will be well."

She gave a sigh of relief. "Good. I just wanted tonight to be special."

Putting his hand on her long skirt, he pulled it up so he could touch the smoothness of her calf. "So far...it has been most wonderful." He inched his hand up her naked leg. "Are the cameras off?"

"They should be," she said breathlessly.

"Good." He smiled and caressed her lips with his own. "Now, I can return the favor." His hand moved up her leg and over her quivering thigh. "I am going to touch you. I'm going to make you explode like you made me."

Her eyes fluttered shut as his hand stroked across the crotch of her panties. "*Assai*," he groaned. "You are already wet for me." His thumb rubbed gently against her clit and her hips shifted involuntarily. "I love the way you respond to me. So hot and wild."

"Milcham," she gasped, her body already on fire. If she wasn't careful, she would toss her plan out the window and just let him do what he wanted. But she'd thought long and hard about this. She had to be strong.

Reaching down, she grabbed his wrist. "Wait!"

He froze and his amber eyes locked on hers. "What? Why?"

Gently, she pushed his hand away and kissed him. "Because," she murmured, "I have something else in mind."

Milcham sat back and watched as she pulled a small box from her pocket. Leaving her skirt bunched up around her thighs, she handed it to him with a smile. His cock twitched at the sexy picture she made sitting there.

"What is this?"

"Open it and see."

Curiosity filled him as he popped open the lid. A small silver cylinder about two inches long lay next to a tiny remote control. His breathing quickened, and he looked up at Aithne. "What is it?"

"It's called a *Silver Bullet*." She licked her lips seductively, looking remarkably like a sleek, sexy cat. "Can you think what to do with it?"

His twitching cock went to full arousal in an instant. He swallowed, hard. "I…I can guess."

She turned slightly in the seat and put her foot up on the front of the boat. Her skirt fell back, exposing her thong panties to his lustful eyes. "Let's see if your guess is correct."

His heart racing, he picked up the small vibrator and leaned over to her. Gently, he rubbed it against the crotch of her panties. She gasped, but when he used his finger to move aside the fabric, her eyes dilated and she cried out softly.

Milcham had to fight not to take her right then and there, but he knew the ride would soon be over. He didn't have time to do anything...yet. Instead, he eased the Silver Bullet behind the fabric, letting it rest between her panties and her soft wet folds.

"Let's see how this works," he said hoarsely. Taking the remote from the box, he flicked the *on* switch.

Aithne jerked and her mouth fell open slightly. Her eyes closed in utter enjoyment. "Oh, God," she whimpered. "It feels so good."

He moved closer to her and stroked her leg. "You sound surprised."

She opened her eyes and looked at him. "I...never used this before." She smiled, so innocently seductive, he fought again for control. "Never had anyone I trusted enough to...give that control to. Just heard about it...from customers."

Milcham's throat tightened. Her trust was worth a thousand lifetimes of pain and loneliness. He bent and kissed her before he lost total command of himself. Out of the corner of his eye, he saw the end approaching, so he pulled Aithne's leg off the front and draped her skirt back over her legs. She moaned into his mouth as the movement brought the vibrator closer to her clit.

"Don't come yet," he muttered against her ear. "You have to wait until I give you permission."

Her shudder was his only answer.

They drifted into the light, and Milcham nodded to the ride jock. "Send us again," he ordered hoarsely as he bent his head back to Aithne's sweet lips. "We haven't finished our ride." They both ignored the man's grin as they stared into each other's eyes.

"Milcham," she whispered as they headed back into the dark. "What are you doing?"

"Loving you, *assai,*" he answered. He continued to kiss her as they made their way again through the garishly lit tunnel. His hand came up to cover her breast, and she arched into him with another soft sigh. In answer, he flicked the switch on the remote to a faster speed, watching her tremble slightly before she grabbed at his hand.

"Please, Milcham," she whispered. "I can't...I can't take much more."

He rolled her nipple between his fingers. "Oh, but you will. You don't want to be punished, do you?" His teeth nipped at her lower lip, making her jump.

"Punished?" she gasped, her hips undulating against the vibrations on her clit.

His hand moved from her breast to between her legs, cupping the vibrator against her tightly. "I will punish you with such pleasure you won't be able to stand up," he whispered in her ear. "What I will do, you cannot imagine. So don't come, Aithne. Don't come."

His words were meant to inflame. To send her over the edge into oblivion. Between them and the vibrations against her clit, she couldn't stand any more. The heat inside her that had started with her pleasuring Milcham coiled tighter and tighter until it did explode. His mouth swallowed her screams, his hand held her down as she shattered, letting her convulse again and again, until she was a limp puddle in his arms.

She drew a ragged breath when he released her mouth. He chuckled and turned off the vibrator, but instead of removing it, he reached down and very gently pushed it inside her sensitive quim.

Aithne cried out as the new sensation set off more tremors inside of her. "Milcham," she croaked out, her voice hoarse from her climax. "What are you doing?"

He chuckled again, and his hand massaged her soft folds. "I'm punishing you, *assai.* I'm punishing you."

Chapter Ten

Aithne stared up at him with dilated eyes. He was going to kill her with this pleasure. "I can't," she whispered. "It's too much."

"I will be the judge of that," he said with a touch of his old arrogance. Gently, he smoothed down her skirt and pulled her to him. "Is it uncomfortable?"

The Bullet was cool and smooth inside her, but it wasn't painful. "No, but Milcham—"

"Hush, *assai.* You disobeyed me. You have to take your punishment now."

They rolled into the lights of the carnival. The ride jock grinned. "Another round, Boss?"

Milcham shook his head. "I think we will move on to something else." He helped the unsteady Aithne from the boat.

Aithne followed him mutely, wondering how the evening had been wrenched from her control. She wasn't unwilling. In fact, the opposite was true. It was just no matter how she tried, Milcham was too alpha of a male to give up control for long.

Putting his arm around her, he nuzzled her neck. "Are you all right?"

She chuckled weakly. "I'm not sure yet."

"Now you know how I felt on the Ferris wheel."

Leaned against him, she sighed. "So do you know where we are going next?"

He grinned down at her. "I have a few ideas."

The next few hours were the strangest and most achingly pleasurable of Aithne's life. Milcham was determined to bring her to the brink as many times as possible, yet he never allowed her the full release again. Her lips were almost bitten through, trying to control herself.

He took her on the Tilt-A-Whirl, and they swirled and kissed and laughed. Just when she'd almost forgotten about the Bullet, he turned it on, making her screech with surprise, and him roar with laughter. The movement of the ride and the vibration in her quim brought her quickly to the edge, but just before she could find satisfaction, he turned it off, chuckling at her heartfelt groan.

Next he dragged her to the Octopus, where each time they sank sharply to the ground, he'd turn the device on, whispering that that's how it would be when he drove deep inside her. His words, as well as the gadget, made her tremble.

Then it was off to the Zipper, where Aithne balked until he promised not to make her go upside down. But once they were airborne and the toy was vibrating deep inside her body, she didn't care about the ride. All she wanted was to come and come hard. When he turned it off, she almost wept.

She had a break when they rode the YoYo Swing. This was a ride that had a chair suspended from chains spinning around in a large circle. Since they were individual chairs, Milcham couldn't stay close enough to make the vibrator work. But he made up for it on the next ride.

The Carousel. One of the most gentle and placid of rides at a carnival, Milcham turned it into an instrument of delicious torture. He smilingly helped Aithne onto a horse, and then climbed on the one next to her. At first it was just a normal ride, but then after a while, each time the horse would begin its downward motion, he would turn on the vibrator. The motion of the horse between her legs and the tickling sensations inside her were almost more than she could stand. By the time the ride was over, she was wild with need and could barely walk.

One look at her and Milcham knew he had to end it now. Her face was covered in a sheen of perspiration, and her eyes were dilated so much you could barely see the green.

He pulled her into the Round Up. A ride that uses g-force to spin you so fast, when the bottom of the ride drops out, you stay in place. He stood next to her, watching her closely, and waited until the ride was at its zenith before turning the tiny vibrator back on.

He knew the second she was going over the edge. The g-force held them in place, but he forced his mouth to her ear. "Come for me, *assai.* Now! And here...you can scream all you want!"

She did, her orgasm ripping through her with such strength she screamed his name over and over again. She convulsed against the wall, her face taut with pleasure. Because she couldn't move, it was if she was being restrained, adding to the enjoyment. It went on and on for as long as the ride lasted. Then, when it slowed, he turned the toy off and caught her in his arms before she fell into a heap on the ground.

She was so shaky he had to carry her out, but everyone who saw them thought it was the ride that had done her in.

His own need beat at him as he carried her over to a nearby bench and sat with her in his lap. He kissed her gently. "Did you enjoy your punishment, Aithne?"

She whimpered and bit his chin, none too gently. "You know I did. But *you* enjoyed that a little too much!"

His eyes flared at her bite. "Ahhh, don't you understand watching you was as pleasurable for me as it was for you?"

She shifted, the rock-hard erection he still sported poking at her hip. "I guess we should take care of that."

Milcham smiled. "Should I carry you back to our trailer? Or did you have another adventure planned for us?"

She giggled, getting some of her strength back. “I’ve heard about having sex on a roller coaster,” she offered. “I’m game if you are.”

His body throbbed. “Too many people, *assai*,” he answered hoarsely. “But someday...I promise you.”

She leaned her head on his shoulder. “Then it’s your choice.”

He thought quickly. Where else could they make love without having too many prying eyes? He wanted to bury himself deep within her body. Feel her writhing beneath him. His gaze swept over the sparkling lights of his carnival. Then he smiled.

“I have the perfect place.”

“This next ride will be a private one,” Milcham informed the ride monkey who stood below the Rocketship. It was an attraction using a long rocket-shaped car that lifted into the air and spun and dipped. “Take us high, and keep it at a low speed. We want to look at the lights of the carnival.”

The man grinned as he cast an amused glance at Aithne. “Y’all having a good time tonight?”

She giggled, completely at ease with herself and Milcham. “It’s been fabulous, Timmy.”

He grinned shyly. “Good. The boss works too hard. You’re good for him. He needs to have some fun.”

“I’m standing right here,” Milcham grumbled.

Timmy chuckled and opened the door to the rocket. “Here you go, sir. I’ll keep it going until you wave it down.”

Milcham followed Aithne into the narrow car. “Looks like an oversized Bullet,” he muttered with a grin.

She giggled and sat on the bench. “I have to take *my* Bullet out.”

He straddled the seat and pulled her into his arms as the door closed behind him. "No!" He leaned in close. "It will be my pleasure to do it for you."

Her eyes widened and then she gasped as his hand moved up her leg in a familiar tickling motion. "Again? I don't think I can..."

His eyes heated. "This time, we will do it together." His mouth crushed down on hers as the rocket shot off the ground.

Aithne was pressed back into the seat with Milcham's big body on top of hers. His lips slanted over hers in an almost desperate kiss. The kiss was deep and carnal and so very possessive. Suddenly, she was as frantic for him as he was for her.

Her arms wrapped around him as she twisted her hands in his long hair, pulling him even closer to her. Her surrender fanned the fire within even hotter. Their tongues danced and tasted and fought for supremacy, but neither one would give in.

Milcham felt the change in her. From purring kitten to raging tigress, his already over-stimulated body could barely take it when her hands moved from his hair to his ass, pulling his throbbing cock into the vee of her thighs.

He groaned and his control slipped. With a quick flick of his fingers, he had her skirt undone. He tossed it onto the floor and her sodden panties were next. He continued his assault on her sweet mouth as he toed off both their shoes.

He had to stop kissing her for a moment, to get his own jeans off, but soon they joined her clothes in the heap and his mouth was moving voraciously over hers again.

Shirts were next, and within just a few seconds they were both completely naked. He ran his hand up her curved waist to a plump breast. "You have me so hot," he murmured against her kiss-swollen lips. "Lying here, knowing we are fifty feet off the ground with people all staring at us. And soon I am going to be deep inside you making you scream again."

She gasped and moved under him. "Milcham…make love to me, please. I don't want to wait any longer."

Her breathy voice made him go even harder. Shakily, his hand made its way back down her body. Very gently, he caressed her until her legs spread of their own volition and she moaned again. His finger pinched her clit and she cried out, her nipples contracting with the erotic sensation.

"Let me get this out of our way," he murmured soothingly. Careful not to hurt her, he reached in her already dripping channel and pulled out the little toy. She gasped again and clenched down on his fingers.

He tossed the vibrator on the pile of clothes. Almost roughly, he kneed her legs farther apart. "I have wanted to fuck you since I got your note," he growled in her ear. "Hold on, *assai*. This time I won't stop until we are both flying into the sun."

With one thrust of his hard muscular body, he buried himself balls-deep in her heat. They both cried out at the utter rightness and pleasure that enveloped them. There was no hesitation, no stopping. Milcham clutched her tightly to him and pounded into her. Her legs wrapped around his plunging hips, making their contact even more dramatic, and he could barely take the extra sensation.

Sweat dripped from his forehead as he continued his thrusts, feeling the sweet, slick clutching of her body as she moved with him. Her nails raked at his shoulders and he grunted as the sensual pain added to his enjoyment. He felt himself getting closer and closer and desperately tried to hold on until she could join him.

Aithne was lost in a bubble of heat and sensation. It was like the small rocket was a cocoon of sensual delight, and Milcham and she were all that was important in the world. His body, so hard and strong, kept moving in and out of her, massaging her hyper-sensitive nerve endings until she wanted to scream from the pleasure-pain of it.

When he reached down to hold her even closer to him, his penis swelled deep inside of her. The awareness sent shockwaves of sensation roaring through her, and without warning, her climax hit her so fast and hard, she could barely take a breath to scream.

She came apart in his arms like a wild thing, her body shaking uncontrollably. Her spasms sent him into his own orgasm, and with a roar, he poured himself into her. His body continued to move as he shuddered above her, until finally he collapsed on top of her, his chest heaving and his heart pounding.

They both lay still, somewhat like shipwreck victims washed up on shore. The Rocketship whirled lazily in a circle, giving a surreal feel to the afterglow.

Finally, Milcham moved, turning them so Aithne lay sprawled over the top of him, her head on his chest. Reaching down, he grabbed his shirt and spread it across her body to give her some warmth. He held her tightly as his lips caressed her hair. Gently, he stroked her back as he fought the overwhelming emotion that threatened him.

"*Sto cadendo nell'amore con voi, il mio prezioso,*" he whispered softly, unable to keep it in any longer. *I am falling in love with you, my precious one.*

She yawned and rubbed her cheek against his chest. "What does that mean?"

Closing his eyes, he sighed. He couldn't tell her. It wouldn't be fair. He'd be leaving soon. He bent and kissed her forehead. "It means...you make me feel wonderful."

Aithne smiled and cuddled closer. "It was the most amazing night of my life. Thank you for being with me."

His jaw clenched as he pulled her closer. "There is nowhere else I would rather be."

The motion of the ride lulled them gently, and after a few minutes, Milcham knew by her soft even breathing and relaxed body that Aithne had fallen asleep. Smiling, he closed his own eyes. He'd rest for a moment and then wave down to Timmy. Then he'd take his sweet woman home with him and hold her throughout the night.

His stomach clenched. How many more nights would he have with her? Time was slipping away from him, and for the first time in almost a thousand years, he didn't look forward to returning to his walled city and renewing fire. Because when he did, he'd lose Aithne...forever.

He awoke to the sounds and smells of bacon frying. Rolling over to his side, he blinked his eyes. Aithne stood at the stove in his shirt, humming quietly to herself. For a long moment, he just looked at the picture she made, his heart racing.

This was how he wanted to wake up every morning. The realization poured through him with the strength of a rushing river. So fast and achingly certain.

He wasn't falling anymore. He'd fallen. He loved her. Had loved her from the very beginning, though he'd fought against it. And why had he fought so hard? He closed his eyes in shame. Because she wasn't what he'd expected.

He'd looked for a mate like he would interview a new employee. Milcham had a list of qualifications, and if the woman didn't make the cut, he might enjoy her as a bed partner, but that was as far as it went.

What he should have done was what Yahweh had advised him to do right from the beginning. He was to seek not with his mind, but with his heart. To find a woman he could love. Not for just a moment, but for eternity.

Was Aithne that woman? She was strong and smart, beautiful and caring. She was loyal to her friends and her family, she worked hard to be independent, yet she didn't mind too much when he acted the caveman. And she was adventurous...in *and* out of bed. Milcham had been human long enough to appreciate that.

But was she his true soulmate? He had to be sure. And until he was, he couldn't share his feelings with her. Though he was afraid now that each time he looked at her, each time he kissed her sweet lips, he told her that truth whether he wanted to or not.

The scent of coffee wafted under his nose and his nostrils twitched. He took a deep breath and opening his eyes again, saw the object of his thoughts standing before him holding a coffee cup.

"Good morning," she said, her cheeks a pretty pink.

He chuckled. No matter how many times they were together, she still was shy around him. He looked at the cup. "Is that for me?"

She sat beside him. "If you're a good boy."

Grinning, he pulled her carefully against his chest. "And how do I show you if I'm a good boy?"

Her eyebrow went up. "How about a good morning kiss *before* you steal my coffee."

He pulled her head down to his and brushed his lips lightly over hers. "Good morning."

"Well," she huffed in an amused tone. "If that's all you got."

Milcham narrowed his eyes, and plucking the cup out of her hand, set it on the counter. In a single motion, he rolled her back beneath him on the bed. "Then let me try again."

Aithne's laugh was smothered by his kiss. It was deep and long, but filled more with tenderness than the lust she was used to receiving from this man. Granted, his cock twitched between her legs, but it was what she sensed in his kiss that warmed her. For the first time, she knew he was kissing her with something more than just his body.

When he lifted his head, their eyes met, and she knew something had changed. She lifted a hand to cup his cheek. “Are you okay? You seem...different.”

He stiffened slightly then calmed. “I am...just very relaxed. It was an enjoyable night.”

She caressed his bristly cheek. “The best.”

With a grin he rubbed his morning beard gently across her soft cleavage. She squealed and grabbed at his hair to pull him off of her. “What’s that for?” she giggled.

“Call it payback for the Ferris wheel.”

Aithne’s mouth dropped open. “Excuse me? You paid me back plenty. In the Tunnel, on the Zipper, on the Caro—”

He stopped her with another kiss. “But I ached through those as well. So I figure you still owe me.”

“What do you have in mind?” she asked with a smile. She half expected him to pull her farther beneath him and start loving her all over again.

“I would hope,” he said somewhat hesitantly, “that we can spend more time together. I enjoy your company. I miss you when we are apart.”

Her eyes filled. Here was the openness she’d longed for. Was this what was different about him? Had he finally realized they belonged together? Her heart swirled with emotion. She knew now, without even realizing it, she’d handed her heart into his keeping.

She was in love with him.

Aithne buried her head into his chest, praying one day he might feel the same. Had she finally found her twin-flame? “I love being with you, too.” She hugged him to her. “And we have plenty of time to spend together. I’m not going anywhere.”

Milcham swallowed as he held her tightly to him. She may not be planning to move on any time soon, but unfortunately he was. He had no choice.

Chapter Eleven

"He said it was *what*?"

The short, motherly looking woman blinked at Aithne over the vat of pink floss. Her apron was speckled with the sticky candy, and there were trails of it in her graying hair as well.

"He said it was arson, dear. I thought you knew."

Aithne tried to keep her voice even. It wasn't Tabitha's fault Milcham had lied to her. Okay...not lied. But he sure didn't tell her the truth. "Alexander said it was gasoline that started the fire?"

Tabitha nodded as she swirled the white paper cone into the pink spidery floss until a large puffy ball formed. She handed it to the last customer, a gap-toothed little boy, and accepted his wadded up money.

"That's right, honey. One side of the tent was completely doused in the stuff." She shook her head and closed her window. "It's a wonder you made it out alive."

Aithne sat down hard on the stool next to the vat. "I can't believe it. Who would want to burn me out?"

"That's a good question." The woman turned off the floss machine and started scraping at the leftover candy. "We've all been told to keep an eye on you."

"Excuse me?"

"Now honey...don't get your knickers in a twist. The boss, he just wants to know you're safe."

Aithne thought back over the last week since the fire. She hadn't realized it until now, but there had been someone with her every hour of the day, and then Milcham was with her at night. No wonder he'd wanted her to move in with him. Her temper rose. "He should have told me."

"Gotta agree with you there." Tabitha gave a loud groan as she leaned over the machine. "Oh...does my back ache today."

"Tabitha!" Aithne leaped off the stool. "Go put your feet up. I can clean this up."

The woman blinked wearily at her. "Now when I invited you in for a spell, I wasn't expecting that."

"I know...and we had a grand time reading the cards for you." Aithne giggled. "Remember to look for that guy who is good with his hands."

Her friend laughed. "I do like the way you do tarot. But you aren't here to pick up after me."

"I get the fact you were just watching out for me, like Milcham wanted." Aithne firmed her lips. "But I'll be fine. You head off to bed, and let me take care of this."

She could tell the idea of soaking her tired feet was a very tempting one to Tabitha—as was the idea of one glorious night free from cleaning. The woman sighed as her resolve crumbled. "If you're sure?"

"Positive." Aithne helped her untie her apron and shooed her out the door. "Straight home and relax. Gypsy's orders!"

Tabitha laughed. "I'll see you tomorrow, honey. And go easy on the boss. He meant right."

"I'll go easy on him," Aithne snarled as she watched the older woman stagger towards the back lot. "I'll go real easy!"

Turning, she tied the apron over her clothes and set to cleaning. Temper made her hands fly, and she quickly cleaned out the sticky vat of floss. As she scrubbed, she thought of all the reasons Milcham might keep the truth from her. She could understand him wanting her to be safe, but why wouldn't he just tell her about the arson?

Her heart dropped like a stone when she thought of something. She bit her lip to keep from crying. Could it be he just wanted someone to screw? And the fire was a convenient way to get her into his bed? Was that why he seemed so distant at times? It wasn't emotional...just physical?

Fury rose up inside of her again, adding to the hurt. She deserved better. She'd waited for a century, knowing someday she *would* find her twin-flame. She'd fallen in love with Milcham, dreamed of making a life with him, but now...

She finished wiping out the vat and was looking for a place to dump the extra rapidly hardening floss mixture when the door opened.

"Hey, beautiful!"

Aithne turned to see Milcham's smiling face. His gaze shot around the small stand and he frowned. "Where's Tabitha?"

Immediately, she knew why he was asking, and her anger sparked even hotter. "I sent her home. She was tired."

"You're here alone?"

"Yes. So what?" Maybe he would tell her the truth.

He frowned deeper and then came into the booth. "I...I just don't like people taking advantage of you."

Her fury grew. "Tabitha wasn't taking advantage. I offered."

His eyebrow rose at her tone. "Even so, I'll talk to her in the morning."

"*You will not!*" she spat at him. "There is no reason for me not to do this for her. She's a nice lady, and I wanted to help."

"Easy, *assai*," he soothed, coming closer. "It's all right. No big deal."

She backed away, trying to control herself. She was angrier than she could ever remember being. Why was it the men in her life felt she couldn't make decisions for herself? Why did they insist on keeping the truth from her? First her brother and now Milcham. It was all just too much.

"Are you ready to go home?"

Her head jerked up, her green eyes lit with temper. Home? If all he wanted was sex, he could take his offer of home and stuff it. She'd been so wrong about him. He didn't care about her at all.

"I've been thinking, Milcham. It's time I got a place of my own. When we are in Raleigh, I'm going to get a trailer."

His mouth dropped open. "*What?*"

"It's time we gave each other a little space. I want to be alone, so I'm going to buy a trailer."

Milcham stared at her. She wanted to be alone? Rage and hurt that she wanted to leave warred within him. He was so shocked at the thought, he missed the anger on her lovely face. Responses tumbled through his mind, but all he could come up with was, "I...I don't think that would be a good idea."

She tossed her head. "I think it's a great one! I don't want to be with you anymore."

His own eyes went dark amber as his own temper exploded. "The hell you say!" He grabbed her arm. "You are going to stay with me! And that's final!"

Without warning, she tossed the contents of the floss mixture at him. "Leave me alone!"

He gasped and staggered backwards as the sticky mess splashed all over the front of him. It coated his hair and face, and his once pristine white shirt was suddenly covered in pink spider webs of candy floss.

He cursed and wiped the liquid from his eyes, leaving his long eyelashes to harden into sweet spikes. "What the fuck did you do that for?" he roared.

She seemed as shocked at herself as he was, but recovered quickly. "You're a liar and a bully and a...liar!"

Milcham wanted to use his flame. He wanted to explode. Not just to melt the damn candy off, but he was so angry, he needed to just let go. Battling back the temper, he stared at the furious woman in front of him. He couldn't decide whether to spank her ass, or kiss her until she shut up. Suddenly, her words caught him. "What did you say? What are you talking about?"

She stomped her foot and tossed the canister at him. Pushing past him, she left the stand. "I hate you!"

His heart iced painfully at her words. "Aithne!" he shouted as he raced out the door after her. He grabbed her again. "Why are you so angry? What have I done?"

She struggled against him, tears dotting her lashes. "Were you ever going to tell me, Milcham? Or do you think I'm too stupid to know?"

"Aithne!" he ordered as he tried to hold her still. "You're not making sense. What is it I'm supposed to have done?"

"You didn't *do* anything." She jerked herself free and rubbed at her arms. "That's the problem!"

"I don't believe this!" He paced away from her and then back. He could see curious carny folk coming out of the different stands and tents, but was too furious to care. "I can't fix it if you don't tell me why you're angry."

Aithne glared at him, loving him despite her fury. Maybe that's why she hurt so much. His actions showed her exactly what he really thought of her, making all her rosy little daydreams about the two of them into nothing but ashes.

"Aithne!"

"I trusted you!" she shouted at him. "I believed you wanted the best for me...for us! Now I find it's all a lie!"

"So help me," he growled. "If you don't tell me what's wrong, I'm going to spank that cute little ass of yours!"

Her stomach jumped. The thought of Milcham standing behind her with a paddle suddenly became vivid. But she pushed it away and shook her head. "You're a liar!"

"Tell me!"

Her chest heaved as her tears finally overflowed. "Were you ever going to tell me what really happened to my tent?"

Milcham froze. He stared at her beautiful, angry face and groaned aloud. She'd found out about the arson. He cursed the person who'd let it slip, but then cursed himself even more for keeping it from her. No wonder she was angry.

"Assai—"

"Don't call me that," Aithne screamed, putting her hands over her ears. "I'm not. I'm not. If I was precious to you, you wouldn't lie to me."

His heart pounded in his chest. "Aithne, I'm sorry. Please, let me explain."

"What can you say to explain this, Milcham? What reason would you have to keep this from me?" Her eyes narrowed. "How about this? It was just an excuse so you could get me in your bed? You never really cared about me. You just wanted sex!"

His head jerked up, suddenly understanding her pain and fury, even if it was totally illogical. "No! *Assai*... It was never like that. This I swear."

"How can I believe you?" she wept out. "Someone torches my tent, and you use it to move me in with you, but don't tell me about it?" She shook her head. "Am I that good a lay?"

There was no way to answer that one without getting another vat of candy thrown on him, so he ignored it. "Aithne, I should have told you. I'm sorry. But you're not thinking straight. If I had been using you as you say I was, why would I keep the knowledge it was arson from you? If all I wanted was sex, wouldn't I use the origin of the fire to frighten you into staying with me? Into my bed?"

He took a careful step closer as she frowned at his words. He had to make her understand. "The only reasons I moved you in with me were to keep you safe *and* because I wanted you with me. The fire terrified me. When I saw you lying unconscious, and I realized I'd almost lost you, I couldn't bear it. I...care too much. All I could think about was having you close to me. Period. I wasn't thinking about sex. I was thinking about being with you."

She was finally listening, but the anger and hurt were still in her eyes.

"Besides, I didn't know it was arson when I brought you into my trailer. Alexander and Jarrod discovered it when they were mopping up. Remember when they brought your purse?"

She nodded.

"That's when they told me. I would have told you when they left, but you'd already been through so much. I wanted you to sleep that night. Then—" he grimaced when he tried to run his hand through his sticky hair and it got stuck, "—I just didn't. You were so happy with me and..." He trailed off with a sigh. "I am a fool."

"Yes...you are."

"But Aithne," he went on, hoping desperately it wasn't too late, "it was never because I wanted a bed mate. I wanted you, yes. But...only you. Please...if you believe anything, you must believe that."

"Why?" she cried. "I want to believe you, but why should I? You lied to me. Everyone in the carnival knew but me. Did it ever occur to you I'd be safer knowing someone tried to burn me out?"

"I will keep you safe." His voice was arrogant, but his eyes begged her to understand. "I didn't want you to worry! Everything I did...I did for you."

She swore loudly, making his eyes widen in shock. She never used that type of language, even in love play.

"We've had this discussion before, Milcham," she shouted at him with even more fury. "I will make my own decisions, remember? It's the one thing I demanded of you. Who do you think you are to take that away from me?"

His control snapped. He grabbed her by the arms and shook her. "Who do I think I am?" he shouted. "I'm the man who loves you, damn it!"

Her eyes went impossibly wide, and she stilled in his arms. Her mouth opened and shut several times before she managed to croak out, "*What*?"

Milcham swore under his breath. He had not planned to tell her how he felt. Somehow, she constantly made him ignore his own rules. This would change everything. He struggled for a moment, and then gave up. He pulled her against his sticky body and tipped her startled face up to his.

"I am in love with you, *assai*. So much I would use any excuse to keep you with me. I didn't mean it to happen, but it did. When I pulled you from the fire, I think I knew then, but I have never been in love before so I fought my emotions. But I tell you true. I love you."

Aithne could only stare at him. Her mind was a complete and total blank, all the fury and pain draining out of her as if it never was. After several long moments passed, she managed, "You...love...me."

He pressed a sticky kiss on her parted lips. "I do. More than anything in this world."

She blinked, warmth coursing through her. It was gentle at first, and then it grew. Little by little it filled her. Her heart pounded in her chest, and a laugh welled up inside of her. It was then that she recognized it. Joy. Pure, unadulterated joy.

He loved her.

"Aithne?" His voice penetrated her dazed mind, and now she could hear irritation in it.

She met his gaze and saw the familiar arrogance, but this time, she saw something else. Vulnerability. She couldn't help a smile. This big, strong, gorgeous hunk of a man was afraid of what she was going to say.

"Damn it, Aithne. Speak to me!"

With a glad cry, she leaped into his arms, pressing wild kisses all over his candy-coated face. After a brief, frozen second, he responded, lifting her against him and holding her close.

She pressed her cheek against his. "Oh, Milcham," she whispered. "I thought I was the only one."

Milcham went very still, his arms tightening around her. His heart beat in tandem with hers. "*Assai*," he murmured, hardly daring to hope. "Please. I need to hear you say it. Please."

She leaned back, her eyes sparkling with happy tears. He drew in his breath at the look on her face. Cupping his cheek in her hand, she smiled mistily.

"I love you, Milcham. I love you so much."

His own eyes flared with joy and love. Holding her close, he gave a whoop of happiness and whirled her around in a circle. "She loves me!"

The crowd that had gathered to watch their fight now broke into cheers and applause. If nothing else, carny folk enjoyed a good show.

"Stop, please," she laughed. "I can't breathe!"

Milcham halted, yet refused to let go of his precious armful. One hand snaked up into her hair and grabbed a handful of it as he stared deep into her loving green eyes. "You're mine now."

Her own hands slid into his sticky locks, holding him just as tightly, as she answered him with a saucy grin. "And you're mine."

Their lips met and everything around them disappeared. Immediately, they were both wrapped in a cocoon of light and love and heated desire. The kiss was a declaration of all that was left unsaid, yet deeply felt, as they pressed closer together sharing their first true embrace of love.

They stood there, their arms wrapped around each other, as the night stars twinkled overhead. Their kisses grew more heated, more filled with passion until someone in the crowd called out, "Get a room!"

They pulled apart and stared at each other, ignoring the now laughing group. Milcham touched her face with gentle fingers. "You have my love, Aithne. Please, come back to the trailer. I want to touch you. I need you."

Her heart swelled. Never before had he said those words. He was too self-possessed...too solitary. To be needed for herself was as important a gift to her as his *I love you* had been. She turned her face to kiss the palm of his hand.

"I need to be with you too, Milcham. Take me home."

His amber eyes flared gold, and after a quick kiss, he lifted her into his arms. Turning, he walked rapidly through the whispering crowd to the trailer. Suddenly, he stopped abruptly and looked down at her. "You're as sticky and covered with candy as I am. Do you want to stop at the showers first?"

Aithne smiled, slowly and seductively, feeling his body tighten against her in reaction. Reaching out, she trailed her finger through the floss coating on his cheek. She kept her eyes on his as she put her finger in her mouth and sucked...hard.

"We can," she murmured in a sultry voice. "Or...I can lick it off of you."

He groaned and almost ran towards the trailer. "Lick now...shower later."

High above the carnival, a dark figure rained down curses as it gnashed its teeth. It had been so sure the female wouldn't forgive the Phoenix his lies. But she had, and even worse, the two had admitted their love for each other. Now, it would be even more difficult to keep them apart.

The demon wrung gnarled hands, whimpering fearfully. It had tried to prevent this by burning the woman in the fire, but the Phoenix had rescued her. The demon had even whispered in the candymaker's ear, telling her to reveal the truth about the arson. It had thought it would be the end of them, but instead the opposite had happened.

For some reason it was very important that the Phoenix and the woman be torn apart from each other, but no matter what was tried, it seemed to fail. The Master would not be pleased.

Suddenly, a dark cloud swirled up from the abyss to envelope the demon, and pain speared through its scaled body. The creature screamed in agony as two red eyes appeared in the dark, and sharp claws rent the leathery wings.

The demon tried to scrabble away, but the cloud was merciless. It tore and ripped and stabbed as the creature was slowly pulled into the gloom.

The punishment had begun.

The Ancient One slowly pulled himself from the putrid darkness and stared down at the dimly lit trailer where the lovers lay intertwined. "No more," he hissed, his hatred overflowing. "I have stopped you before, and I'll stop you again. This union will never take place." He smiled evilly. "I will not allow it."

It was much later when they finally made it to the shower. They tickled each other and laughed like children as they washed each other's sticky bodies. They had left a good portion of the floss mix on the bed sheets, but it didn't matter to them. All they cared about was being together.

Aithne sighed when his hand cupped her breast. "You make me feel wonderful. It's even better now. How can that be?"

Milcham nibbled gently on the back of her neck. "We know our love is shared. It is...extraordinary."

She turned to face him, putting her hands on his hard chest. "I've never told another man *I love you*. I was waiting. For you."

He smoothed back her tangled hair. "You are the first woman I have ever wanted to say these words to." He kissed her, lingeringly. "I wasn't sure I ever would find the right one."

She searched his face, her green eyes suddenly serious. "Am I your twin-flame, Milcham?"

"I...I don't know, Aithne. I want you to be, but things are more complicated than you know."

"I don't understand."

He pulled her against him, delighting in her silky body against his. "I know you don't. I would ask you give me time. I have to tell you something, and I am afraid to."

Aithne pulled away from him, fear touching her face. "Is there...someone else?"

He wrapped her long hair around his fist and held her so she couldn't move. "No! Never!" He shook his head. "It is you I love, *assai*, only you."

"Then what—"

He stopped her with another kiss. "Please...let me tell you in my own way."

She sighed and melted against him. "Now I am worried. Don't take too long. Okay?"

He nodded. "I promise."

She smiled and ran her hands over his wet body. "I guess you'll have to make me forget my worry."

His breath caught as she wrapped her hand around his awakening cock. Suddenly needing her, he pulled one of her legs up to around his waist, sliding his hard length deep inside of her. When her head fell back in surrender, he feasted upon her slim neck, nibbling and sucking.

His throat ached with a combination of fear, love and desire. Could he tell Aithne the truth? Would she accept what he was? If she didn't, could he let her go now that he'd loved her? Could he go back to his lonely life of before?

And what if she did accept who he was? What then? Could he chance her dying in the fire that gave him life, if she wasn't deemed worthy? Would he even be able to try it?

He buried his face against her, his heart breaking. Either way, he could lose her. Unless he was given another miracle, these precious moments may be all he'd ever have to remember her by.

Chapter Twelve

Milcham wiped the sweat from his face and stared around at the almost empty fairground. He'd be glad to get out of this town. It was like they were jinxed. It had been one thing after another. Permit problems, then one of the games had been accused of cheating. Then, to top it off, just before they were to pull out, Jarrod had gotten into it with one of the locals and been arrested.

Alexander had gone into town to get him and pay whatever fine the corrupt local government would demand, but it still pissed Milcham off. He hated those who dealt unfairly or were judgmental. It was one part of carnival life he despised.

Luckily, Alexander's temperament was much more conducive to working with the locals. Over the last year, Milcham had made use of his talents more and more often. He knew that when he left to go home, Alexander would be the one he'd leave in charge.

He bent and picked up his ax, walking towards the truck to store it as he thought about his trip. He wasn't looking forward to it. He'd have to leave Aithne, and he wasn't sure how long Yahweh expected him to stay in the walled city. In fact...for all he knew, he might not be allowed to leave again.

Either way, he knew it wasn't fair to expect Aithne to wait for him, no matter how much she said she loved him. And as for telling her... Milcham sighed. The thought of how she might react scared him to death. If he told her at all, he'd wait until the last possible moment. He didn't want to lose these last few days with her. He still struggled with calling her his twin-flame. Not because he didn't love her. He did, more than he thought he could love any female.

But if he did finally admit she was his soulmate, he would want to take her home with him, and he was terrified she might come to harm there. The flame that gave him life might cost Aithne her own.

He found himself looking around for her, before he remembered she'd gone into town to pick up supplies while Alexander bailed Jarrod out. He didn't like her out of his sight, but he trusted both men to keep an eye on her. Though...he wouldn't be telling Aithne that anytime soon. She was too independent for words.

Turning, he went back to the ride he was dismantling. If they were lucky, they'd be out of here by nightfall.

"Son of a bitch sheriff."

"Calm down, Jarrod." Alexander glanced across the cab at his friend.

"It's over now," Aithne agreed soothingly. "Let it go."

Jarrod slammed his hand against the dash of the truck. "You shouldn't have had to pay a fine."

Alexander sighed. He drove carefully down the darkened road towards the fairgrounds. "If that's what it took to get you out of there, it was worth it."

"But it was that damn kid who took the money. Not me!" Jarrod glared at his friend. "I even had witnesses."

"Yes, and if that one local hadn't admitted she saw the kid take the money, you would still be in jail," Aithne responded. "I love you to death, Jarrod, but you can't go around manhandling people. Even if they deserve it."

"I didn't manhandle him." The big man sulked. "I just pulled him away from the gate."

"And tossed him on his ass," Alexander put in. "You don't know your own strength."

"I knew it. Didn't care."

Aithne rolled her eyes. Sitting between the two men in the truck seat, she sensed the anger and frustration rolling off them both. She didn't need her gift to tell her they were both furious at the whole situation. "It's over and done with. They got what they wanted, and we got Jarrod. But I wasn't able to get supplies, so we'll have to stop in the next town for them."

Jarrod looked ashamed of himself. "Sorry, girl. But we needed to get out of there and fast."

She smiled. "It's okay. Let's just get home so we can help Milcham. Then we can get out of this area. No more surprises!"

"Amen," Alexander agreed fervently.

"Hey!" exclaimed Jarrod. "Did you see that?"

Aithne peered out the window. "What?"

"I don't know." He rolled down his window and stuck his head outside. "But it was big. It flew right over us."

"Probably an owl." Alexander kept his eyes on the narrow, winding road. They were less than a mile from the fairgrounds and he too was anxious to be back.

"I know what a fucking owl looks like." Jarrod glared at them both. "And this wasn't it! I don't know what it was, but it wasn't a bird."

Something swooped by the front of the truck, making Alexander veer to the right. "Damn it! What the hell was that?"

"I told you I saw something!" Jarrod growled. He craned his neck to look out the small back window. "Think *that* was an owl?"

Alexander ignored the jab. "It was huge, and I swear its wings were leathery." He glanced at Aithne. "Don't suppose you know any vampires in this area," he said only half-jokingly.

Aithne bit her lip. "It wasn't a vampire. I can still sense them. Haven't seen one of the brethren since Charleston." She leaned forward and hesitantly looked into the sky. "Besides...vampires can't fly. At least most of them can't."

Jarrod turned back around, but his eyes didn't stop searching the dark. "I thought all vamps could fly."

She shook her head. "All vampires have special gifts given to them at their turning. Different gifts for different vamps. Aidan has superhuman strength, is very fast and can read minds." She grinned in memory. "Dawn says it's why he's such a great lover. He knows exactly what she—"

"TMI, girl," grumbled Jarrod. "Don't need to know about your brother's sex life. Need to know about flying vamps."

Aithne giggled at the werewolf's discomfiture. "Flying is a very rare gift. I've never heard of a vampire who could in this century."

"There it is again!" Alexander shouted as the figure sped towards them. It crashed into the top of the truck, making the dark-haired man fight for control of the wheel.

Jarrod swore and Aithne stifled a scream. It would be of no help, and she refused to be one of those women who screamed in the middle of a crisis for no good reason.

The thing hit them again, this time from the right. It plowed into them so hard, Alexander lost control of the truck, and its tires squealed as it veered across the road to the steep incline on the other side.

"*Damn it!*" Alexander roared as he fought the wheel. "Hold on!" They all heard an inhuman screech of laughter, and the vehicle was hit again, this time sending it careening over the side of the mountain.

Jarrod shouted Aithne's name as he used his were-strength to rip the truck door open. Wrapping a strong arm around her, he threw himself and her from the cab.

"*No*!" Aithne screamed as she flew through the air. She watched as if in slow motion as the truck went over the side of the cliff, plummeting to the ground below. "Alexander!"

Jarrod and Aithne hit the ground hard, the big man scrabbling for a handhold on the side of the bushy hill. He grabbed onto a small bush and heaved Aithne to the top, pulling himself up after her.

"Are you all right?" he asked frantically.

She nodded and struggled to her knees. Her face was scraped and her arms were bleeding from the impact, but she wasn't badly hurt. She stared at Jarrod's bloody face and then crawled over to the edge. "Oh God...he went over the edge! We've got to get to him."

Jarrod staggered to his feet. "I'm going down."

"Me, too!"

Together, they carefully made their way down the hill. It wasn't as steep as it looked, but they both knew the car had rolled on its way down. They were terrified of what they might find.

"Keep an eye open for that damn bird," Jarrod yelled as they scrambled down the steep slope. "I don't know what the fuck is going on, but it caused this."

Aithne nodded, more frightened of what might have happened to Alexander than the unknown creature. When they finally made it to the base of the cliff, she sucked her breath in at the sight of the mangled truck. It was on its side, with the driver's door to the ground, jammed between two huge boulders.

Jarrod let out another shout and rushed over to it. Aithne followed him, her heart dropping when she saw the still form of Alexander lying half under the torn and smashed metal.

"Alex?" Jarrod dropped to his knees and put two fingers to his pulse. His jaw worked hard. "Come on, man! You're not giving up on me!"

Aithne joined him, brushing the black locks out of her friend's eyes. "Please, Alexander," she begged tearfully. "Wake up."

His blue eyes fluttered open and then closed again. He groaned, and a ribbon of blood trickled from his mouth. Aithne pressed a fist against her mouth to keep from screaming at the pain she saw in his face.

"I gotta get this off of him," Jarrod snarled. He leapt to his feet and put his shoulder to the truck. He heaved and Aithne watched as his muscles bulged and knotted, but while he was able to move it slightly, even his werewolf strength couldn't move the truck because of the rocks holding it on either side.

He panted against it for a moment then swung back around to Aithne. "I can't do it alone." He pulled out his cell and tried it, then tossed it to the ground with a curse. "No fucking signal."

"What do we do?"

"I need you to run and get Phoenix. We need him...now!"

Her eyes widened in confusion. "But—"

Jarrod didn't give her time to argue. "Damn it, Aithne. Trust me! Go! He's the only one who can save Alex now!"

Without another word, her face wreathed in fear and confusion, she turned and started up the hill. Jarrod knelt back down next to his friend.

"Hang on, buddy," he muttered. "Help's on the way."

Milcham wiped his hands on a rag then glanced at his watch. They should be back soon. It had been almost three hours since they left, and Alexander knew enough not to hang about after a gig.

He bent and packed the last of the tools in the truck. When they got here, he was going to send Alexander and Jarrod on ahead. Then he was going to take Aithne somewhere special. He grinned. He was going to find the biggest and fanciest hotel in the area and treat them both to a night in a real bed that didn't move.

Room service, candlelight and champagne. He wanted it all for her. He'd even go buy roses so he could cover their bed with them. His body stirred at the mental image of Aithne lying naked among the petals. He'd kiss her from the tip of her nose to the bottoms of her feet. Then he'd make love to her. Over and over again until they both collapsed from exhaustion. And when they woke up, he'd start all over...

He frowned and stilled. Had someone called him? He listened for a couple of moments, but heard nothing. Shrugging, he turned to walk towards his trailer.

"Milcham!"

He whirled around, his gaze searching in the darkness. His muscles clenched in worry. It was Aithne's voice he heard, he was sure of it. He started towards the front gate, and it was then he saw her.

She was stumbling up the road, her hair hanging in her face. Her blouse was torn off one creamy shoulder, and he could see dirt and blood staining her skirt. His anger went to flashpoint in seconds. He was there, beside her, before she drew her next breath to scream his name.

He took her into his arms. "Aithne! *Assai*! What happened? My God! Are you all right?"

She clawed at his arm. "I'm fine. We have to go! It's Alexander! Truck wrecked! Please!"

Milcham didn't understand it all, but the fear and panic in her eyes made him head for his own vehicle without any other questions. He tossed her in the cab and slid in beside her. "Where?"

Her breath hitched. "Half mile down the road."

He started the truck and floored it. It fishtailed wildly, but then he got it pointed in the right direction and headed out the fairground's gate. Once they were on the road, he glanced over to her. "Talk."

Aithne wiped away her tears. "Something pushed us off the road. It flew...and it was huge. It kept hitting the side of the truck and wouldn't stop. It pushed us over the side. Jarrod pulled me out, but he couldn't get to both of us." She broke off, fighting her emotions. "The truck went all the way to the bottom and Alexander is trapped. Oh, God...I think he's dead!"

Milcham's jaw tightened and he drove faster. The idea he may lose his quiet, dark friend was more than he could stomach.

Aithne went on, "Jarrod sent me to get you. He said you were the only one who could help him. I don't understand. Shouldn't I go get a rescue crew or something?"

Coming around the last corner, Milcham pulled over to where he could see the broken guardrail. The truck squealed to a stop. He didn't answer as he helped her out. His heart pounded at the choice he might soon have to make. "Let me see if it's as bad as you think. If it is, we'll send you to town."

She frowned at that, but seconds later she was too busy scrambling back down the hill to worry. She led Milcham to where Jarrod sat with Alexander's head in his lap. The wolfman looked exhausted, but his face brightened when he saw Milcham.

"Boss! Thank God. I tried, but I couldn't move it." He eased out from under the limp man. "It's my fault. I couldn't get to him. I—"

"Shut up, Jarrod." Milcham took one look at the scene and went to his knees to check Alexander. One touch and his heart sank. The man's skin was cold and clammy, and if there was a pulse, he couldn't feel it.

Shooting back to his feet, he knew there was only one thing left to do. He stared over at Aithne who stood watching him, confusion in her eyes. He wanted to explain, but in the end, all he could say was...

"*Assai*...I am so sorry."

Aithne blinked at his sorrowful words. She was even more confused as he moved a distance away from his fallen friend. Was Alexander dead? Were they too late?

Then...without warning, there was a flash of bright red-gold light. Thinking the truck had exploded, she cried out and covered her face with her hands. Expecting to be peppered with debris and hot metal, she waited, but nothing came her way. Instead of the pain she was expecting, there was a sudden surprising sense of warmth and light.

Slowly, Aithne removed her hands from her face. Her eyes widened and she took a step backwards in utter shock. The radiance and heat didn't come from the truck. She closed unbelieving eyes and then re-opened them.

Where once a man stood, now floated a being of brilliant light and beauty. Wings, outstretched and flapping gently, shot trails of fire as they shone with all the colors of the rainbow. The large, bird-like body blazed with tendrils of flames that undulated around him as if they were alive. Sharp, taloned claws settled gently onto the ground as he came to rest next to the destroyed truck. He was enveloped in a sphere of white gold light that gave off heat, yet it didn't burn.

"Milcham..." she whispered.

As if he heard her, his head turned her way. Changed to one of a bird of prey, with a sharply curved beak, he had a crown of scarlet fire. His eyes stared at Aithne, glowing so golden, she thought she could get lost in the liquid warmth.

Her knees gave out on her and she sank to the ground. Suddenly, she understood. It hadn't been an angel she'd seen in the fire in her tent. And it hadn't been Milcham either. At least, not in the form she knew him as. He wasn't the man she thought he was.

The man she'd fallen in love with. The man she'd given her heart, soul and body to wasn't a man at all. He wasn't even human. She knew exactly who stood before her on the dark mountainside.

Milcham was the legendary Phoenix.

Chapter Thirteen

One look at her shocked face, and Milcham knew he'd lost her. Aithne valued truth, and even if she'd been able to accept him for what he was, he was very much afraid she would never understand why he'd kept it from her. He wanted to go to her and wrap her in his flaming wings to comfort her, but he knew he didn't have time. Alexander's life hung in the balance, and if he was to save him, he must act immediately.

His eyes glowed at Aithne for one last moment before he turned and flew over the top of the destroyed vehicle. Hovering there, he grasped the mangled cab in his talons, and using his strong wings, lifted it off the ground and Alexander's crushed body. The steel groaned alarmingly, and Milcham was suddenly afraid the whole thing would fall apart and plummet down on Alexander again.

Quickly, he nodded to Jarrod, and the big man rushed over to pull Alexander out from under the floating truck. Once he could see that his friend was safe, Milcham dropped the truck back to the ground. The sound of metal grating on metal made them all cringe.

He flew over to where Jarrod crouched, his hands touching Alexander worriedly. The wolfman looked up at the Phoenix. "I can't feel a pulse."

Milcham touched him carefully, but the flames from his wings set the man's clothes to smoking, so he quickly backed off. Concentrating, he morphed back into his human form and then again knelt down.

"Can you...can you do anything?" Jarrod muttered. His dark eyes were moist.

"If he's not too far gone." Milcham took a deep breath, and concentrated on producing tears. At first his eyes stayed dry then he happened to glance up and see Aithne's frozen, shocked visage. The realization she was lost to him broke his heart anew, making him tear up immediately. Soon tears were streaming down his cheeks. Leaning over, he let them fall on Alexander's face.

The tears sizzled on the injured man's skin then were absorbed immediately, disappearing as if they had never been. Alexander's flesh took on a glow as if lit from the inside out. Then...all the scratches and bruises healed...right before their astonished eyes.

"You cry and people can get...better?" Jarrod's face was a study in amazement.

"A Phoenix's tears have healing properties." Milcham checked Alexander's pulse and frowned. "But it is the internal damage I am concerned about."

He continued his weeping, letting his copious tears drench his fallen friend's body. Soon, it was very apparent that any bodily injuries were healed, yet Alexander still didn't move or breathe.

"Damn," Milcham murmured. "There must be more I can do. He wouldn't heal if he were already dead."

"Perhaps if he...tasted your tears."

They were the first words Aithne had spoken since he'd shifted. Their eyes met, and while she didn't look away, he knew immediately something had changed between them. Again, he wanted to go to her, but as before, he didn't have time. It about destroyed him, but he concentrated instead on what she had said.

"Feed him my tears?"

“You said it was the internal stuff you were worried about,” reminded Jarrod. “She means give him something internally.”

Milcham shrugged. He’d never done it before, but he’d try anything to make sure Alexander opened his eyes and smiled at them again. Cupping his hands, he thought again of losing Aithne, and his eyes flooded with moisture. The tears flowed into the shallow bowl of his hands.

Jarrod gently opened Alexander’s slack mouth and they watched as Milcham poured the liquid in. They waited breathlessly, each praying it wasn’t too late.

Minutes ticked by and they all sat frozen, their eyes fixed on Alexander’s still form. After a while, Milcham’s shoulders slumped. He looked over at Jarrod and tears again wet his cheeks. “I’m sorry. There’s nothing more I can do.”

Jarrod shot to his feet. “No!” he shouted. “He can’t be dead.”

Aithne put her face into her hands and wept.

Milcham felt so helpless. His best friend was dead, he’d lost his only love trying to help him, and he could do nothing about either of them. In all his long life, he’d never known such grief.

“No!” Reaching down, Jarrod grabbed Alexander’s limp body and shook it. He pressed his friend’s head to his wide chest and dropped to his knees. Then, lifting his gaze to the moon, he howled.

The hair on the back of Milcham’s neck stood up. The cry of a male werewolf in grief, passion or killing rage was one not easily forgotten. He wanted to join him and scream out his frustration to the sky.

“Can’t...breathe...here!”

They all froze. Aithne’s face popped out of her hands. Milcham stood abruptly, and Jarrod jerked Alexander’s head away from him.

“What the hell...?” the werewolf snarled. He stared in shock at the weary, smiling eyes of his now conscious friend.

"It's almost worth going through all that to see the look on your face," Alexander chuckled weakly. "But next time I'm lying at death's door, do you think it could be Aithne's arms I'm lying in? At least I'd be able to die pillowed against her beautiful breasts and not your hard, hairy chest!"

"Alexander!" Aithne crawled over to him and threw herself into his arms, almost knocking him flat in the process. "We thought you were dead!"

His arms wrapped shakily around her. "I was. I was in the light on the way to the other side when you pulled me back."

Relief poured through Milcham in a sweet flood. He hadn't been too late after all. His throat clogged with emotion as he watched Alexander hug Aithne. He wished his dealings with her would turn out as well.

Jarrod clapped his shaky friend on the back. "Damn it! You scared the hell out of me!"

Alexander winced. "Easy there, buddy, or you'll send me to the other side again." He looked at Milcham over the top of Aithne's head, noting the new gray in his boss' hair. "How can I thank you? I was dead and you brought me back." He glanced down at the weeping woman in his arms. "I won't forget what it cost you to do this."

Milcham's eyes dropped to Aithne's ebony head. His gut clenched in fear and need, but he ignored it. "I...I didn't want to lose you, either. It wasn't a difficult choice to make."

"I'm sorry, Boss," Jarrod grunted, realizing for the first time what his request had done. "I didn't know what else to do. You were all I could think of."

Milcham nodded. "I don't blame you." He shrugged. "If anyone, I blame myself."

Alexander pulled gently out of Aithne's arms and wiped her tears. "I'm okay now. Let me get up and see just how healed I am."

Jarrod pulled Aithne to her feet, while Milcham did the same with Alexander. He stretched and took a few test steps. "Damn...I guess coming back to life makes you a little stiff."

"Wimp!"

Alexander grinned at his friend. "At least I'm here to whine." He walked carefully over to his truck. "Now...do we know what the hell happened?"

The wolfman shook his head. "All I know is it was the biggest fucking bird I've ever seen."

"A bird?" Milcham stared at the men.

Alexander shrugged. "It flew. That's all I can tell you. But I could have sworn I heard a laugh when it pushed us over the side."

Jarrod's eyes widened. "Shit! Now that you mention it, I did, too."

"I did as well," Aithne said quietly. She still wouldn't look at Milcham. "But everything happened so fast."

"Do you think it was deliberate?"

Alexander patted what was left of his truck. "It came at us at least three different times, so...hell yes, I think it was deliberate."

"It wanted to push us off that mountain," Jarrod agreed.

"But why?" Aithne bit her lip. "Why would anyone want to hurt us?"

"That's what I'm going to find out. But I want to get us out of here first," Milcham said grimly. He walked over to stand near Alexander. "What about your ride?"

The dark man shook his head. "Insurance company is going to have a field day with this one."

Milcham grinned. "I can always just incinerate it for you. Save you the trouble."

Alexander laughed and then coughed as the motion hurt his abused chest. "Ouch! Guess I'm not a hundred percent yet." He stared at the heap of metal. "Can you lift it to the top of the mountain? I'll get a truck to tow it into the next town and then I'll decide what to do."

Milcham glanced at Aithne and sighed. Her face was as closed up as a rosebud. He wasn't even sure she'd let him explain anything, so one more demonstration of his power wouldn't make any difference. He nodded. "Sure. Move back so I don't burn you again."

Alexander frowned. "Your fire burns me?" At the other man's nod, he shook his head and his voice dropped. "But...then why didn't it burn Aithne when you pulled her from the tent? She was enveloped in it when you came out."

Freezing in his tracks, Milcham gaped at his friend. He was right. His fire hadn't affected Aithne, yet it had singed Alexander immediately. So...what the hell did *that* mean?

"I...I don't know," he managed. "But unless she gives me a chance to explain everything, I may never find out."

Alexander sighed. "I'm sorry. If I had been more careful—"

"Don't!" Milcham shook his head. "This wasn't your fault. I don't know exactly what did it, but I don't think it had anything to do with you."

"You know what that flying thing was?"

Dread welled up in Milcham. "Let's just say, I hope I'm wrong."

It was much later when Milcham got back to his trailer. He'd sent Jarrod and Aithne back to the fairground to finish packing up and drive the trailers into the next town, while he and Alexander lifted the truck to the top of the highway and waited for a tow truck to come along to take it away. The two men had spoken little, Alexander seeming to realize Milcham's thoughts were elsewhere...with Aithne.

They'd arrived in the town of Fayetteville long after everyone else had gone to bed. After a brief, heartfelt embrace, the two men had separated. Milcham watched as Alexander wearily trudged to his own home and climbed inside. He knew Jarrod would make sure his friend had a hot meal waiting for him.

Now, as he stood outside his own home, he was scared to enter. If it was empty, he wasn't sure what he'd do. Aithne had become so much a part of his life, the thought of being without her made him physically sick. If she left him, it would be like having a piece of himself go missing.

He paused, his hand on the door handle. A piece of himself? He groaned inwardly as anguish flooded his body. What a fool...what a jerk he was. Why had he taken so long to accept it? To admit it to himself? He'd fought the idea from the beginning, but he knew now as sure as there was a sun in the sky.

Aithne was his soulmate.

He rubbed at his tired, grainy eyes, realizing he may be immortal, but he was an idiot. His twin-flame had been standing right in front of him, and he'd refused to acknowledge her. And now...now that he knew? It might be too late.

Steeling himself, he opened the door and stepped inside. His heart fell to his feet when he saw the small trailer was empty and dark. There was no meal on the stove and no welcoming smile from the woman who meant more to him than his own life. His shoulders sagged and his eyes smarted.

She was gone.

Aithne sat on the edge of the bed and stared at the limp curtains on the motel's window. She felt totally numb. The pain of finding out the truth about Milcham hadn't even penetrated yet. She'd just done what he'd ordered her to do and gone with

Jarrod to finish packing up the carnival. But when they'd finished setting up the trailers, she couldn't even make herself step inside the one she shared with him. Instead, she'd asked Jarrod to take her to a motel.

The wolfman protested, trying to excuse Milcham's secrets, but she hadn't listened. He'd found her a cheap motel on the outskirts of town with small individual cabins and she'd rented one gladly. She wanted—no needed—to be away from her lover's mesmerizing presence so she could think things through. Tears crept slowly down her cheeks as the frozen feeling wore off and miserable, painful reality set in.

Milcham was the Phoenix. An immortal being, thought of as the most beloved animal created by God. That fact all by itself was enough to make her lose her breath. Her shock had been so great she couldn't have said a word if her life had depended on it. Watching him use his powers had been awe inspiring.

She'd grown up with the legend of the Phoenix. Her mother loved stories and fables and told them to Aithne and Aidan every night as they went to sleep. The story of the just and loyal Phoenix was one of them.

Aithne knew, of course, the Phoenix had been the one animal to stand firm in the garden and refuse to disobey the Lord. She also knew God had rewarded him with immortality because of it.

But what she didn't know...what no story ever shared, was the Phoenix was also a man, walking amongst humans, searching for his other half.

And it was this truth that hurt so badly. It was obvious she wasn't it. Oh...she might be good enough to play with for awhile. Maybe he even loved her...in his own fashion. But if he really thought she was his soulmate, he would have told her his true identity long ago. What really wounded her was both Alexander and Jarrod knew. Jarrod had explained they'd seen him come out of the fire when he'd rescued her from her burning tent, but it didn't matter to her. She felt betrayed by all of them.

Scrubbing at her eyes, she was tired and angry and hurt and wanted just for a little while to forget about the whole mess. She knew that she and Milcham would have to talk, but for now she just wanted some time to herself.

The knock at the door surprised her. Thinking it was the motel owner, she walked over and peeked out the curtains. When Aithne saw who it was, she stiffened. Was she ready for this? The knock came again...louder and she shuddered. Her emotions were drawn so tight, she felt like she'd snap in two.

"Aithne," came his beloved voice. "Please, *assai*...I must talk to you."

Tears threatened again, but she bit her lip and forced them back. She knew he was stubborn enough to stand out there all night long. It looked like she would be talking to him, whether she was ready or not.

Pulling the door open, she took a deep breath. "What do you want?"

He showed her a bag of fast food and two cups that smelled deliciously of coffee. "I was worried about you."

Refusing to answer him, she stared past his broad shoulder. If he wasn't going to be honest with her, she was finished with him.

Milcham sighed. "I would ask you give me time to explain, *and* I worried you may be hungry."

She fought with herself for several long moments. Part of her wanted to slam the door in his handsome face, while the other part wanted to leap into his arms and sob out her pain and fear. Terrified the second part would win, she stepped back quickly and motioned him in. "How did you find me?"

Breathing a sigh of relief, Milcham walked inside. Being allowed in was more than he'd expected. "When you weren't in our trailer, I woke Jarrod up and made him tell me." He walked over and put the food on the table, then turned to her. "Eat or talk...your choice."

Aithne wrapped her arms around herself and walked over to the window. "You want to talk...talk."

His jaw tightened, but he nodded. He had everything planned out as to what he was going to say, but now...staring at her angry face, all he could say was one thing.

"I love you, Aithne."

She squeezed her eyes tightly closed as a sob wrenched from her throat. "Don't! Please don't lie to me anymore!"

"I'm not lying!" He took an involuntary step towards her and then stopped. She was holding herself so tightly, he was afraid she'd shatter if he touched her. "Please, *assai.* I have never lied to you about how I feel."

"Just about who you are."

He ran a frustrated hand through his messy hair. "I didn't lie to you. But I know I didn't tell you everything. I do have a reason. Will you give me a chance and let me tell you what it is?"

"Will you leave if I say no?"

His lips twitched into a sad grin. "No."

"Then I don't have any choice...do I?"

Milcham swore out loud. She wasn't going to make this easy. "Then let me tell you this first. I've never told anyone about myself. Ever."

That seemed to catch her attention. "What?"

"It's true," he gritted out. "I have kept my true identity from everyone since I left my home to travel the earth. I was not allowed to share this secret. It was forbidden."

"With anyone?"

Milcham paused for a moment then his eyes met hers. "I am only allowed to share this with the one woman who I consider my twin-flame."

She flinched as if struck and his gut clenched. "*Assai*...please...you don't understand. I was going to tell you."

Aithne's heart was bleeding. She'd asked for the truth. But it hurt so much to actually hear it. "Don't...please."

"It's true," he insisted. "The other night, after you found out about the arson, I told you I had something to tell you. Remember?"

She nodded slowly. "I remember you said you were afraid." She searched his face for the truth. "Is this what you meant?"

"Yes."

"Of what?" She shook her head. "I don't understand."

"Aithne," he gritted out her name almost angrily. "Do you think it's easy to tell the woman you love that you aren't human? That you are almost as old as the earth itself? Do you think words can express the loneliness of immortality or the pain of seeing your friends die of old age while you stay young and healthy?" He paced over to the other side of the room.

"I have been searching for my twin-flame for almost eight hundred years. Eight long, lonely centuries. Longing to find the one woman I could call my own. I'd grown weary of looking. Had accepted that I would go back to my walled city alone." He turned and his golden eyes burned into hers.

"And then I met you."

Aithne's breath caught in her throat. The look in his eyes made her chest ache and her eyes swim with tears.

"I didn't expect to fall like this. With a woman whose gifts and beliefs I didn't understand and had trouble accepting. You were so different from what I had anticipated, I fought our attraction...ignored my feelings for you." He took a step closer. "It was only when I almost lost you that I admitted to myself how I felt." He shook his head. "But even then, I couldn't believe you could be the one."

"Why? Am I so bad?" Her throat ached with unshed tears.

"No. God, no." He came closer and brushed the hair back from her face. As she watched, his eyes filled with tears and using his finger, he caught one and dabbed it gently at a cut on her cheek. It stung slightly and then the pain went away. Turning, she looked in the mirror over the dresser and she could see the cut had disappeared.

"*Assai*, you are perfect. That is why I was so afraid." Gently, he treated the other wounds on her face with the same healing touch. "Once I realized I was completely and totally in love with you, I wanted to tell you. But if you weren't my real soulmate...if this was just an overwhelming attraction, I wasn't sure what would happen to you."

"You think that...I'd be punished?"

Milcham framed her face in his hands, rejoicing that she wasn't pushing him away. "I worried...yes. But I knew I needed to tell you anyway. I love you in a way I've never loved in all my immortal life." His gaze fell. "But I didn't know how you would react. I was afraid you'd turn away from me. So I made the decision to tell you just before I have to leave to go back to the fire."

"Back to the fire?"

He sighed again. "My thousand years are almost up. Soon, I have to leave this place. To keep my immortality, I must return to the walled city and be born again." He brushed his lips over her forehead. "I admit it. I was selfish. If you were to turn away from me, I didn't want to lose even a minute with you. I am truly sorry."

She pulled away and walked over to the bed. "And then we had the accident and you didn't have a choice but to show me who you were."

"Yes." He'd expected her to be much angrier. Would have preferred it to the pain he saw in her eyes. The knowledge he'd hurt her almost killed him.

"Saving Alexander's life was more important than keeping the truth from me."

Milcham flinched, but he nodded. “I love you, Aithne, and I want you to be with me, but if I had let him die, I would never have forgiven myself. I had to do what was right.”

Aithne took a deep breath. Her jumbled emotions made it hard to think. “But why would you think I’d turn away? Milcham...my two best friends are supernaturals. I’m not afraid of them.”

He blinked. “I...I never thought of it that way. I just kept thinking you would look at me with disgust in your eyes.”

“That’s what upsets me the most,” she said quietly. “I loved you and you didn’t trust me. You even trusted Alexander and Jarrod before me.”

“*Assai.* Them finding out was an accident. The only reason they know is because I couldn’t let you die in the tent fire. They saw my Phoenix form carry you out. I know now, I should have told you too, but like I said. I was too selfish...too afraid I would lose you. Please...forgive me.”

She was silent for a long moment and then she sighed. “I want to, Milcham, but I don’t know if I can. It seems like everything has been against us from the beginning. First, you thought I was evil, and so we both pushed each other away. Then, you hid things from me. I’m tired of fighting.” She rubbed her eyes tiredly. “Besides...where do we go from here? The man I love is immortal and I’m not. It’s not like we have a future together. I thought we did, but...”

The irony made her pause. When she was Aidan’s familiar, she was as good as immortal. But then Dawn had taken her place and she’d left to find her own twin-flame, happy to be human again. Her chance at some type of immortality was gone.

Now she found that not only had she discovered her soulmate, it was the loss of her hated immortality that would eventually separate them.

Chapter Fourteen

Milcham's heart pounded. This was it. What he'd waited for almost a millennium to do. "What if I told you we could have a future together?"

Her emerald eyes met his. "What do you mean?"

"*Assai*...I was sent to this world to find my other half. My soulmate. You know this. I believe I found her, in you. It was only my fear and selfishness that prevented me from telling you who I was. But it was never because I didn't love you. I did. I do."

"I still don't understand."

He walked over to her and carefully took her hands, unsure of his reception. "I want you to come with me when I go back to my home. Let me share all that I truly am with you."

Her lips parted. "Come with you? Back to your special city? Can I do that?"

His heart beat even faster. "Yes." He touched her cheek with a gentle finger. "You are the only one I have ever asked, Aithne. You are who I want to spend eternity with."

"If we go to your special city, we can be together...forever?"

"The city is the first step. If you are happy there, then, if you still wish it, I will tell you how we can share our lives together."

She frowned at him. "Why can't you tell me now?"

Milcham's gaze slid away. He still cringed at the thought of telling her about the fire. He would work up to it. Once she was in his beautiful home, perhaps it would be easier for her to understand. "It is best to let you see things a little at a time."

There was a pregnant silence. Then, fury coloring her face, Aithne jerked away from him and paced to the door. She flung it open and turned to him. "Get out!"

His eyes widened. "What?"

"You still want to keep things from me? After everything we've been through? You haven't learned anything at all, Milcham!"

His jaw clenched as he understood her meaning. "I do this to protect you, *assai*."

Aithne tossed her head. "Like you did about the arson? Or keeping your identity from me?" She glared at him. "If that's the way it is, then...*no*! I don't want to go with you."

Milcham was so astonished by the refusal, he staggered back away from her. "You say no to me? I have never offered this to another woman...and you say no?"

Her eyes flashed. "While I am humbled to know I'm the only one," she hissed sarcastically, "if you can't be honest with me, I don't want any part of it. I deserve better, Milcham." She pointed out the door. "Please leave."

Anger, sorrow and pain filled him as he stared at her. The woman he loved was turning him down. In all his years, he'd never imagined this scenario. But she stood with her chin raised, her beautiful eyes filled with tears, and he knew she meant every word of what she said.

As if in a dream, he walked towards the door. How could it end this way? He'd found his mate just to lose her again? As he passed Aithne, he could smell the sweet scent of her perfume, and his heart ached with grief. He remembered all the long lonely years of his past, and he thought of all the years ahead without her. Suddenly, he couldn't bear it.

Turning, he pulled her into his arms, burying his face in her fragrant hair. “I can't,” he choked out. “I won't leave you. Don't ask this of me. I love you, Aithne. I can't walk away from you. I'd rather stay here with you and become mortal than leave you, knowing what we mean to each other.”

Aithne was pummeled by the force of his emotions. He wasn't hiding them now. What he felt was all over his face, in the shaking of his body pressed against hers. In the tears touching her cheeks. Her own love expanded and went out to intertwine with his. Slowly, her arms went up and encircled him.

He shuddered. “Tell me what to do, *assai*. How can I make this right?” He pulled away from her and looked down into her face. “You want to know everything? I'll tell you. Just please...don't ask me to leave.”

Burying her face in his chest, she let the tears flow. He'd finally opened all the way up, letting her see his beautiful soul, just like her hungry heart needed. This was the gift she'd been looking for her whole life.

“*Assai*,” he whispered, framing her wet face in his hands. “Tell me it's not too late. We love each other. We can fix this!”

She shivered at the wealth of emotion in his voice. The wall of her anger and pain fell away, crashing to her feet. Leaning up, she kissed him tenderly. “I love you, Milcham. Don't leave me. Don't ever leave me.”

Her breath whooshed out of her as he crushed her to him. His mouth slanted over hers with so much feeling, her knees immediately turned to water. His tongue dove deep between her lips as if he was parched for a drink of her. Lifting her in his arms, he carried her over to the bed. As they fell down upon it, he continued to whisper words of love in her ears.

His hand moved up to cup her breast and she gasped. “Tell me you want this,” he murmured. “If it is too fast—”

She stopped his words with a hard kiss. “Love me, Milcham. Show me how forever will be with you.”

Milcham's eyes glowed with happiness. Bending, he tasted her lips again. He shuddered at the flavor. Always delicious, always sweet. He smiled against her mouth. This was not the fancy hotel he'd dreamed of, and instead of a delicious meal, they would have cold hamburgers and stale coffee, but it didn't really matter where they were...the lovemaking would still be glorious.

Their clothes melted off, piece by piece. They kept their eyes on each other, desire simmering as their nakedness was revealed. Aithne ran her hand down his chest to the throbbing evidence of his need for her. His loud groan made her hunger even more for him, and it was as if it had been years since they'd made love together.

He kissed her. Her lips, her cheeks, the indent of her chin. All were treated to his loving touch. His mouth moved down her neck to her shoulders, and he gave a growl when he saw torn flesh caused by the accident. She watched as tears welled up and then fell on her bruised skin. A momentary pain, and then the cut was gone, smoothed away as if only a bad memory.

"I am so sorry you were hurt," he whispered as his tongue tasted the crown of her breast. "I would do anything to keep you safe. Anything."

She arched against him. Her body softened, her legs shifted, opening to bring him deep inside of her.

He smiled at her movements then sucked her nipple into his mouth. Her cry of delight sent tremors of heat through him. His cock pulsed against Aithne's flat stomach, and he wondered suddenly what she would look like heavy with his child.

The thought almost sent him over the edge, and he had to pull back to regain control. He concentrated instead on touching her soft body, marveling she was in his arms and all was as it should be. His hand moved to between her legs and when she moaned again, he drove two fingers deep within her heated channel.

Aithne screamed when he touched her, bucking against him. He covered her mouth with his as he used his fingers to fuck her. He teased her, pulling all the way out, and then pushing deep inside of her again, all the while tickling her clit with his thumb.

Her body was ablaze. He'd brought her to peak so quickly, Aithne didn't have time to do anything but ride the river of fire. She desperately wanted him inside her, but the thought of him not touching her was more than she could contemplate. She didn't have words to ask for more, so she just moved against him, trying to entice him in the only way she knew how.

When his mouth moved again to her breast, she couldn't take any more. Her body imploded, streams of red heat shot through her, all ending up where Milcham's fingers danced in her quim. She cried out his name and climaxed, her mind blanking of everything but the sensations in her body and the love in her heart.

Milcham hurt...he was so hard. His cock ached like a sore tooth, and he could barely manage to wait until Aithne had come before he removed his hand and replaced his fingers with his throbbing cock. When he slid deep into her, they both cried out again.

There was nothing like having your lover's body held tightly against yours...surrounding you. He kissed her again and then began to thrust, fast and sure into her still trembling body.

Her legs came up around him, and his balls pulled even tighter. His cock drove against her sensitive clit, and he wanted to make her explode again.

Her nails bit into his shoulders, and leaning forward, she sucked his flat masculine nipple into her mouth. He growled at the exquisite feeling and reaching down, grabbed her butt, grinding himself against her.

Her body tightened around him, squeezing him, just like he'd longed for. Holding back his own pleasure, he waited for her. When her eyes flew open and she screamed again, he let go of his control and joined her.

Wrapped tightly in each other's arms, they shattered, spinning out of control, the burning heat of their climaxes mirrored in each other's body. The white hot light of pure love danced around them until they slowly, gently, drifted again back to earth.

They lay...content in each other's arms. All the anger and pain erased for the moment. After what had happened earlier, neither was eager to end the happy afterglow of their lovemaking.

But, eventually, Milcham stirred and kissed Aithne's smiling mouth. "Thank you, *assai.* For giving me another chance."

She brushed the hair out of his eyes. "I do love you, Milcham. And I want to be with you. I just want to know the truth from now on."

He sighed. "It will not be easy, but yes...I will tell you everything. I just hope you don't judge me too harshly."

Her brows furrowed. "Judge you? Why would I judge you?"

Rolling, he moved so she lay on top of him. He flipped her dark hair behind her shoulder. "I am not the same being that left the walled city, centuries ago. I have changed, and some of it wasn't for the better. Being human in this world is much harder than I thought it would be."

"In what way?"

"There are—" he swallowed hard, "—many temptations out there."

Aithne smiled. "You don't have to be perfect, Milcham. All you have to do is try your best."

He pressed a kiss against her soft lips. "Thank you for that. It took me years to understand that was what Yahweh meant when he sent me out. In my walled city, it was very easy to be good and righteous, but in the real world..."

"Not so easy?"

"Almost impossible. I did try. I still do. But I am not the same creature that left home eight centuries ago. I don't know how I will be received."

She touched his cheek. "Don't you think that God already knows what you've been through? Your struggles and successes? He does see all. He won't be surprised."

"No," Milcham said slowly, as if he were just thinking it through. "But because I have changed, he may treat me differently."

"How? What happened when you left the first time?"

Milcham sighed. "I had lived in my city for over five millennia. At first it was paradise and I loved it, but then I realized something was missing."

"What?"

He dropped a kiss on her nose. "I was lonely. Everyone in the city had someone to love. A mate to call their own. Everybody but me."

Aithne heard the loneliness and her tender heart wept for him. "What happened to the female Phoenix? The stories never speak of her."

Milcham's eyes darkened with remembered pain and anger. "She...she decided to fall with the others. Nothing I said made any difference. When Eve tempted me, my mate was right beside her." He sighed. "Walking away from her was the hardest thing I ever had to do in my life."

She hugged him. "I'm so sorry!"

Wrapping his arms around her, he hugged her back. "If I had not stood firm, I wouldn't be here with you today. I cannot be sorry about that."

"Still...five thousand years is a long time to go without."

His cheeks reddened. "In my city, I didn't care. But once I became a man, my body had...needs. I found it wasn't hard to have those needs taken care of."

Aithne tweaked his nipple gently and he jumped. “Don’t know if I want to hear about all that.” Then she sighed. “Yes...yes I do. I have to ask. There was no one else?”

He chuckled. “There were other women I cared about. Some who meant a great deal to me. But none so much I wanted to tell them about myself.” He cupped her face in his big hand. “You alone hold that honor, *assai.*”

She smiled, her heart melting again. “I love you, Milcham.”

He groaned and kissed her. It was a long time before he took his mouth from hers. “There...there is more of the story.”

Aithne snuggled against his chest. “Tell me.”

“When I pleaded with Yahweh to allow me to search for a mate, he agreed, telling me only I would have to return at the end of my thousand years to be reborn. I went to sleep that night rejoicing. I was excited about seeing the world.”

“What happened?”

Milcham’s eyes glowed hot amber. “During the night, the Ancient One came and convinced Yahweh he should be allowed to tempt me. He said only through temptation and challenge would I truly appreciate my mate when I found her.”

Her eyes widened. “You’re talking about Satan?”

“Yes. And he has done everything he could to make my existence difficult. From the beginning, he put women in my path. Those that didn’t know how to love or care for anyone but themselves. For a while I fell for it, but then I learned who I could trust. But he never stopped.”

Aithne blinked as understanding hit her. “That’s why you thought I was evil. You thought Satan...the Ancient One sent me.”

“I was wrong...and I am sorry for it. I had been taught over the centuries what you can do is a sign of wickedness. I know better now.”

She put chin in her hands. “So what did you do for all those centuries?”

He grinned. "I have explored the world. I spent a great deal of time searching for my mate in the animal world, but I realized after a few hundred years, I wasn't an animal. Even though I may take the form of one...I am more."

"You are definitely more!"

He kissed her again. "Knowing this, I began to look in the human world for my mate."

"And I was the first woman who made you take a second look?"

Again Milcham thought briefly of the few minutes a century ago when he'd had that extra special feeling. Now that he had Aithne, he knew it had been very similar.

"There was one other time," he said quietly. "But it turned out to be nothing. I forgot about it quickly and moved on." He frowned again. "I thought at the time, it might be another temptation. The Ancient One has become more active in recent years. And I think he has moved from tossing inappropriate women in front of me to something more insidious."

"What do you mean?"

Milcham didn't want to tell her, but he'd promised. "I don't want to scare you, *assai.*"

She leaned up on an elbow, her green eyes intense. "Too late. Tell me what you're thinking."

He sighed. "I think the Ancient One realized that you were my soulmate, and he took steps to make sure we didn't get together."

She was too intelligent not to understand what he meant. She sat up with a gasp. "You mean he caused my tent fire?"

Nodding grimly, he pulled her back into the curve of his arm. "As well as the men who attacked you." He gave her a quick hug. "And...if I'm not mistaken...I don't think it was Alexander who was supposed to die in that accident tonight."

She went very still. "You think Satan wants me dead?"

Rolling over, he pulled her back beneath him, knowing it would comfort her to have his body over the top of hers. “I told you it was frightening…but yes…this is what I believe.”

“Because he doesn’t want me to go with you to the walled city?”

“Yes.”

“I don’t understand. Why does Satan care if you succeed or not? What’s it to him?”

Milcham traced her lips with his finger. “He hates me,” he said simply. “I was the one creature in the garden who resisted his temptation. I am a favorite of Yahweh. When I was given this opportunity to go find my beloved, he saw it as a chance to destroy me…once and for all.”

“But he didn’t succeed, did he? I mean we found each other, and you want me to go back home with you.”

“He is a deceiver, Aithne. He will use our own fears against us. He whispered in my ear that you wouldn’t accept who I was, and I almost fell for it. When I saw the trailer was empty, I came close to packing up and leaving immediately.”

Her eyes burned at the thought she might have lost him forever. “I’m so sorry. I needed time to think. That’s why I left. It wasn’t for good.”

He held her tightly. “In the end, I couldn’t leave either. I had to try to make you understand. Yet even then, my fears got in the way.”

“Then tell me now about the city, Milcham. What will happen there?”

His jaw clenched. “The city is in a place beyond time, *assai.* We will get there by what some would call magic.” He kissed her as if he needed the contact. “When we arrive, I will show you how wonderful it is.” His eyes shone in remembrance. “It is the most beautiful place on this earth.”

“I can’t wait to see it.”

"I'm not sure if the Lord will greet us or not. He comes and goes as he pleases. But this I do know. On the last day of the thousandth year of my life, I must be reborn."

Her eyes searched his as her heart beat faster in her chest. Suddenly, she knew whatever he had to tell her would change her life irrevocably. "You...will die and then come back to life?"

He nodded. "I will build my nest, and at dawn, I will sing my song to Yahweh and the sun. Then I will be consumed by fire to be born again. In this way, I am made immortal."

"And what about me?" she whispered. Somehow hearing the tale of his joyous rebirth made dread well up inside of her.

He looked at her, his amber eyes serious. "If you wish to join me in immortality, you too must enter the refiner's fire. You too...must die."

Chapter Fifteen

Aithne's face went as white as snow. "Fire?" she whispered, terror rising up inside of her. "I have to be burned in a fire?"

He nodded slowly. "If you wish to be my mate, you must be consumed by fire and born again."

Aithne fought against the sickness that rose in her throat. Fire. Her worst nightmare. The one thing in all the world she feared more than anything. She'd thought the tent fire was a nightmare. But this? Would she be able to walk into a burning fire on her own? A thousand thoughts raced through her mind, but she couldn't speak at all. Knowing what she faced made her mind blank and her mouth go dry. But even with all the fear invading her soul, she knew she would go with him. She loved him too much to do anything else.

Watching her, Milcham knew something was wrong. She'd gone so pale, he was afraid she would faint. "*Assai*...talk to me. Why does this upset you so?"

She stared at him. "I just went through a horrible fire. It...scares me."

He sighed. "There is more."

"What?"

"There are rules I have to follow. As you know, I could only tell the woman I believe to be my soulmate who I am. But I must also tell her what might happen when she leaps into the flame with me."

"I don't think I'm going to like this."

Milcham was pretty sure she was right. "I'm sorry. But you must know the truth before we go any farther. If you are my soulmate, you will be reborn in the fire as I am. After that, I'm not sure of the details. I only know you will be immortal."

"And if I'm not?"

He held her tightly. "If you aren't my true twin-flame, the fire will consume you, and...you will die."

"You aren't kidding me, are you?" She pressed a hand over her stomach and he worried briefly she was going to be sick. "No." She answered her own question before he could. "You're saying if I'm not who we think I am, I'm going to burn to death.

Her fear was apparent. Milcham could see all the emotions flicker across her face. Thinking quickly, he realized all he could do was try and make her more confident in what was ahead. Wrapping his arms around her, he rolled off the bed with her.

She squealed and grabbed his neck. "Milcham! What are you doing?"

"Proving you don't have anything to worry about."

"I don't understand."

"When you leap into the fire with me, my flames will protect you." He looked at the bed and grinned. "Unfortunately, I seem to singe other things, and since I intend to use the bed again, I moved us."

Aithne went very still. "But you burned Alexander! I saw you!"

He nodded. "Yes. But I got you out of your tent by holding you in my arms. My body protected you. I can only believe it's because we are meant to be together. Please, Aithne...you must trust me."

Her lips quivered as she stared deep into his eyes. He held his breath as she fought her fears. Finally, closing her eyes, she buried her face in his neck and nodded.

His eyes glowed in relief and gratitude. She was still terrified, but she trusted him to take care of her. Her trust was a gift in itself. He wouldn't let her down.

At first, Aithne felt nothing. Then, so slowly she almost missed it, the warmth came. She sensed it at her fingertips and toes first before it covered the rest of her. Soon, her entire body was cocooned in a bubble of heated comfort.

Cautiously, she opened her eyes. Her whole body glowed. Gasping, she turned and looked at Milcham. He was there, looking right at her, his golden eyes filled with love and passion for her. But, when she looked again, he changed. His human face melted into his Phoenix one. His blond hair caught fire, and the arms that held her so carefully turned to burnished wings of purple and gold.

"You're beautiful." It was the first thing that came out of her mouth. In response, the Phoenix's eyes burned even brighter and without warning, he caught fire, filling the room with golden light.

Aithne cried out in fear, but she immediately realized she wasn't burning, nor was she hurt in any way. She watched in awe as tendrils of scarlet fire wrapped around her body, licking at her with its warmth. Joy bubbled up inside of her. Milcham had told the truth. His fire didn't hurt her. Not in the slightest.

She laughed out loud and threw her arms around him. "I love you," she shouted, her heart overflowing with happiness. "I love you!"

The Phoenix smiled and tossed her in the air to land squealing again in the curve of his wings. She could sense his utter happiness. Then his wingtip touched her cheek gently, and he began to sing.

In his human form, Milcham had a fine voice and was teased by the other carny folk that he was on the wrong side of the desk when it came to entertainment. He was often asked to sing for his supper and enjoyed doing so. But nothing had prepared Aithne for how he sang as the Phoenix.

As soon as he opened his beak, the most glorious song poured from his throat. While the words weren't human, she could understand them. Tears streamed down her cheeks as she listened.

He sang of his love for her. Of their life together and the future that lay so golden before them. He told her exactly how he felt in every sweet, liquid note he offered her. When the song finally ended, she was sobbing in his arms. Never had she been loved so much...so completely. She was so caught up in what she was feeling, she didn't even notice when he shifted into a man.

When he laid her back down on the bed, she stared up at him, her emerald eyes drenched in tears. He bent and kissed her gently. "I love you Aithne...in any form. As a man or as the immortal Phoenix. I have spent every moment on this earth searching for you, and I know now, I never want to be without you. Say you will come with me. Back to my walled city to be born again with me in Yahweh's renewing fire. I swear I will protect you and take care of you. You'll want for nothing as my mate." His gaze moved over her face with a vulnerability she'd never really seen before. "Please, *assai*...I need you. Will you come with me and be mine...forever?"

Her throat was so clogged with tears, she couldn't speak. She thought of Aidan and Dawn and how she would miss them. Her mind flashed to Alexander and Jarrod and all the friends she'd made here, in the carnival. Could she leave them forever to go live in a place beyond time?

Then the man standing above her smiled, and Aithne's heart melted. She knew that those worries were unimportant. She was in love with Milcham, and she would follow him anywhere. Lifting her arms to him, she pulled him down to her.

"To be without you would be a much worse death than I can imagine," she whispered. "Please...take me with you. Not for immortality or for the riches of your wonderful city. But because you are my soulmate, my twin-flame. The man I've been searching for my whole life. Because I need you just as much as you need me." Her tears overflowed and she smiled as he kissed them away. "But mostly because I love you, Milcham...Phoenix...whatever you want to call yourself, more than my own life."

Pulling her under him, Milcham held her tightly. His heart beat so hard with joy it was almost painful. "Then it will be so. We will go together to test the fire, but immortality or not, I couldn't love you more than I do right this minute."

She smiled and moved invitingly under him. "Then show me again, my eternal lover. Show me what I have to look forward to for the next thousand years."

No more was said as he buried himself deep inside her willing body. They spent the rest of the night showing each other that their twin flames of passion would never go out.

"And you know that payroll needs to go out by the fifteenth," Milcham said as he looked at the papers in his hands. "I've left you my power of attorney, so you shouldn't have any problem writing checks." He looked around at his messy desk. "I know I'm forgetting something."

Alexander sighed from where he sat taking notes on the other side of the desk. "Are you sure this is necessary? I mean...maybe you will be able to come back."

Milcham's jaw tightened. Part of him wanted to come back to this human life very much. Living here with Aithne held great appeal to him. But he looked forward to going home as well. "I don't know what the future will bring, my friend. We must be prepared for the possibility I am not allowed to return. I won't leave the carnival hanging in that way. Someone must be able to make decisions."

"And you're sure I'm the one, huh?"

Grinning, Milcham handed over the accounting books. "You are the best one for the job. You've been helping me run this place for months now. And we both know your temperament is much better suited for a lot of the management jobs around here."

Alexander snickered. "Hey...you can't help having a temper. And Aithne doesn't seem to mind."

Milcham chuckled. "Yes, for being a gentle woman, she gives as good as she gets. I am a lucky man."

"I'm just glad it turned out all right." Alexander shook his head. "I wasn't sure she'd talk to any of us for a while."

Milcham remembered the look on Aithne's face when she first realized the other men knew his secret. "I hope to never put her in a position like that again."

"How does she feel about leaving everything behind?"

"It is a miracle." Milcham was still awed by her choice to accompany him. "She loves me enough to go with me. To leave all that she has ever known. Even after everything I did, she trusts me."

"Love and trust go hand in hand." Alexander smiled sadly. "I don't know if I'll ever find someone like that."

"Of course you will. Your soulmate is out there as well."

Alexander shook his head. "Women like Aithne are not easy to find. One who won't mind, that you aren't...normal. Hell, it took you eight hundred years. What chance do I have to find someone in a single lifetime?"

"The right woman won't care you can communicate with the dead, my friend. She will love you anyway."

"It's not...just talking to ghosts anymore, Milcham." Alexander stood abruptly and paced over to the small window. "I'm not sure any woman could handle what I can do now."

Milcham could hear the pain and frustration in his friend's voice. "What are you talking about? What's changed?"

Alexander turned to him. “Have you ever done to someone else, what you did to me?”

“Heal them? Of course. Many times.”

“No, I don’t mean just heal them.” Alexander ran his hand through his dark locks. “I mean...you brought me back from the dead.”

“You were farther gone than any other I have healed,” Milcham said carefully. “But I don’t have the power of resurrection. Only Yahweh has that. You weren’t dead. At least, not completely.”

“But I was partially dead,” Alexander insisted. “And if you hadn’t brought me back, I would have died.”

“Yes.” Milcham gazed in concern at him. “What are you getting at, Alexander? What has happened to you?”

“When I...died...went to the other side, or whatever you want to call it, something happened to me. I came back...changed. I’m not the same man I was.”

“You went through a frightening experience. Of course you’ve changed.”

Alexander slammed his fist into the wall. “That’s not what I mean.”

“Okay...okay,” Milcham soothed him. He rose from his seat. “Tell me then. Can you still speak to your Ethereals?”

“Yes, that’s still the same. But that’s not all I can do.”

“I don’t understand.”

Alexander sighed. “It’s easier to show you than to tell you. Watch.” He moved away from the wall to back in front of the desk.

Milcham stared at his friend. At first he saw nothing. Alexander just stood before him, his azure eyes dark with a mixture of fear and worry. Then suddenly, so slowly Milcham’s eyes couldn’t register what he was seeing, it happened.

Alexander went transparent.

Gasping in astonishment, Milcham closed his eyes and then reopened them. Alexander gradually faded until all that could be seen was a faint outline of his body.

"I can disappear completely," came Alexander's disembodied voice. "But I thought you'd like to see this first."

"You're...invisible." Milcham sat down hard on his chair. "How can this be?"

Little by little, Alexander regained his solid form. "I was hoping you could tell me."

"I have no idea. This is new to me as well."

"It's not all."

Milcham swallowed. "What else can there be?"

"You'd be surprised," Alexander muttered. Leaning down, he put his hand on Milcham's desk. "Watch."

They both stared at his lean hand. Without warning, it vanished. But this time, instead of becoming invisible, it pushed through the papers and melted into the desk itself. Alexander moved and the limb moved from side to side in the desk as easily as if the hard wood was water.

Milcham shook his head. "This is impossible."

Alexander's lips quirked into a smile. "As impossible as a man who is the immortal Phoenix?"

"You can turn invisible *and* you can walk through walls?"

"If I want." He pulled his hand from the desk and flexed it. "Feels weird, but it doesn't seem to damage anything."

"You think I had something to do with this?" Guilt rose up in Milcham. Had he done this to his friend?

Alexander surprised him with his answer. "No, it's not your fault. I think it happened when I went into the light. I came out of it like this. Other than saving my life, you didn't have anything to do with it. Maybe I need to look at it as another gift. I don't only talk to the dead, I can act like them, too."

Milcham thought about all the times a gift like that would come in handy. “You could use it for good, you know. Perhaps you can help others. Not just the Ethereals anymore.”

“Maybe.” Alexander gave a little grin. “I guess I was hoping you’ve run across this somewhere in your travels, but it is a little weird.” He laughed and his face brightened. “You should have seen me the first time it happened. I was reaching for the door to the trailer and I fell right through. Jarrod screamed like a girl. Then he immediately wanted me to try out my new skill in the women’s shower room.”

Both men broke into laughter. After a while, Milcham sobered. “I am sorry I can’t be of more help.”

Alexander shrugged. “Now you can see why finding a lady of my own will be difficult. What woman would want a man like me?”

“Hey!” Milcham came around the desk and clapped his shoulder. “You’d be surprised at who is out there. When the time is right, you *will* find her. This I know.”

The dark man smiled. “And is this a prophecy from the Phoenix? Or just the belief of a friend?”

Milcham thought of the love he and Aithne shared. Somehow he knew deep in his soul Alexander would find the same. “Both, my friend…both.”

“Are you sure you want to give up everything you know and go live in a place you’ve never seen before?”

Aithne smiled as she helped Jarrod blow up balloons on the dart game. “As long as I’m with Milcham, I don’t care where I live.”

Jarrod growled. “Won’t you miss everyone? I mean…there won’t be any humans in the city, will there?”

"I don't know who will be in the city, and of course I'll miss everyone. But Milcham and I hope we can come back, at least to visit. You're not getting rid of us that easily."

Jarrod grumbled under his breath. "I still wish you were both staying here."

Aithne leaned over and gave the big man a hug. "We don't know what's going to happen, Jarrod. But be glad for us. We are both so happy."

The werewolf was silent for a few minutes. All that could be heard was the sound of balloons filling with air. Then he looked at her. "Have you told him about Aidan yet?"

Aithne's beautiful mouth tightened. In the last few days she'd been thinking a lot about Aidan as well as what she should tell Milcham about him. Her past hadn't even crossed her mind before—it was just that...in her past. But after he'd been less than honest, worry about whether she should tell him about the first years of her life began niggling at her. She'd had to examine her own heart, and it had taken several days of soul searching, but knowing how Milcham had reacted to things in the past, she'd made a tough decision. And she had to admit to herself she was still struggling with it. She cleared her throat. "He knows I have an older brother. That's enough."

He stopped blowing up the balloons and turned to look at her. "You got so angry with him about not telling you about being the Phoenix; do you really think it's okay not to tell him about your brother?"

She turned and glared at him, pushing back the worry he was right in his concern. "There is a huge difference between the two. I've never had to lie to him because Aidan and what we were to each other is in my past. It's over and done with, and I'm human now. Besides, they will never even meet. But Milcham was and is the Phoenix. That isn't just his past, but his future, one I'll be a part of. I had a right to know."

Jarrod shook his head and turned back to the board. "You're fooling yourself, girl. Your past made you what you are today, and he has a right to know about it. You shouldn't hide from what you really are."

Her eyes flashed at him. "Is that so?"

He nodded grimly. "I may not be as smart as Milcham or Alexander, but I know what's right and you keeping your past from him isn't."

"So I shouldn't hide what I was, huh?" Guilt that he was somehow right fueled her anger, and she reacted defensively, turning the tables right back on him. Tossing the inflator nozzle down on the ground, she stomped her foot. "Maybe you should practice what you preach."

"What the hell is that supposed to mean?"

"It means...you've been hiding since you got here. When are you going to come clean about *your* past?"

Jarrod froze where he stood. "That has nothing to do with this!"

She tossed her head. "Maybe not, but if you're going to start berating me about my actions, you better not be doing the same."

"You have no idea what you're talking about!"

Aithne sighed. "Aidan and I knew some werewolves over the years. And I know something about them." She reached over and jerked his shirt sleeve up to show the tattoo of a wolf, high on his left arm. Howling at the moon and surrounded by lightning bolts, it was a beautiful piece of art.

"I know this is a sign of leadership in a wolf clan. And, if you are a leader and you aren't with your people, then one of two things happened. You either rejected them or you were denied your place in the pack."

His face filled with fury and pain. "It's none of your business!"

"No," she agreed, her eyes bright with tears. "It's not. It's *your* past. But I'm your friend, Jarrod. I love you and I know you're hurting. I know you don't agree with how I'm handling my past and Milcham, but if you want to talk...I'll listen. No matter what."

She could see him struggling, and going on instinct, she wrapped her arms around him. "Is it so bad, really?"

His massive arms engulfed her, and he shuddered. "You can't tell anyone."

"You've kept my secret...I'll keep yours."

He pulled away and went to stand next to the side of the booth. His face was drawn and tight. "You're right. I was next in line for my clan leadership. My father was old and ready to die, so I set about finding a mate and getting myself prepared to take over when he finally passed beyond the moon."

"Go on," she urged.

Jarrod cleared his throat. "I found a mate. Her name was Benasia. She was sweet and beautiful, and I fell hard for her. We planned out our life, and I thought all was perfect." Pacing over to the other side of the stand, he turned and looked back at her.

"My father died, and after we sent his soul to the moon goddess, I came forward to accept my place as leader and finalize my mating with Bena. As you may know, there are often challenges to a new rule, and I wasn't surprised when I too was tested." He rubbed his eyes. "It was who challenged me that was the surprise."

"Who was it?"

Jarrod's chocolate eyes were full of remembered anger. "It was Theos. Benasia's brother. I couldn't believe my mate's family would turn against me."

Aithne's heart hurt for her friend. "What happened?"

"As is our custom, clan members are to encircle their choice. Most surrounded me, but someone was missing. Bena had chosen her brother."

"But...but..." She didn't need him to tell her what a betrayal that was. It was the same in the vampire world. Going against your own—it was beyond wrong.

"I was infuriated. I went to them and tried to force her to my side." Jarrod looked at Aithne, and she could see the confusion that still touched his eyes. "She wore my first mark. She was my mate in everything but name. I loved her." He turned away and stared out over the empty carnival.

"When I grabbed her, he attacked me. Not even waiting for the ceremony to start, he went for my jugular. I didn't think, I just protected myself."

Jarrod looked back at Aithne. "I killed him with one blow."

"You killed her brother?"

He scrubbed at his face as if he could erase the memory of what he saw. "Benasia went crazy. She threw herself on her brother's body and cursed me. Then she told the whole pack the truth of why her brother had challenged me."

"Why? It doesn't make sense."

Jarrod stared at her with eyes as bleak as a northern winter. "She screamed it so all could hear. He wasn't just her brother...he was her mate as well." He flinched when Aithne gasped. "But that isn't all. She told me she hated me, had always hated me. There was only one reason she had agreed to become my mate."

Sickness curled in her stomach. "Oh no, Jarrod. Not that."

He nodded grimly. "Yes...even as she received my mark on her body, she carried his pup in her belly. When he saw her coming forward to become my mate, he lost it. Couldn't handle the thought of her being with me, so he issued the challenge."

"What happened to her?"

"Their relationship was an abomination. One of the things not tolerated by clan. My people attacked her, ready to tear her apart. I couldn't let them." His eyes misted with memories. "I'd loved her. I told them as their leader I would decide her fate."

He looked at Aithne. "I was going to have her locked up until I could decide what to do with her, but before I could say anything, she attacked me from behind, driving a knife deep between my shoulder blades." He squeezed his eyes closed. "It was made of silver."

Aithne went to him, holding him tight as the horror of what he'd been through coursed through her. Jarrod kept talking, as if the bitterness of the memory had to be purged. "I collapsed and in the confusion, she escaped. But when I recovered, my clan had turned from me. They said I had been blinded by emotion and was too weak to lead them. They gave leadership to my cousin instead."

"I am so sorry," she murmured to him. "They were wrong. It takes strength to have compassion."

"I left as soon as I was able," he went on. "I chose not to fight for my place in the pack. I couldn't stay there. Everywhere I turned, I could see my shame in their eyes."

Aithne pulled away and looked up at him. "It wasn't your shame, Jarrod. It was theirs. Whether you would have decided to have her killed or not, making snap judgments is never smart. They accused you of too much emotion, when it was them who were out of control."

"Either way, I decided to leave my clan and strike out on my own. It was the hardest thing I ever did." He sighed. "It's why I worry about you going off on your own."

"I'll have Milcham," Aithne said quietly. Again she had to force down the worry of what her mate-to-be would do if he found out why she'd kept her past a secret from him. Again she told herself that what had happened between her and Aidan had no bearing on her future with Milcham.

"I just don't want you to get hurt," the wolfman said, interrupting her turbulent thoughts. "You know how lonely being alone can be."

"Yes, I do. But Milcham isn't going to walk away from me. He loves me. And I won't do anything to ruin that."

"Telling him the truth won't ruin it. It will free you both."

Aithne swallowed and shook off the worry she felt. "I'm not going to even think about it." She hugged him again. "Both of us have painful pasts. Neither of us wants to talk about them, so we won't. We will only go forward from here."

Jarrod kissed the top of her ebony head. "I hope so, girl. I hope so." He sighed and prayed to whatever gods were listening that Aithne wasn't making the biggest mistake of her life.

Chapter Sixteen

"Milcham...where are you taking me?"

He looked over at her pouting lips and chuckled. "That will not get me to give away my surprise, *assai*."

Aithne sighed and put on one of the small emerald earrings he'd insisted on buying her that day. Looking in the mirror, she admired how they were the exact same color as her eyes. He did have good taste. As he did with lingerie. He'd also chosen the emerald lace corset set she was wearing. It was clingy, sexy and easily removed, and his eyes glowed like candles when he'd first seen her in it. She'd half-expected him to tear it off, but so far he was controlling himself. "But I can't dress properly if I don't know where I'm going."

Laughing, Milcham went to the closet, pulling out his choice. "It is said a little black dress goes anywhere."

Putting her hands on her hips, she studied him. He'd been so much more open and demonstrative with her since their argument earlier in the week. His eyes were clearer and he smiled more. It was as if a huge burden had been lifted from his shoulders.

They'd finished up all the business at the carnival, leaving it in Alexander's capable hands. With Jarrod to help him, Milcham was sure everything would go smoothly. They'd packed a few things, then headed to the airport where Aithne found, to her amusement and Milcham's disgruntlement, that he'd never flown in a plane before.

He quickly reminded her that being a creature with wings he'd never needed to avail himself of another form of transportation. It was then she realized it was only because she was with him they were taking this journey at all. If he'd been alone, he would have magically flown to his walled city home.

Now, as she looked at him standing so smugly by their hotel bed, she was thankful all over again he loved her and she was going home with him.

"Aithne?"

She walked to him and put her arms around his trim waist. "So, if you want me to wear that little scrap of a dress, you must have something special in mind."

"I do."

"And since this is New York City...maybe you are taking me to see a Broadway play? Or an exclusive restaurant?"

He laughed and slapped her gently on the butt. "I am not telling you. It is a surprise. Now get dressed."

Heaving a mock sigh, she let her shoulders sag as she walked away from him. "Okay," she sniffed in a tearful voice. "Be that way."

She gave a muffled shriek when he spun her around and tossed her on the bed. "Milcham!"

He came down on top of her, nipping at her lips and running his hand up her semi-naked body. He cupped her breast through the tiny bra and squeezed it lovingly. "You looked so sad. I thought you needed to be reminded of how much I want you."

She narrowed her eyes when she saw the twinkle in his. "Oh! You didn't believe me for a second, did you?"

"Nope."

She ran her fingers down his side to the large bulge growing between his legs. "And I suppose this means you want to have your way with me?"

He gave a growling laugh. "*Assai*...I always want to have my way with you!"

"Well, here I am all dressed in this sexy outfit, lying on this huge bed, with you on top of me. I wonder what you'll do with me now?"

Brushing his mouth gently over hers, Milcham answered the question the best way he knew how. His tongue swept over her lips in a teasing kiss, then dipped into the warmth of her mouth to taste her unique sweetness. Clasping her tightly to him, he moved his hard body sensuously against her. "I will show you exactly what I am going to do to you, but..." He slapped her ass again, rolling them both off the bed. "Not now, or we are going to be late."

He grinned when she pouted. "None of that," he ordered, tossing the dress to her. "Now go cover up before I do what I want to do and we never leave this hotel room."

Giggling, Aithne sauntered into the bathroom. "You don't know what you missed."

Adjusting himself, Milcham groaned. "Oh yes, I do."

An hour later Aithne stared out the taxi's window in wonder. The tall buildings around her looked like they touched the sky. She'd been in a lot of towns since Aidan was first turned, but they'd never made it as far as New York City.

"Are you enjoying yourself, *assai*?"

She turned and grinned at him. "This is an amazing place." Turning back, she gawked at the stream of people pouring out of Grand Central Station. "There are so many of them."

Milcham leaned over and looked to where she was pointing. "Yes, this is one of the busiest places in the world."

She slanted him a look. "You've been here before?"

Nodding, he took her hand in his. "Several times, but not recently. As you noticed...too many people."

"And yet...here we are now."

Milcham grinned as he thought of the surprise he was planning. "I thought you would like to see the sights."

She pounced on that. "You're taking me sightseeing?"

He laughed aloud. "Tomorrow. Tonight, I have something else in mind."

Aithne leaned over and bit him gently on the chin. "It must be special. You shaved again."

They pulled up in front of a brightly lit storefront. Milcham paid the driver and then helped Aithne out of the taxi.

"Where are we?" she wondered out loud.

Milcham was grinning so wide he thought his cheeks would split. "You'll see." He glanced up at the sign above the store. The Gregory Marx Gallery was one of the most prestigious in the city, but Aithne was too busy looking around to see exactly where she was. He wondered how long it would take before she would figure it out. After handing his invitation to the man at the door, he ushered her inside.

She was frowning as she gazed around the crowded room. "I don't understand. Why are we..." Her voice trailed off, and she gasped, coming to a complete standstill.

"Aidan?"

There was a glad cry from across the room. A tall dark man, standing next to a slender redhead opened his arms.

"Aithne!"

The shout freed her from her shock, and with a sob of joy, Aithne launched herself into the man's arms. Milcham felt a stab of jealousy when the man hugged her tightly and lifted her from the ground. His eyes began to glow.

"I would suggest you douse the light unless you want all of New York to see you aren't quite human," a dry voice to his right said quietly.

Milcham blinked. Turning, he saw the same redhead who seconds before had been across the room. "How did you...?"

"It's part of the gift." She smiled and held out her hand. "I'm Dawn, and you must be Milcham."

He bowed quickly, not taking his eyes from the two dark heads across the room. "I am pleased to meet you."

"Did your trip go well?"

He thought of the crowds at the airport and the narrow, uncomfortable seats on the plane and almost sneered. "It was adequate."

"This was a wonderful idea, surprising them both."

"Thank you for sending us the invitation." Milcham frowned as he watched Aithne and her brother touch their foreheads together. His senses expanded suddenly. Why did he have this feeling of wrongness?

Dawn didn't notice his stillness. "I know she told us all about you, but it's very cool to finally meet you. A Phoenix. I bet you can tell all kinds of stories about your life."

"Not a Phoenix," he said absently, trying to figure out what was bothering him. "I am *the* Phoenix."

"That's right...I forgot. Sorry. I'm just so super curious, and I've got tons of questions. I hope you can stay long enough for us to get to know everything about you. I wonder...will Aithne become a Phoenix, too? And what about your kids?"

That brought Milcham's head around. "Kids?"

Dawn blushed. "I'm sorry. It's just since Aidan and I can't have children, I was hoping for a nephew or niece to spoil."

"I'm sorry. I don't know what will happen." Milcham frowned and looked back at Aithne. "I am not sure if she will turn into something different, and as far as children are concerned...up until now, I too have been unable to father a child. I hope Yahweh lifts that ban from me when Aithne and I are truly mated."

"Good," giggled Dawn. "Then I can send you a drum set for your firstborn."

Milcham smiled, but his heart wasn't in it. The senses the Lord had given him were telling him something wasn't right. He stared around the room. Was Aithne in danger again? Was the Ancient One lurking about?

His eyes went back to his lover and her brother. They were so alike, he'd have thought they were twins. The same eyes, the same shape of the face. He frowned again. But something was wrong. He took a deep breath and allowed his mind to expand even farther. When his inner being touched Aidan, Milcham staggered back in shock. This was the wrongness he was experiencing. His heart screamed out in disbelief and pain. He turned back to Dawn, his eyes burning.

"What is he?"

"Little sister…it is so good to have you here."

Aithne buried her face in her brother's chest. She hadn't realized until just that moment how much she'd missed him. His familiar arms held her lovingly, making her eyes fill with tears. "Oh, Aidan. I've been longing to see you."

"You could have come home, anytime."

Aithne shook her head. "No. You and Dawn needed time to yourselves. I would have been in the way."

"Never in the way," he rebuked her. "You are family." He gazed over Aithne's head at the tall, muscular blond standing with Dawn. "And it looks as if our family is growing. Is that your Phoenix?"

She stiffened. "Oh, God…Milcham." Suddenly, all the joy of seeing her brother disappeared. Jarrod had warned her this would happen, but in her arrogance she'd assumed she had everything under control. It never occurred to her Milcham would surprise her with a trip to see Aidan. Now her secret would be revealed. His generous gift could destroy them.

"What is it?" Aidan dropped his forehead to hers in an instinctive effort to soothe. The traditional gesture made her tear up even more.

"I've made a huge mistake." She sighed deeply. "I didn't think I would see you again. I thought we would go straight to the walled city."

He understood immediately, and his eyes darkened. "You didn't tell him about me. Or about us." He pulled away from her. "You are ashamed of what you did for me?"

"No! Never!" Her lower lip trembled. "It's just... He just had some really weird views about my gift of reading the cards, so I think I was afraid to tell him about what we were to each other. And it was all in my past, so I'd convinced myself it really didn't matter. I never expected you two to meet, so I didn't worry about it."

"Aithne!"

She closed her eyes. "I know, I know. It was foolish."

"From the look on his face, he's already figured it out."

Aithne turned to meet Milcham's horrified gaze and flinched. "Oh Aidan," she whispered. "What have I done?"

"Be brave, little sister." He hugged her close to him. "If he loves you, he will accept it."

She gave a shiver, remembering their first meeting and how he'd railed at her. His view on evil was very strong. "I don't know, brother. I just don't know."

Dawn blinked up at Milcham. "What do you mean...what is he? Didn't Aithne tell you?"

"She...did...not!"

She flinched at his obvious anger. "Hey! Keep your voice down. I'm not going to allow you to endanger the man I love just because you're surprised."

Milcham turned and stared down at her, but he softened his voice. "He is not human. I sense...something else."

Dawn opened her mouth, but then shut it. "This isn't my story. You should talk to Aithne."

"If she had wanted me to know, she would have told me," he said in a quiet, furious tone. He stared across the room at the siblings. "She kept this from me."

"She probably had a reason."

"We are to be mated! There is no good reason!"

Dawn grabbed his arm with surprising strength. "I'm going to say this one more time. This is a very important night for me. I'm sorry you didn't know what you were getting into, but I'm not going to let you ruin it and jeopardize both of them because you can't keep your temper!"

He fought back the urge to throw something. "At least tell me what he is!"

She sighed. "*If* it will help you to calm down." She pulled him with her as she moved towards Aidan and Aithne. "Aidan is a vampire."

Milcham's stomach rolled in disbelief. He had hunted vampires a century earlier in Europe. They were killers with only one function in life. To maim and destroy humans. How could Aithne's brother be one of the cursed undead? None of it made sense. His eyes locked with his lover's as Dawn drew him closer.

He was furious, Aithne could tell. His eyes only glowed like that when he was aroused or angry. Her heart sank. Would he understand? Or would he walk away from her?

"So..." Aidan broke the uncomfortable silence. "You are the Phoenix."

"I am," Milcham answered shortly. "And you are a...Aidan."

"I am the only Aidan." Her brother smiled, deliberately misunderstanding him. "As you are the only Phoenix. Our mother used to tell stories of you."

Aithne shivered as Milcham's hot gaze moved over her. "So she told me."

"Milcham—" Aithne began.

"How old are you?" he interrupted, ignoring her.

Aidan raised a dark brow. "I have lived for over a century in this form. Is that what you wanted to know?"

"How many have you killed? How many have died to satisfy your lust for blood?" Milcham's voice was very quiet, but it was full of rage.

Both women gasped. Dawn's hazel eyes flashed with her own fury. "How dare you!"

Aidan went completely still in a way only a vampire can. "You insult me...brother."

"I am not...your brother."

Aithne put her hand on Milcham's arm. "Please, don't." When his angry gaze came back to her, she flinched again, but went on bravely. "You don't know anything about him, Milcham. You made the mistake once of judging me and were wrong. Why do you think I didn't tell you about my brother? I knew you'd do the same thing."

"Don't turn this around on me!" he fumed. "You kept this from me. You, who were so angry I didn't tell you who I was? How could you?"

"I think it's time to take this elsewhere," Aidan growled quietly. "I will not allow you to turn Dawn's showing into a mockery." He took Dawn's hand and kissed her gently. "We will be back soon, love."

"I want to go, too!"

He shook his head. "This is your big night. You can't walk away. We will be back soon."

Dawn glared at the three of them. "If you aren't back in a half an hour, I'm coming to find you."

"We will," he soothed. Then he bowed mockingly at Milcham. "Follow me."

Milcham followed silently as his brother-in-law to be led him through a door and up a narrow flight of stairs. They didn't stop until they came out on to the roof.

Aidan walked over to the side and then turned. “Now, say what you have to say.”

“You are a vampire?”

“Yes.”

“One that has existed for over a century?”

“One hundred and twenty-nine years, to be exact.”

“And you exist by killing innocents to drink their blood?”

“No.”

The abrupt answer surprised him. “Of course you do. It’s what all vampires do. I hunted your kind many years ago, because of your bloodthirsty tendencies.”

Aidan almost smiled. “Did you destroy those that killed humans?”

“Most gladly.”

“Good!”

Again, Milcham was surprised. “You are pleased I killed your kind? What kind of vampire are you?” He answered his own question. “Never mind. It matters not. You are an unholy demon. Give me one reason not to kill you, too!”

Aithne gasped and stepped between them. “No, you can’t. He’s my brother.”

“A brother you didn’t tell me about!”

“I should have. I’m sorry. I was afraid of how you would react.”

Aidan snorted. “And well she should be. I thought the Phoenix was the most righteous of all the creatures in the garden, not the most judgmental.”

Milcham’s conscience twinged, but he ignored it. “You are evil. It is so written.”

“And you, my soon-to-be brother, have got a lot to learn about my kind.”

“You didn’t want to kill Jarrod and Alexander.” Aithne trembled in protest. “They both aren’t really human. Jarrod is a werewolf and Alexander…we don’t know what he is.”

"They are not written in the manuscripts as unholy. They do not live for centuries on the blood..." His voice trailed off and his face whitened. He swung back around to Aithne. "He is over a century old."

She knew what was coming. "Yes."

"Then...how old are you?"

Chapter Seventeen

She lifted green eyes to meet his amber ones. "I am one hundred and twenty-four years old…chronologically. Twenty-four…physically."

Milcham staggered backwards, confusion and disgust written all over his face. "You…you're not a vampire. I would have sensed it."

Aithne put out her hand to him. Now she knew she was fully human. Her heart was breaking. "No…I'm not. But I am as old as he is. I was immortal, but I'm not now."

"I don't understand."

"Allow me, little sister," Aidan ordered gently. He turned to Milcham and his eyes glowed angrily. "I did not become a vampire by choice. When I did, I refused to live off the blood of another human being. I would not do to someone else what was done to me." He reached out his arm and drew Aithne into his embrace. "I was ready to die, but Aithne wouldn't let me. She forced me into drinking from her. She became my familiar, one whom I feed from, and I had no other until I met Dawn."

He smiled darkly. "Dawn is my world. As soon as I met her, I knew she was my twin-flame, the other half of my soul. I love her completely. She took Aithne's place and my sister was freed from her position as my familiar. She became human again."

Milcham rubbed his eyes. "You're telling me you don't kill humans?"

Aidan chuckled. "You are behind the times, Milcham. Things have changed since you hunted vampires. We exist all over the world, mostly at peace in the human world. In flocks, or on our own, we don't need to hunt. Blood is easy to find."

"This is insane."

"No more insane than a bird who can be reborn in the sun."

Milcham ignored that dig and turned to Aithne. "Why didn't you tell me? You knew I had a right to know."

She bit her lip. "It was in the past, Milcham. I'm human now. I didn't even expect you to meet him, so why stir up trouble?"

"You were furious I didn't tell you who I was. How can you justify not telling me who and what you were?"

Aithne's eyes filled with tears. "At first I didn't think it mattered. Truly, I didn't. Then, once your secrets came out, I thought about telling you, but I was afraid. Afraid of how you'd act. But I see now how wrong I was. I'm sorry. I'm so, so sorry."

Milcham paced away from them both. "I can't believe this. I thought I would be the freak in the family."

"Every family has their skeletons," Aidan said mildly. "Ours are not so bad."

"Are you crazy!" Milcham exploded. "You're the living dead, your mate lets you drink her blood, and the woman whom I thought I loved wasn't human for over a century. Those aren't skeletons. That's a whole fuckin' graveyard."

Aidan lifted an ebony eyebrow. "You are right, sister. He does have a temper."

Aithne's eyes flashed. "See! This is why I didn't say anything. You called me a witch just because I read tarot cards. I knew you would never understand why I did what I did. I knew you would stop loving me."

She took a step closer to him and poked him in the chest. "But, hear me now. I love you, but I wouldn't change what I did for Aidan for anything. He's my brother. All I had left in the world. I would have died for him." She looked back at her sibling. "Just like he did for me."

"Aidan?"

Dawn's voice made them all jump. The redhead poked her head out of the roof door. "I know it hasn't been a half hour yet, but I need you."

The vampire moved immediately to her side. "I am done here anyway." Aidan gave Dawn a loving kiss and then turned back to them. "Brother, I made the same mistake with my lady. I didn't tell her what I was until it was almost too late. Fortunately, she loved me enough to forgive me." He glared at Milcham. "Don't judge what you do not know. Don't be foolish and throw away love that is precious and forever just because you don't understand."

Milcham gave a growl and turned away to stare off at the city lights. Aidan sighed. "Tell him, Aithne. Tell him our story. If he is going to judge us, let him know everything."

The door closed, leaving them alone. There was nothing but the sound of the wind as it whistled through the metal bracings on the roof. A few moments later, he felt her step to his side.

"Will you be able to forgive me?"

He had to answer her honestly. "I don't know," he said, shaking his head. "You're a hypocrite, Aithne. You got so angry at me for not telling you everything, yet you did the same. And not to tell me about this?" He shook his head again. "It is a lot to accept."

She nodded, a single clear tear tracing down her cheek. "You're right. I am a hypocrite. I really did believe it was different because it was my past. I talked myself into it, because I was so afraid of how you would react. Can you understand that?"

He nodded slowly, remembering their first meeting. "I can understand, but I have trouble accepting. I changed. You saw it. Yet, you still didn't tell me."

She touched his sleeve. "Can you honestly say if I told you I let my brother make me his familiar, it wouldn't have mattered?"

Milcham was silent for a long time as he struggled with the question. Everything in him was horrified with the whole idea. "It is not something...I can easily accept." Suddenly, he turned to her and grabbed her by the arms. "Why, Aithne? Why would you allow him to do that to you? He was already one of the undead. Why couldn't you let him die?"

A slap across the face caught him by surprise, knocking him back several steps. He whipped his head back around to see Aithne, her breasts heaving in anger, glaring at him.

"Damn it, Aith—"

"Don't you ever say that again," she snapped. "He is my brother. I love him. If it wasn't for him, I wouldn't be here. He saved my life. Don't you understand? I would have done anything to help him. Anything!"

She paced away, and then turned back abruptly. "You don't understand. You never will, because you don't have a family of your own."

Pain shot through him. "I thought I did...in you!"

"I love you, Milcham. But I'm not ashamed of my brother, even though I may have acted like it. Aidan is the bravest and kindest man I know. He gave his life for me."

"You said that before. What do you mean? Is that what he wanted you to tell me?"

She sighed. "Dawn is the only other one who knows. We swore we wouldn't tell anyone what happened to us."

"I'm listening."

Aithne shivered. She hated talking about this. It made her feel exposed and frightened, still, after all these years. "My family lived in a small town in California. My father owned the local bar, but it wasn't a bad place, more of a pub where a man could get a beer and a good meal after he got off work." She chewed her lip.

"My mother worked in the kitchen, but Aidan and I helped my father in the front. I never had any trouble. People were respectful of me, especially when my father and Aidan were around."

Milcham thought of the strength he'd seen in the vampire. He wouldn't want to come up against him in a fight, supernatural or not.

"Life was good. We lived over the top of the bar, but we were saving to buy land to build a house on. We weren't rich, but we had what we needed to be happy."

When her eyes darkened, he had to fight the urge to take her into his arms.

"One night, a gang of men came in. It was after closing time, and I was in the kitchen with Aidan cleaning up. Mother was out in the front with Father putting the chairs up so she could mop. Father tried to tell them we were closed, but they just laughed at him. They shut and locked the door behind them." Aithne swallowed.

"Aidan and I came to the door just in time to see one of the men attack my father. But instead of hitting him, he picked him up and threw him against the wall. Then to our horror and shock, he bit him, right on the neck."

Her eyes gazed out over the bright sparkling city. "I can remember my mother screaming. Blood was everywhere, and when the man looked up, we saw he had fangs instead of teeth."

"Aithne, my God." He stared at her, horrified. Were all of her family vampires?

She went on quickly. "Aidan picked me up and tossed me in a nearby closet. One we kept the money in, so it wasn't easily seen. He told me not to say a word, no matter what I heard. I fought him, but he locked me in." Her green eyes glistened with tears.

"He got back in time to see Father beheaded, so the vampires could more easily feed. Our mother was on the floor, her clothes in tatters, still screaming as the remaining vampires feasted on her. Aidan picked up a chair and broke it over one of the vampire's heads. Of course it didn't stop them."

She wiped away the tears that were now streaming down her cheeks. "He fought them. Actually killed two before they overwhelmed him." She closed her eyes and shuddered. "I could hear him shouting at them. Telling them they were beasts and monsters. Then, I heard the leader say he was too impressive a human to kill. They needed a man of his strength in their flock. So they didn't finish him off, they decided to turn him instead."

Milcham's guts were churning with a mixture of guilt and anguish for her. To hear all of that going on, and not be able to do anything? "*Assai*, I'm so sorry."

She didn't hear him, her thoughts back in the painful past. "When he awoke later and found out what they'd done, he was sickened. I could hear him screaming at them, hating them for their actions. When they left, he refused to go with them. Aidan was strong enough, even from the beginning, to defy them. He told them he would rather be dead like his family than be monsters like them."

Aithne took a deep breath and looked up at him. "They were angry. Apparently it isn't good form to refuse your sire anything. So they tied him up and left him behind."

"They never found you?"

She shook her head. "Aidan kept them so busy they didn't look for anyone else. I sat in that cupboard for almost two days listening to them kill and torture my family."

His heart broke again for her. "How did you get out?"

Aithne's face went white. "When they left, they didn't just walk away. Aidan had to pay for refusing them. So they bound and gagged him and left him in the bar." Her eyes blinked back more tears.

"Then they set the place on fire."

"Sweet Yahweh, no!" Milcham breathed.

"I smelled the smoke and was able to kick my way out of the cupboard. The whole building was on fire." Remembered horror reflected in her eyes. "Flames were everywhere. I crawled on my hands and knees out into the front of the bar and found Aidan, unconscious. I untied him and...to this day, I don't know how I did it, but I pulled him through the backdoor and out of the fire."

"The vampires?"

She shook her head. "Long gone. They figured he was as good as dead, so they didn't stick around for the show. People came to help, but it was no use. Everything burned in the fire, even my parents' bodies."

Suddenly, Milcham remembered her face when he'd told her about how she would have to die in the fire to be with him for eternity. The fact she'd trusted him and agreed to go with him gnawed at his gut. He swallowed back the sickness he felt. "No wonder you had reservations about becoming immortal."

Aithne nodded bleakly. "When my gypsy tent went up around me, I was paralyzed in fright. I couldn't believe it was happening again. You saved me, and I thought it was all over. No more fire worries." Her lips trembled. "Then you told me about what I would need to do. And I'm still frightened."

He pushed back the instinctive need to soothe her. He had to find out everything. "What happened after the fire in your home?"

"Aidan was so ill. Being turned isn't easy, and because he hated the creature he'd become, I had to watch him every minute so he wouldn't suicide by walking out into the sunlight. I knew he was starving, but he refused to eat anything." She laughed sadly. "We were living in our barn, and he wouldn't even go near the horses, because he was afraid of what he might do."

She walked over and stood by the edge of the rooftop. "I knew we couldn't stay in town. People would wonder about

Aidan and his strange behavior. But he was so weak he couldn't even sit a horse. Finally, I took matters into my own hands."

Aithne stared back at Milcham. "He was my brother and he was dying. I couldn't let that happen. He'd protected me from those monsters, and in doing so, became one himself. I owed him everything."

"Go on."

"When he was lying asleep, so weak from lack of nourishment he couldn't fight me, I slashed my wrist and held it to his mouth. He still fought me, but his nature took over after he tasted the blood. He fed." She smiled grimly. "Afterwards, he was furious with me, because he'd wanted to die. But I wanted him to live more. I talked him into letting me be his food source until we found the creatures that had killed our parents and done this to him. Then...if he wanted to die, I'd let him."

"And did he? Find those monsters, I mean?"

Emerald eyes lit up with satisfaction. "Yes. It took us several years, but after we left Sonora, we tracked down and killed them all." She smiled again. "By that time, Aidan was used to being a vampire. He still refused to feed on anything else, so we just kept going as we were. It wasn't until several years later that we realized there were benefits to me as well."

"Immortality?"

She nodded. "When I was his familiar, I didn't age, just as Dawn doesn't now. I also have quicker reflexes, am stronger, and my senses are acute. I still have a few of those gifts."

Milcham's mind snapped back to her last statement. "Where did you say you lived?"

"It was a small town, in the mountains of California. Sonora."

Realization stabbed through him like a pointed spear, piercing his heart. "This was in the summer, just before it got cool again."

Her eyes widened. "Yes...it was the end of August. I remember the raspberries were ripe. How did you know?"

He groaned and closed his eyes. To him it was as clear as if it had happened yesterday. He remembered walking past the remains of a burned-down building. Someone had told him it had been a bar and the owners had died in the fire. It was just after that he'd felt the call. Anger and sorrow warred within him.

Going to Aithne, he trapped her face in his large hands. Fearful green eyes looked up at him. "I was there."

Her mouth dropped open. "What?"

"Remember how I told you there was one other time I experienced that special pull I now know with you?"

She nodded.

"Sonora was where I sensed it. I was there just a few days after the fire. I knew you were close, but as I searched for you, it just up and disappeared, like it never was. I thought at the time the Ancient One was fooling me, but now I see it was more than that. The feeling disappeared when you became Aidan's familiar."

Aithne grabbed at his wrists. "Are you telling me Satan deliberately killed my family and made my brother a vampire so I would do what I did and be taken out of your reach?"

Milcham bent and put his forehead to hers in an unconscious mirroring of what Aidan had done earlier. "I don't know if it was deliberate or not, *assai*. But what I do know is evil forced you to make a decision you never should have had to make, and by doing so I lost you." Grief filled his voice. "A hundred years wasted."

"Are you sure?" Aithne sounded stunned. "I can't believe it."

"I have never forgotten that day or that sensation. When I first met you, I noticed it again, but because I disregarded it the first time, I didn't think it meant anything the second. Now I know it was you...both times."

"Oh, my God."

He sighed and pulled her into his arms. "It means you were always meant to be my soulmate, Aithne. You should have told me about Aidan and your past, just like I should have told you about being the Phoenix, but in the end, it changes nothing."

"About what Aidan and I were to each other...it's a bond that will never be broken. I know that now. I should have never tried to hide it."

"It is not an easy thing for me to accept. As you said, I'm not used to shades of gray. But this I do know. Your brother saved your life. Perhaps the Ancient One sent those men to kill *you*, knowing I was on my way. Aidan kept you alive for me then and through the years until we found each other again. I may be slow, but I'm not stupid. Yahweh has offered you to me twice. The first time you were snatched away from me, and this time, although the enemy has tried again, I will not allow it. I won't let you go."

She buried her face in his shirt. "I love you so much. I'm sorry for being such a coward."

"I forgive you, *assai.* I love you, too. I will not throw this gift away. Not after I have searched for you for so long."

He bent his head and kissed her, shuddering as her lips parted eagerly for him. She tasted so delicious he was suddenly ravenous for her. His tongue dove deep into her mouth, touching each nerve ending and sending him spinning out of control. His whole body tightened when she teased his lips with her own.

His heartbeat raced as she melted against him. He cursed himself for even considering putting her aside. She belonged to him, heart and soul, and would until the end of eternity.

Aithne gasped and clutched him to her. All the anger and hurt of before disappeared. They'd both been wrong, but that was behind them now. Now...all they had to think about was how much they loved each other.

His body grew even hotter under her hands. It was like he had a fever and she was the cause. His heat warmed her, making her ache deep inside. She craved his touch like a drunkard craved drink, and she sent a grateful prayer up to heaven he'd forgiven her fear and stupidity. She moaned when his hand moved up her silken thigh. "Milcham..."

"I find that I don't want to wait for our nice hotel bed," he murmured. "I wish to put my seal on you. I want you to walk back into that room with the look of a woman well pleasured."

Her face turned pink at the thought. "Here? On the roof?"

He smiled slowly. "I have something even more interesting in mind."

She stared at him a moment, and then smiling, she slid her arms around his neck. "Really? Just what do you have planned?"

"Hold on."

Chapter Eighteen

Aithne's eyes widened as he suddenly burst into flame. His eyes met hers and she took a deep breath, knowing somehow he was testing her. Lifting her chin, she nodded. His eyes glowed even hotter, and then without warning, he shot up into the sky.

She gave a shriek and held on tightly to him. He grinned down at her, his head and body still in human form, while his arms had changed to powerful luminescent wings of fire.

"*What are you doing?*" she cried. Glancing down, she saw the city retreating below.

Milcham laughed. "I have always wanted to do this. I have heard about a Mile High Club we can join."

Her eyes widened. "We can't go that high!"

He bent and kissed her. "No, *assai*...but we can pretend." He dipped and twirled, laughing as she shrieked out his name. "I will keep you safe, Aithne. Even if you were to fall, I would catch you."

"I don't *want* to fall!"

"Then hold on to me. You know I will never let you go."

Getting into the spirit of things, she wrapped her legs around his waist. "Promise?"

"Promise."

She wriggled against him. "I hope we are high enough. Anyone below can see right up this short skirt."

Milcham frowned for a moment then chuckled. "People on the ground will think we are two birds, high in the sky, and it's a good thing. That short skirt is now up around your waist. I wish I could touch you, but..."

"You just keep flying," Aithne said quickly. "Just tell me what to do."

His eyes glowed hotter. "Unsnap the crotch of your corset set. Then undo my trousers."

She rolled her eyes. "One handed?"

His mouth quirked into a smug smile. "I happen to know you are very good one handed."

Aithne giggled. Holding on tightly to his strong neck, she eased her hand down between their bodies. His muscles contracted in his chest as his great wings beat rhythmically to keep them aloft. She met his eyes as she slowly undid his belt and unsnapped the top snap of his suit trousers.

"You were supposed to do yours," he muttered hoarsely.

"I will," she promised him. "I just want to play first." Carefully, she unzipped him and slipped her hand inside. His heartfelt groan made her smile, and the sudden faster flapping of his wings was proof he wasn't unaffected.

Gently, she pulled his cock free of his pants, stroking it until it was hard and throbbing. Small beads of pre-come would appear but then were swept away by the wind. She knew only a few strong pumps would signal the end, so she kept her strokes even and slow. Up and down, up and down, with a hard squeeze when she reached the base.

It wasn't long before his hips were jerking against her, and his panting breaths could be heard even over the beating of his wings. "For the love of God," he muttered as she squeezed him again. "I can't take any more."

"I would think you should say...for the love of me," she whispered in his ear. "Do you love *me*, Milcham?"

He gave a little growl and then twisted slightly so she was lying more on top of him. "You are my everything, *assai.* I want to be with you forever. I love you." He kissed her then, his mouth pressing against hers with all the love he had stored up inside of him. "Join our bodies...*now*! I want to be inside of you."

Breathlessly, she nodded and unsnapped the clasp at the crotch of her corset. It immediately sprang apart, exposing her damp folds to the coolness of the night wind. She gripped his throbbing length in her hand and guided the head of his penis into her wet channel. They both moaned at the feeling.

Milcham's body was already red hot. His inner flame had been kept dampened, but when his cock slid inside her silken heat, he lost control and immediately they were enveloped in an even brighter cocoon of flame.

Aithne cried out but didn't pull away. Instead, she dropped her head to his chest and wrapping her legs even tighter, brought him deep inside of her. She clenched down around him, and his fire built even hotter.

Bending his head, he caught her lips in a desperate hungry kiss as their bodies moved in rhythm together. He pumped in and out of her, heated motions that fanned the flames in both of them. Motions that matched the beating of his wings, so each thrust went deeper and deeper into her trembling body.

She whimpered into his mouth, sucking lovingly on his tongue. He stopped breathing when her quim squeezed down hard on his pulsing shaft. He sensed the beginnings of her climax, and his own rose to meet her. Pumping wildly, he forgot everything but the ensuing pleasure of their bodies.

They both exploded together, a firework of red, orange and yellow fire in their minds. They both shuddered and shook. Aithne cried out his name as she spasmed in his arms. Unthinkingly, he wrapped his wings around her as his own orgasm overwhelmed him.

Without the beating of his strong wings, they plummeted from the sky, a scarlet-gold ball of light tumbling to earth. It took several long moments for Milcham to realize what he'd done, and then he shouted into Aithne's ear. "*Assai*...hold on tight to me!"

Once she was gripping his neck again, he opened up his wings, grunting at the effort of breaking their fall. He heard her give a muffled cry of fear. As if in slow motion, the ground rose up to meet them. His wings beat hard, filling with air as he put the brakes on their descent, slowly regaining control. Once he had them completely stopped, he kissed the top of Aithne's head and flew them back up high enough so they were just a shadow in the sky.

"I am sorry. Forgive me."

Aithne shivered in his arms. "I guess we won't do that again!"

"I didn't think I would lose total control." Milcham shook his head. "I should know better. Each time I touch you, I am lost to everything else."

"I think we should stay grounded next time," she agreed.

He kissed her again. "But it was wonderful."

She giggled. "It was. One to remember, that's for sure."

He laughed and flew lower. "I think we have had enough of the Mile High Club for one evening."

Aithne gazed out over the brightly lit city. "It is beautiful up here."

His eyes twinkled. "If you can promise not to stick your hands in my pants next time, I'll take you up once more before we leave."

"I think I can agree to that, if you take care of me elsewhere," she said with a sultry look. "But until then...where to now?"

Milcham came to rest on the top of the gallery roof. "Back to the party. I know you want to spend time with your brother." He closed his eyes and morphed back fully human. Wrapping his arms around her, he kissed her gently. "And I have some apologies to make."

She wrinkled her nose at him as she slid down his body to stand before him. "As Aidan said, he made the same mistake I did. He won't be too hard on you."

Milcham shook his head and stepped back to set his clothes to right. "I bet Dawn didn't threaten to kill him." He handed her a handkerchief.

Aithne looked up from where she was pulling down her corset, gladly taking the proffered cloth. "No...but he wanted to die without her."

"He did?"

She nodded as she tidied herself. "She left him. Wouldn't even speak to him when she found out he'd been feeding off of her. Stupid fool wouldn't feed from me, so he was slowly starving to death." Her eyes flashed with remembered anger. "Dawn came back to him just in time."

He watched as she snapped her corset panties closed and smoothed down the black dress. "If I was gone, and you knew your only means to survival was to have sex with Jarrod, would you?"

She froze, her gaze lifting to his. "What? *Ick*...no...of course not."

He grinned at the look on her face. "Perhaps he felt the same way. He had found the only woman to sustain him. Another would be...intolerable."

Aithne frowned. "I never thought of it that way."

He pulled her into his arms. "You never were in love before." Their lips met in a slow, gratifying kiss. When he raised his head, he looked down at her with satisfied eyes. "I couldn't be with another woman now that I've found you. We are a part of each other. Forever."

She smiled. "Forever."

He took a deep breath. "But until then, let us return to the party. You look just the way I wanted you to. Totally pleasured."

Aithne blushed and took the arm he offered. “And you look suitably disheveled. What do you think Aidan will say when he finds out you just fucked his sister on the roof?”

Milcham missed a step and glared at her when she giggled. “If your brother is the type of man to own a sex toy shop, I doubt he will be all that surprised.”

She squeezed his arm. “I’m an owner too, don’t forget.”

His eyes glowed lightly. “I haven’t. And I hope to see some of those toys when we get back to the hotel tonight.”

Aithne was right. While Aidan did lift a dark eyebrow at their appearance, he said nothing. Perhaps he was remembering the time when she had walked in on Dawn and him in the middle of the apothecary. His pants were around his knees, and Dawn was stark naked on the counter. Aithne had rolled her eyes and just kept walking through, but she could still remember the looks on both their faces.

It didn’t take long for Milcham and her brother to pair off and disappear into a corner together. She wasn’t sure what they were talking about, but at least they hadn’t come to blows.

She and Dawn spent the night catching up. It was the second night of Dawn’s show and already, she was considered a success. There were *sold* stickers on most of the pieces. The two talked girl-talk between times when Dawn had to glad-hand different people. Clients, agents and other artists all wanted a piece of her.

They didn’t even see their men until they were approached by two good-looking guys in suits. Perfect smiles and perfect hair, they wanted to take both women out for a drink.

Instantly, Aidan and Milcham were there to put their claim on their women. One look at the tall, dark, brooding vampire and the fiery-tempered Phoenix, and both interlopers beat a hasty retreat. The women almost collapsed in giggles at the look on their faces.

Soon after they decided it was time to go. Dawn had had enough of smiling and they were all hungry. They had a late night supper at Sardi's before separating to go to their own hotels.

The next evening, after Aithne and Milcham had spent the day sightseeing, they met the others for a show. Aithne was overjoyed at the bond she could already sense forming between Milcham and her brother. It was as if Aidan being a vampire didn't even matter anymore. Once her amber-eyed lover had accepted the situation, nothing more needed to be said.

They had tickets to see *Phantom of the Opera*, and she enjoyed herself thoroughly. Being with the man she loved as well as her family was the best thing next to heaven. When she thought about how she might have missed this, she wanted to kick herself all over again.

As if he could read her thoughts, Milcham pulled her into his arms and dropped a loving kiss on her trembling lips. "*Adore...assai voi.* I love you, precious."

She wrapped her arms around him and kissed him deeply, wondering how she had ever existed without him.

Two days later, the couples sat in Tavern on the Green. The men were bickering companionably about who the next Super Bowl winners would be, and Aithne and Dawn were talking about the shopping they had done that day.

Aithne bit her lip in consternation. "But, Dawn...I'm going to a walled city. I probably won't need that gown designed by Prada. Where would I wear it?"

Dawn rolled her eyes as she sipped a spoonful of lobster bisque. "No one *needs* a dress by Prada. Besides, even if it's only Milcham who sees it, it will be worthwhile."

Aithne glanced at her soon-to-be mate who was arguing madly about who the best quarterback was. "It was so expensive."

"Geesh, Aithne. You have more money than Midas, and I'll bet Milcham's not doing too bad either. Don't stress over a stupid dress."

Put that way, it did seem foolish. Aithne forked up a bite of her stone crab cake and savored the flavor. "You're right. Now I wish I'd bought that green negligee as well."

Dawn giggled and reaching under her chair, handed her a gaily wrapped package. "I thought you might change your mind."

"Dawn!"

Milcham broke off his discussion of the finer points of instant replays to stare at the present. "What is it?"

Aithne blushed becomingly. "Nothing I can open here."

"Ah, come on," Dawn giggled. "Let him see. It's really for him, anyway."

Milcham snatched the gift from Aithne and pried off the top. "For me? Wow! I haven't gotten a gift..." His voice trailed off when he saw the delicate lingerie inside. He looked up at Aithne and his eyes glowed. "It *is* for me. Who do I thank, you or Dawn?"

"Put it away!" Aithne buried her face in her hands as Dawn laughed.

Grinning, he obeyed. "I do this with the proviso you will wear this our first night together in the walled city."

"Milcham!"

Her brother chuckled, his dark laughter turning heads. "It is my turn to embarrass you next. Then everyone in the restaurant will know our names."

Milcham laughed and kissed Aithne. "Eat your appetizer. I'll put it away for later." He waggled his eyebrows at her as she blushed again.

"What time do you leave tomorrow?" Aidan asked as he watched Milcham feast on his seafood cocktail. "Will we have time to see you?"

Milcham shook his head. "Unfortunately, no. The only flight I could get leaves around noon. I know you will still be in bed."

"Where is this walled city?" Dawn asked curiously. "You've never really said."

"It isn't somewhere," Milcham tried to explain. "More like sometime. Think of Shangri-La, or Brigadoon. Places that truly exist, but cannot be found."

"Does your home have a name?" Aidan sipped at his red wine.

Milcham shook his head. "No. It is just my home." He looked over at Aithne and smiled. "And now hers."

"When will we see you again?" Dawn queried. "Soon, I hope."

The blond man sighed. "I don't know what will happen. We may be required to stay. My hope is that Aithne and I can return to the carnival and live there. We can go back to the city as we choose."

"But if it is so beautiful, why would you wish to leave?" Aidan sat back as the wait staff brought their main courses.

Milcham waited until Dawn and Aithne had been served roast prime rib of beef and Gremolata salmon. "It is a beautiful place." He sighed when his Mediterranean seafood risotto was set before him. "But after so long out in the real world, I think it would lack the stimulation we would need." He watched as Aidan was served a large piece of filet mignon, cooked very rare. The staff left and he went on. "I must face the fact that I am more human than animal now."

"Don't you think God will take that into account?" Dawn asked as she cut off a sliver of her meat and fed it to Aidan.

Stabbing his fork into a delicate freshwater prawn, Milcham shrugged. "I don't know that either. I have not spoken to Yahweh since I left so many years ago." He looked up into three shocked faces and laughed. "Did you think I had daily communication with him?"

"I guess I thought you had talked to him...sometime," Aithne said slowly. "You haven't discussed anything?"

"I pray to him, of course. And I do know he answers prayers." He lifted Aithne's hand to his lips. "He gave me you, after all."

Aidan smiled indulgently at them. "Just so." He sliced off a piece of the bloody meat and popped it into his mouth. He couldn't eat much, but not eating would raise suspicion. "But to go so long without conversing with him. I can see how that could be wearing."

Milcham chewed thoughtfully. "There were many times I wished for more of his guidance. But I managed."

Aithne grinned. "I'll say you did. Do you know Milcham saw the pyramids being built?" Her eyes sparkled with excitement. "And he was there when gold was found at Sutter's Mill. *And* he watched Michelangelo paint the Sistine Chapel!"

"Hush...*assai*," he cautioned as a diner at a nearby table turned and gawked at them. "And I didn't see the pyramids...I was told about them by a friend of mine who happened to fly by when they were being constructed."

Dawn stared at him with her mouth open. "You have seen so much."

Chuckling, Aidan reached over and closed her mouth. "Up to now, I've always been the oldest of the bunch. But now...I feel like a youngster."

"Age isn't all it's cracked up to be," Milcham said quietly. He ran his hand through his gray-streaked hair. "In my city, I was very lonely. It was loneliness that sent me out into the world."

"Then thank God for it," Aithne murmured as she leaned against him for a moment. "Otherwise, we would never have met."

He put his arm around her. "I thank Yahweh every day for bringing us together. You make me complete."

Dawn sighed and smacked Aidan on the arm. "Isn't that just wonderful? We knew when she left on her little adventure that she'd find the perfect man."

Aidan snorted. "Instead she found the perfect...immortal." He frowned slightly as he noted Milcham's appearance. It looked as if the Phoenix had aged years in just the few days they'd known him. He took his sister's hand and squeezed it gently. "But I too am glad she left, even though I was concerned at the time."

His sister's eyes filled with tears. "Did you knock down the wall like I told you to?"

His eyes gleaming with his own emotion, Aidan nodded. "We did. It took several weeks for me to convince Dawn, but finally...she gave in."

"All one big room, now," Dawn said with a sniff. "But still space enough for you to come and visit."

Milcham wiped the tears off Aithne's cheeks. "It is our greatest wish to come see you both again. If it is allowed, we will be there."

"Good," Dawn said, a smile lighting up her face. "Because I want to sculpt you."

He blinked. "Me?"

She nodded. "Yes. As both a human and Phoenix. I can see it already in my mind, but I'll need to sketch you to get the particulars. Plus—" she batted her long eyelashes at Milcham flirtatiously, "—I need to see you in your Phoenix form. To get all the details correct, you understand."

Aithne giggled as Milcham choked on a piece of scallop. "You've seen her work—you should be honored."

He turned and glared at her in dark amusement. "If I ever want to let people know what I am, I will consider it, this I promise."

"They will just think it is a play on your name, my brother. A Phoenix, for a phoenix." Aidan inclined his head as he took a drink of his wine. "If you wish, she can sculpt you as she did me...naked."

"Aidan!" Aithne's shocked voice rang out.

Her brother smirked knowingly. "See, I told you she would say my name, too!"

They all laughed and Milcham bent and kissed her soundly. "I am very glad we took this time to meet your family. Even though it didn't start out so well, this visit has been most enjoyable."

Aithne smiled and looked around the table at the people she might never see again. She mentally stored away the memories of the last few days...just in case. "I hope it won't be the last one."

"It won't be, little sister." Aidan's leaf green eyes shown with the strength of his emotion. "You will go to the walled city and find your destiny. And then you will come back here and we will celebrate together."

As one they all held up their wine glasses.

"To destiny," Milcham murmured as he looked into his beloved's green eyes.

"To the future," Aithne whispered back to him. "As long as it's with you."

Chapter Nineteen

"Oh, Milcham...it's beautiful." Aithne gazed in awe at the tall, crystalline walls before her. They stood so high, they looked as if they touched the clouds. The ramparts shimmered with all the colors of the rainbow, giving the impression of the aurora borealis caught in the polished walls. Beautifully carved arches could be seen along the length of the wall. On the top, set about every fifty feet, were sculpted turrets with flags of gold and orange blowing in the wind.

It had taken them three long days to get here. They had traveled on several planes, winding up in Jerusalem. It was then Milcham had told her all their belongings would be put into storage until they knew whether they would be leaving the city or not. She had insisted on carrying a small bag with her.

Once that was taken care of, Milcham had flown them the rest of the way. Because she had to hold onto him as he flew, Aithne's arms tired easily. So they traveled in short spurts and it took another full day to finally cross the otherworldly barrier between the real world and where the walled city lay.

Now, standing before it, she was only sorry they hadn't come sooner. The walled city was everything she'd dreamed it would be, and she hadn't even gone inside yet.

Milcham stared at her in surprise. "But what do you see? Humans see just a sandstone wall."

She raised an eyebrow at him. "Don't be ridiculous. I can see everything."

"You can?"

She turned to him. "Of course. It's like you captured a rainbow and made it into a fortress."

Milcham shook his head in awe. If he had any doubts before, this would have settled it for him. No one but he could see the true state of his city. That was...no one but him...and his mate. Here was more proof Aithne was the woman he'd been seeking.

"Am I not supposed to see it?"

Laughing with utter joy, he kissed her. "It just shows me how right I was to choose you. Only those destined for the city can truly see it."

Her eyes lit with happiness. "I love you."

"Not as much as I love you!" He whirled her in a circle as they laughed together. "I have an idea."

"What?"

He grinned and his arms turned into flaming wings. "Hold on!"

Giggling, she wrapped her arms around his neck, gasping as he shot off the ground.

He flew straight upwards into the sky, then banked and came back to rest on the turret facing the east. The sun was high overhead, and shimmering clouds could be seen in the distance.

Wrapping his strong wing around her, he pointed with the other one. "Every morning, I would come up here and greet the sun with a song," he murmured softly. "Then I would stare out at the human world, wondering what was out there."

Aithne laid her head on his chest. "You had never actually seen it?"

He shook his head. "I came straight here from Eden. I never saw the outside world until I began looking for you."

She liked the way he said that. He'd been looking for *her*. She stared out over the land, the gentle breeze tugging at her hair. "It is so lovely here. I'm just surprised you could ever leave it."

Milcham grinned. "Wait until you see within the city."

She turned in his arms. "I want you to kiss me. Here at the top of the world."

His wings morphed into arms and he held her tightly. "I stood here for centuries, longing for you before I ever knew who you were. It is only right I reap the rewards of all that waiting."

She lifted her face to his and with the gentlest of motions, he touched his lips to hers. In the kiss was all the wonder of their love. The utter rightness of their being together. The certainty of the future before them. The sun bathed their faces in its warmth as they held each other, assured nothing could ever keep them apart again.

When finally they broke away, both had tears in their eyes. "I love you, *assai*," Milcham murmured, his hands framing her face.

"And I love you, my fiery lover," she whispered as she rubbed her cheeks against the palms of his hands. "Thank you for finding me."

He smiled. "Thank *you* for waiting."

She grinned, too. "So...you going to show me where I'm going to live the next several centuries?"

He chuckled and bowed, then wrapped her arms back around his neck. "As my lady wishes. Hold on!"

They spent the rest of the day exploring his beautiful home. Aithne was awed by the lush, verdant forests with trees so high you couldn't see the tops. As they flew over them and then later, strolling beneath them, she was given the impression of the jungle canopies of South America. She could see why having a nest in these trees would be like living at the high point of the world.

The city was much bigger on the inside than it was on the outside. Not only were there huge expanses of trees, but also present were beautiful flower-filled meadows and sparkling waterfalls that flowed into peaceful clear rivers. It was as if Yahweh had brought all the beauty of the Garden of Eden to this special place.

And, like the long-lost garden, there were no houses. Since it was the home of the Phoenix, Milcham had lived in a nest, high in the trees. But that wouldn't do for Aithne, even though she protested she didn't mind. Because she wasn't used to sleeping up high, he feared she'd fall. So, he built a small hut to give them their privacy from the other creatures of the city.

Aithne worried about him as he worked. His thousand years would be up tomorrow, and she could see he was exhausted. His blond hair was shot through with gray, and his handsome face was lined. He moved much slower than normal, and his superhuman strength was muted. He'd explained that in his human guise, he was able to maintain his strength better than in his bird form. If he became the Phoenix, he would barely be able to move.

Still, she worried. He seemed to be intent on making her happy and comfortable here, and no matter what she said, it didn't make a difference. She wanted him to understand it was he who made her world complete...not a house or nest.

Finally, the little hideaway was finished. It was only the size of a small tent, but it had a roof and four walls and a soft cushion of moss for their bed. In Aithne's eyes, it was perfect. But, instead of resting as she wanted him to, Milcham immediately set to building the special nest of spices they would use for the renewing fire. Only after it was finished would he sit down to rest and eat.

They feasted on nuts and berries and ripe fruit, some of which she had never seen before. Then they bathed in the pool to get all the stickiness off of them. Afterwards, she shooed Milcham back to the hut by himself. She had something very special to do for her handsome lover.

Reclining on the bed of moss he'd built, Milcham sighed heavily. Even though he hadn't said anything to Aithne, he was about at the end of his strength. Each time before when he had needed the renewing fire, he'd been here, protected in his city. But this time, not only had he carried his mate-to-be halfway across the world, he'd taken the time to see to her comfort as well. He didn't begrudge her that. He'd just not considered the impact of how tired he would be.

He teetered between relief that the day of his rebirth was at hand and fear about what would happen. He knew he wanted to be his old self again, and by this time tomorrow he would be, but what would happen with Aithne in the mix?

Oh, he wasn't worried she was the wrong woman for him. Every beat of his heart proclaimed that she was his soulmate...his twin-flame. What concerned him was he didn't know what would happen once they entered the renewing fire. Would she make it through? Would she become a Phoenix, too? Could they have children of their own? Where would they live? Here in the city or out in the human world?

He sighed again. So many questions without answers. He knew Aithne trusted him wholeheartedly, and the fact he couldn't tell her what would happen was part of what weighed on him so heavily. She was about to change her life for him, and he couldn't tell her what her new life would be.

Closing his eyes, he smiled as he thought of her delight in seeing his home. Her reaction was all he'd hoped for. Her wide eyes and multitude of questions had made him re-look at his own world. Seeing it through her eyes was very enjoyable.

Milcham frowned as he thought of the crude hut he now lay in. She deserved so much more. He wanted her to have everything. Silks and lace and the most beautiful home he could give her. As his mate, she would want for nothing.

He heard a sudden sound and opened his eyes. All the breath in his lungs promptly disappeared.

Aithne stood shyly before him. Her long black hair curled down over her shoulders and breasts, and her emerald eyes shone with love for him. His mouth dried up completely when he saw what she was wearing.

She had on the negligee Dawn had given her. The same green of her eyes, it was so sexy his body forgot about being tired. His cock rose to immediate attention.

It had a halter top with thin straps that led down to lacy sheer triangles that cupped her breasts lovingly. A tiny lace bow nestled at the bottom of her cleavage. The silk skirt draped smoothly over her hips, flowing like a green waterfall to pool at her small feet. The fabric parted into a slit that reached all the way up to the top of her thigh, where the lace of an even sexier thong peeked out.

She circled slowly, showing him that the back draped low down around her hips so the sides allowed tantalizing glimpses of the curves of her breasts.

"I thought I'd model your gift for you," she said softly.

Milcham tried to clear his throat, but it was too dry. "Ummm...thank you?"

She laughed lightly and walking over to him, sank down next to his naked body. "Glad I packed that one suitcase?"

Milcham suddenly realized this was why Aithne insisted on carrying the small bag with her. At the time he'd been annoyed, but now...looking at the bounty before him, he knew the extra weight was worth every extra flap of his tired wings.

"You are the most beautiful woman in the world," he said with utter sincerity. "You take my breath away."

Aithne blushed. "I wanted to be pretty for you."

He chuckled. "You've succeeded."

Bending, she brushed her lips over his. "I'm glad."

He teased her lips with his tongue as he returned the kiss. "I was happy in this place before, but now...now I can't even describe how I feel with you here."

"I have waited my whole life for this."

"I waited my whole life...for you."

Aithne smiled. "I love you."

He grinned. "I figured you did when I saw the gown."

She giggled. "I have more than the negligee to give you."

Milcham raised a blond eyebrow. He traced a finger down her cleavage, enjoying the silky smoothness of her body. "Really? I'm very happy with this gift."

Shivering at his touch, she smiled, unconsciously seductive. His groin heated in response. "I think," she whispered as she bent over his prone body, "that you'll like this as well."

He shuddered as her lips touched the curve of his ear. "Aithne..."

"Shhh." She nipped gently at his earlobe. "You are tired and need your rest. Allow me to do this for you, my love. I want to."

Milcham sighed as she moved over the top of him. Her silken gown slid over his heated body sensuously as she straddled his thighs. Her lips moved down his throat, nibbling lightly on his collarbone before moving back up his neck to his chin. She swirled her tongue over the roughness of his beard and then captured his hard lips with her own.

The taste of him always made Aithne sure he was the one thing that could truly satisfy her. Dark and still smoky, his mouth teased her back with his forceful tongue and demanding kisses. For so long, she'd allowed him his way, but tonight...this last night she might ever have as a human, she would show him exactly how much in love with him she was.

Tearing her mouth away before she was caught up in his special fire, she bent and traced her way back down his neck and shoulders to the hard plane of his chest. Lovingly, she kissed each muscle knowing they were tired not only from building the hut and nest, but from the long flight as well.

His breath caught when her mouth hovered over his flat nipple. She breathed on it lightly and heard him groan as it hardened into a dark brown bead. Flicking out her tongue, she licked it, rewarded by a quick jerk of his body and another, even louder groan.

Smiling, she nuzzled the dark male nipple, teasing it with gentle nibbles and swipes of her tongue. Soon, his hands came up and grabbed her hair as he tried to move her to the other side. She allowed it, giving his other nipple the same arousing treatment. His cries filled the small building and his enjoyment aroused her as well. The lacy crotch of her panties was very wet.

When she decided she wanted to move on, she reached up and untangled his fingers. When he protested, she shushed him. "Just wait."

Holding his hands next to him, Aithne kissed her way down the center of his powerful body to the flat of his stomach and its shallow indentation. She swirled and sucked at it, making him move restlessly beneath her as his breath became shorter. She nibbled back and forth over his stomach to his sides, loving his shudders and low masculine murmurs. His erect cock bumped against her chin, and her mouth watered with the urge to take him between her lips.

Milcham's body was so tense he felt as if he might break in two if she touched him anymore. He wanted to roll her beneath him and drive himself deep into her welcoming body, his need was so great. A part of him prayed he would be able to keep the form of a man after the renewing tomorrow. The thought of being unable to make love to Aithne in this way was unbearable.

When she buried her face in his groin, he began to sweat. "Please, *assai*..." he growled. "I want you."

"There's plenty of time for that," she whispered. He hissed lightly as she kissed up the side of his jerking cock and down the other, being careful not to touch the sensitive head. "Until then, I want to make you burn."

His eyes glowed. "I am burning. Right. Now."

"Not enough." Her lips slid away from his throbbing erection and down his thigh. She bit the back of his knee, and he swore when she laughed throatily at his reaction. "Hotter," she murmured. "I want you ready to explode."

His mouth dropped open. She wanted him hotter? Any more and he would die. "I am already there," he gritted out, squeezing her hands tightly. "Feel me? I'm ready to burst as it is."

She smiled at his words and licked her way back up to his groin. "*I'm* not ready yet. I want this to be perfect."

He laid his head back on the moss. "It is perfect. *You* are perfect!" He tried to free his hands when her mouth moved its way back up his erection and hovered over its weeping tip. "Damn it, Aithne. Suck me! I need you to put it in your mouth. Please."

Her heart swelled at his words. He was always so self-possessed; he rarely showed her his true need for her. Unless he was in the middle of a climax, he was usually in perfect control. But this time, she'd put him over the edge and she loved it.

Their eyes met as she carefully licked at the broad head of his penis. It was covered in seminal fluid and dark red with frustrated need. At the first touch of her mouth, they both moaned. He tasted darker here. More smoky. Like warm molasses. His hips jerked up when her mouth enveloped him, and he tried to drive himself deep in her mouth.

"I...love...you," he panted, his eyes glowing a hot amber. "God, how I love you."

Her eyes misted, and she blinked rapidly, but never stopped the slow moves of her mouth up and down his cock.

Every touch. Every flick of her tongue was intended to drive him to the brink of ecstasy.

When his grip on her hands became almost painful, Aithne judged she had pushed him far enough. She gave his penis one last loving suck then allowed him to slip from her mouth.

His eyes, which had closed with pleasure, now popped open. "No...*assai*...please."

She smiled and licked her lips to get the last of his juices from them. His gaze followed her tongue hungrily. "Don't worry, my love. I'm not done yet."

Never taking her eyes from him, she stood and then slowly shimmied out of the miniscule panties she was wearing. Then she pulled apart the folds of her gown and sank back down on top of his body.

Milcham stilled as her heated mound came in contact with his throbbing erection. She leaned forward, putting her hands on either side of his head. His mouth watered when one of her lace-covered breasts brushed his mouth. Moving quickly, he trapped it between his lips and sucked...hard.

Aithne sighed above him, arching closer as he pleasured her with his mouth. Her warm folds rubbed up and down his engorged cock and her juices mingled with his own. His balls tightened and burned just at the thought of how he would feel deep inside of her. He switched sides and took the other breast into his mouth, treating it to the same delight as the first one.

His hands went to her hips, and he began pushing the gown aside to get to her warm flesh. Little by little, until all that was covered were the breasts he was teasing. He removed his mouth and blew on each tip, watching as the pink berries hardened and begged for more.

With a sharp tug, he pulled the beautiful negligee over her head and tossed it aside. The sudden movement pushed the head of his penis right to the entrance of her heated quim. Their eyes met again as he throbbed there, the warmth of her channel beckoning to him. She smiled and took his hands again, threading their fingers together and holding them next to his head. Then…ever so slowly…she eased her way down his turgid length.

She was so hot, so ready, it was like sliding into warm, sweet honey. Her quim pulled at him, teasing him even hotter as he groaned out loud. She moved inch by inch, so slowly he wanted to grab her by the hips and pull her down onto him, but his arms were made too heavy from the exquisite sensation of being inside of her.

At last, she took him all the way, and they panted together, both luxuriating in the feel of each other's body. Then, just as slowly, she began to move.

She lifted herself up off of him, almost to the tip of his throbbing length. Then…she eased herself back down again. She did it again and then again, until Milcham was wild with need for her. His cock ached to drive itself deep inside of her, and when she lifted up off of him a fourth time, he couldn't take any more.

Jerking his hands free, he grasped her by the hips and thrust himself up into her, grinding his hips against her wet mound until she cried out his name. His eyes went to solid gold as he slammed her up and down on top of his burning cock. When she screamed and her quim clenched down on him like a silken vise, he shouted out his desire as well and exploded deep within her.

Their climaxes seemed unending as the tremors moved like heated lightning through their bodies. Lights and music and colors danced behind their eyes until Aithne collapsed on his chest, her body still shivering from the strength of her orgasm.

Shakily, he put his arms around her and kissed her sweat-dampened hair. "That," he growled, "was worth every cent you paid for that gown."

She giggled against him. "Just when I didn't think it could get any better."

Grinning, he rolled them so she now lay beneath him. "Each time is amazing, *assai*—we both know that."

She stroked her finger over his hard chest, idly tracing his tattoo. "It may be the last night we have together as humans."

He frowned. "And does that worry you?"

Immediately she shook her head. "No, not really. I've tried to tell you it doesn't matter where we are as long as we are together. And I guess it doesn't matter *what* we are. But I'd be lying if I didn't say I'd miss making love to you."

Milcham kissed her gently. "I know. I will miss this too, but if we do both become Phoenix, then we can still join together. That will never change."

She nodded and peeked up at him from under her lashes. "Does it make me a bad person to pray we can keep these forms?"

He laughed. "No. I have asked for the same thing. I hope we can both change from Phoenix to human as we choose. I also hope we can live in the human world and come back to my...our city when we want to." He grinned and his eyes turned smoky again. "Perhaps...when the children come."

Aithne blinked back tears. "You too hope for children? Really? We never really spoke about it."

He nuzzled her neck. "A girl with your eyes? A boy with your smile? How could I not want this?"

She wrinkled her nose. "I want a boy that looks just like you, and a girl who has amber eyes."

Milcham's heart pounded at the thought. "Perhaps...if we are blessed...Yahweh will give them all to us." He moved within her, his body stirring as he spoke. "And we can practice making them tonight."

Laughing, she wrapped her arms around him. "Yes. More practice, please."

Suddenly, Milcham caught sight of something that hadn't been there before. "Look, *assai*," he said, smiling. "The Lord has brought us some wine to celebrate our homecoming."

She twisted around in his arms, as he pointed to a decanter of ruby red wine and two tall goblets. "How wonderful."

Milcham pulled away slightly and poured two glasses. Then, he handed one to her, tapping his glass against hers gently. "To the beginning of our life together," he murmured. "And to our love."

Aithne smiled. "May it stand strong and last forever." They sipped the wine, never taking their eyes off each other.

"Now...where were we?" Milcham growled as he took the glasses and put them with the decanter. He pulled her back into his arms.

"About here," she answered throatily as their lips met again.

And somewhere...evil smiled.

Chapter Twenty

Milcham came suddenly awake with the knowledge something was wrong. He sat straight up and glanced around the hut. He saw nothing, and Aithne lay sleeping soundly next to him, but he still couldn't shake the sensation. Easing out from under her limp arm, he stood and walked naked to the door of the hut. As soon as he stepped outside, he knew why he'd been awoken.

To the east, a pale light could be seen. It painted the night sky with misty fingers of light and Milcham's eyes widened in horror.

It was the rising of the sun.

What had happened? Normally, his internal clock awoke him well before the event. He still had time, but this was cutting it close.

Whirling around, he staggered to where Aithne still slept. He bent and kissed her, but she didn't stir. Smiling, he kissed her again. They had made love twice, both falling asleep almost before they finished the second time. His poor lady was worn out.

When she still didn't move, he shook her gently. "Aithne...wake up. It is time."

Her eyes didn't even flutter. Frowning, he shook her again, but still nothing. His heart pounded in sudden worry. Lifting her, he tried harder. "*Assai*...it is time to get up. We must get to the nest."

Her head lolled to the side, but she didn't move at all. No blinking of the eyes or stretching in his arms that would signal she was there and ready to face the day. No sweet smile to make him feel as if it was him and him alone she awoke for.

A sickness started in his gut as he checked her breathing, relieved when he felt it, but why wouldn't she wake up?

A twitter from the door made him turn around. A small bird stood there, black eyes blinking worriedly as it danced from foot to foot. He nodded. "I know I'm late, but there's something wrong with her."

Realizing he couldn't take any more time to find out, he bent and lifted Aithne into his arms, groaning at the effort. Even her small nude frame was difficult for him this morning, with his strength nearly used up. Turning, he staggered groggily out the door towards the nest he had built the day before.

Sweat rolled down his face as he moved slowly across the meadow intent on the tall tree which held the sacred nest. It took all the power he had just to put one foot in front of the other. It was as if he were slogging through quicksand, his feet stuck deep into the clinging mud.

But his eyes glowed with conviction. He would make it to his nest, and Aithne and he would be reborn together. There could be no other ending. Not after all they had been through.

His heart was hammering like a jackhammer and his body was drenched in sweat when he finally reached the base of the tree. The nest was about ten feet off the ground, but a ramp was built up to it. Even before, he'd had trouble climbing in due to age and frailty at the time of his rebirth. He was grateful for his forethought now.

He staggered up the ramp just as the first finger of dawn touched the sky. Milcham shouted aloud in defiance. He had made it.

But his joy turned to ashes when he reached the side of the nest. A blue flame shot up to the clouds and barred his way. When he tried to go through, it pushed him back.

"What is happening?" he shouted to the heavens. "Why can't I get in?"

There was a sharp crack of thunder and the smell of sulfur filled the glade. An evil laugh made the hair on the back of his neck stand up. Turning swiftly, he froze when he saw the form of the Ancient One standing at the bottom of the ramp.

"Foolish Phoenix," Satan drawled. "You can't get in because you are breaking the rules."

Milcham shook his head in frustration. "What are you talking about? What rules? I have kept them all."

The Devil cackled with laughter. "Don't you remember? It was one of the very first commands you were given." He pointed to the limp woman in Milcham's arms. "She must choose to leap into the fire with you. You can't force her."

Milcham swore. "I am not forcing her. Aithne wants to do this. She came here with me, didn't she? But something is wrong. I can't wake her up."

The Ancient One examined his long nails. "Well...I suppose that's what comes from overindulgence in wine. In fact—" he peered at Milcham, "—I'm surprised to see you up and about at all."

Realization dawned. "It was you," he breathed. "You gave us the wine." His gut twisted with anger and disbelief. "You poisoned it!"

"Oh no, dear boy," Satan corrected him. "Not poison. It's not allowed. I can't hurt you...remember? It was just a sleeping potion." His face twisted into a mask of anger. "I'd hoped you'd both sleep through the sunrise."

"This isn't right," snarled Milcham. "You have taken away her choice. It's not fair."

The dark one smiled. "There was nothing in the rules about hurting her, Phoenix. Although, she *was* difficult. She has a strong heart and she is loyal."

"Then wake her. Give her the chance to make the choice."

"Why would I want to do that?" his enemy questioned. "I've just spent the last eight centuries trying to destroy you. Losing your mate again will be a delicious irony, won't it?"

Milcham's eyes burned with tears of anger. "It *was* you, wasn't it? A century ago? You took her away from me."

Satan shrugged. "I tried to kill her, but her brother's love was stronger than my hate. Instead, I had to settle for distracting you from her for a while." He sighed. "I lost track of her, thinking she was safely out of the way. Then to my surprise, she showed up at your carnival...human again." He gave a wry glance up to heaven. "I think she had a little help, there." Then his eyes flashed. "I didn't know who she was at first, even used a vision spell to enhance your desire for her, thinking she would be a distraction. Imagine my shock when I realized she was the woman I tried to destroy a hundred years ago."

"You must release her," Milcham shouted. "Time is slipping away. It isn't fair of you to do this. It wasn't what Yahweh intended."

"I guess we'll never know, will we?" The Ancient One smiled. "At last, I have you right where I want you. I have waited eons for this moment."

Frustrated beyond belief, Milcham turned and tried to leap through the blue wall of flame. There was a long hiss of power, and the wall exploded, knocking him and his precious bundle to the ground.

There was a loud laugh and when he looked up, Satan stood above them. Leaving Aithne lying on the ground, Milcham shot to his feet and faced his enemy. "Let her go!" he shouted again.

The Devil laughed again. "No. You have a choice, Phoenix. Go into the fire alone. Save yourself and become immortal again so you can live for another thousand years mired in loneliness. You would always know you made your decision and left the woman you say you love...behind."

Milcham stared at the dark one. Then his gaze moved to Aithne, lying still on the ground. His heart shredded with agony. He loved her. The thought of being without her ripped at his soul. He closed his eyes in anguish, remembering the last time he'd walked away from his mate. As bad as that had been, there was no describing the misery he was going through now. Aithne was his whole world. How could he go on without her?

"Or," came the Devil's insidious voice, "you can choose not to walk into the flame."

Milcham opened his eyes, flinching at his enemy's tone. He stared into the smug, evil face and felt his soul shrink. "What are you talking about?"

The Ancient One bared his teeth. "Don't you know?" He laughed in genuine amusement. "Are you sure I can't tempt you? One last time?"

"That's what this whole thing has been about, hasn't it?" Milcham exploded. "I wouldn't give in to you in the garden and so you want to destroy me. You've been trying for the last thousand years, starting with this challenge."

"You sound so surprised." Satan shook his head. "And this is about much more than you, Phoenix. This is about proving to your God that everyone has a price. No one is beyond temptation. Not even his favorite, the most loyal of all his creations...The Phoenix."

He stepped up closer. "You are running out of time, you know. Stay with your mate. Stay mortal. I'll even make you young and strong again so you'll have that lifetime together. Only choose what you wouldn't choose in Eden." His smile was pure evil as he continued.

"Choose to die."

Icy pain shot through Milcham. It would come to this. He had to pick between his immortality and his life with Aithne. Everlasting and eternal life alone, or the short span of a normal human male's years with the woman he loved. Without the fire, he would be caught in this human body forever, unable to shift into the beautiful form of the Phoenix. He would be grounded, never again able to soar through the skies or feel the warmth of the sun on his face. Stripped of his gifts, of what made him who he was...he would be a mere man. Another one of those who had been tempted by the Ancient One...and fallen.

He stared down at Aithne's still face and then back up at the evil creature who stood before him. There was no way to win this challenge. Not with Satan calling the shots. It was just like before, although this time evil wasn't offering him the fruit, he was offering him... Milcham narrowed his eyes. Just what *was* he being offered? He thought for a long moment, and then it hit him.

He was being offered nothing evil, he realized. In fact, it was just the opposite. He was being offered...love.

Warmth unfurled within him, chasing away the icy pain of failure. His eyes glowed in sudden comprehension. He was wrong. It wasn't the same. Before, he'd turned away from his mate because he refused to do evil. But loving Aithne wasn't evil. It was just the opposite. It was right and good. Even if it cost him everlasting life, he would still be obeying his Lord. He'd been told to go forth and find his mate and he'd done so.

He'd tried to bring her back and step into the fire with her, but he'd been prevented from doing that. But it didn't change the fact he'd found his soulmate. Even if it cost him his life, he wouldn't turn away from her.

She was his everything.

He glared up at the Devil who smirked down at him. "You have finally succeeded in tempting me. I will stay with her, Satan, because I love her."

The Ancient One's dark eyes smoldered with glee. "You would deny your God. Curse him now for not protecting you."

Milcham shook his head. "I will not curse him. *Never*! You may steal away my immortality and take away my home in the walled city, but I will not reject Yahweh." He bent and gathered the unconscious Aithne in his arms. "I have no reason to do so."

He brushed back an ebony strand of hair. “He has given me my mate. All I have ever desired, I hold now in my arms.”

Satan gave a snarl that shook the trees. “You think she will love you now? You will be nothing! The man she loves will disappear with the rising of the sun.”

Milcham glanced over his shoulder at the rapidly approaching dawn. His heart twinged once with the knowledge of his loss, but then he looked back down at Aithne’s face. “What she and I have, a creature like you will never understand.” He jerked his head up and his amber eyes stared at the Ancient One. “I have made my choice. I will stay with her.”

There was a sudden clap of thunder and the wind blew fiercely. In his arms, Aithne stirred and yawned. When she saw him, she smiled. “Is it morning?”

His throat was tight when he bent and kissed her. “It is, *assai*.”

Aithne sat up and looked around her. “What’s happened? Is it time? Is that why we’re here?”

He crushed her against him. “I have something to tell you.”

She held him to her. “What’s wrong?”

The Devil’s evil laugh broke them apart, and Aithne gasped when she looked up and saw him staring down at her. She struggled to her feet, and with Milcham’s help, stood swaying back and forth as she fought against the dizziness that threatened her.

The Ancient One laughed again. “I have allowed her to awaken. Tell her, Phoenix. Tell her what you’ve done.”

Gritting his teeth, Milcham turned Aithne to face him. “Last night the wine we thought was sent by the Lord was in fact sent by this creature...the Devil.”

Her eyes widened. “Satan?”

He nodded. “Yes. And in that wine was a sleeping herb. It caused us both to oversleep. I finally awoke, perhaps because my immortal body refused the brew, but the sleeping potion put you into an unnatural sleep, and try as I might, I couldn't awaken you." He touched her face. "I tried to carry you into the flame, but it wouldn't accept you."

"But I wanted to go with you," Aithne cried in pain and frustration as she realized what he was saying. Fury filled her mind and soul. It wasn't fair. "I wanted to."

"I know you did. But remember...I promised Yahweh you would make the choice on your own. You had to know the risks, and if you were unconscious, I couldn't prove you had chosen this path with no reservations."

Tears welled up in her eyes, and she turned angrily and faced the enemy who had destroyed her family and now taken her love from her. "This is your fault. You knew I wanted to go with him."

"Fair or not, he made his choice without you."

Aithne's hand itched to slap the satisfied look off his ugly face. Milcham, as if sensing her anger, pulled her back to him. "It is all right, *assai*. We will be together."

She wiped her face. "I know...I know. But it isn't right. I will grow old, and you will live forever. I will take whatever time we have together, but it still isn't fair."

Satan cackled loudly behind them. "But that's just it, my dear. He won't live forever. He isn't the Phoenix anymore. He is only an ordinary man who soon I will gift with strength and youth. He chose to become mortal so he could stay with you. The man you think you love is no more."

Her mouth dropped open, and she swung back around to Milcham. "Tell me he lies! Tell me you didn't do this."

Milcham swallowed and shook his head. "I can't. I would rather be human with you than immortal without you." He cradled her wet face in his hands. "I love you."

Aithne stared at him, her mind numbed with shock. He'd given up his immortality for her? Some small part of her was awed he cared so much he would sacrifice himself, but the rest of her was appalled. She couldn't...wouldn't be the cause of this.

"You can't," she choked out. "Milcham, you must get in the fire. You are the last of your kind. You can't die."

"He can't." Satan rocked back and forth in satisfied delight. "He has made his choice. He won't break his word, you know that."

She ignored him and put her hands on his broad chest. "Please, Milcham. I love you. I want us to be together, but not like this."

"He is right, *assai*," her lover said quietly. "I have made my choice. I will be fully human when the last finger of dawn touches the sky."

Aithne looked over his shoulder, noting the slow lighting of the eastern horizon. She wouldn't accept it. He was the most important thing in her life, and while he might be happy as her husband, he would never be fully whole again without the Phoenix part of him. His very soul would wither away and die. And she was pretty sure the Devil knew exactly that. She looked back at the dark form behind her.

"You know what will happen to him, don't you?" she queried softly. When his eyes glowed with unearthly delight, she flinched. She was right, and she loved Milcham too much to allow that to happen to him. Even though she wouldn't be allowed to be with him in this beautiful place, she knew what she had to do. Turning back, she caressed his strong jaw with a trembling hand.

"I love you," she whispered.

"And I love you. We will have a good life, I promise you."

She sighed and took a step backwards. "You made the choice not to go into the fire, so you can't change your mind, right?"

"Yes."

"Fine." She leaned up and kissed him. "Remember how much I love you."

"I don't understand," he growled. "What are you doing?"

Aithne took a deep breath. "Changing your mind for you." With all the superhuman strength she had left, she pushed him, hard, right into the wall of blue flame. Caught unawares, he tumbled through it with no resistance at all, his naked body landing in the nest of spices.

She heard an unholy shriek behind her and before she could think a step farther, Satan grabbed her by the arm.

"No!" he screamed. "This cannot be. You foolish girl. What have you done?"

The wind whipped around her, but she felt no fear. Aithne gazed at her lover who was clambering upright. "I made sure the man I love will live forever."

In the nest, Milcham jumped to his feet. He looked shocked beyond belief at her actions. Aithne knew he had made his choice to stay with her because he loved her, and by pushing him through the fire, she hadn't respected that. She watched as he tried to climb out of the nest and came up hard against the wall of blue. Their eyes met, his a furious gold as he pounded his fists against the azure barrier.

Aithne gave a sob of relief. He couldn't get out. She could see him beating his hands against the transparent wall but to no avail. He wasn't able to leave the nest, which meant she'd saved him. There would be a Phoenix living here in the walled city for the next thousand years.

"Do you know the trouble you have caused me?" Satan spat at her. "I have planned this so very carefully. Every step of the way. I had contingency plan after contingency plan mapped out. Women, liquor, every temptation known to man I threw at him. And while he may have staggered a bit, he never fell. He was never tempted beyond redemption." He shook her hard. "But this time, he chose you over his God. This time I had him."

"You're wrong," Aithne said joyfully, tears streaming down her cheeks. "You'd already failed. You may have tempted the Phoenix, but his choice was the right one. You forgot perfect love casts out all fear and hatred. He would have stayed for me because he loved me. But I loved him so much I chose to let him go. One love spring-boarding off of another. The sign of two soulmates...of true twin-flames is they would give up their lives for each other."

The Ancient One screamed his fury to the skies, knowing she was right. He had failed because he had forgotten the strongest and most important emotion in the universe.

Love.

"I may have failed with the Phoenix," he snarled, dragging her close to the flames that separated the lovers, "but I won't fail with you. Not again." He grabbed her by the hair. "You two will never again know each other's touch. You may have saved him, but you have condemned yourself."

Quickly, he pulled back her head, and before the horrified eyes of the man on the other side of the flame, he sliced Aithne's throat open with his sharp claws.

Chapter Twenty-One

Her eyes flickered in shock and pain as she choked and grabbed at her throat. Scarlet liquid pooled between her fingers, and she dropped to her knees.

Satan laughed insanely. "I have killed you for taking away the one I truly wanted dead. But even now, I've won. He will have to watch as your life blood drains away and awareness leaves your eyes. A better ending I could not have written myself."

Aithne could hear her enemy's words coming as if from a great distance away. Her eyes were fixed on Milcham. His mouth was moving, but the wall prevented her from hearing him. She tried to smile at him. Even though she hadn't wanted to die, the knowledge she'd saved him soothed her soul.

"I...love...you..." she tried to say as she collapsed into a heap on the ground. Her eyes flickered shut.

"No!" Milcham shouted as blood continued to pour from the gaping wound in his beloved's neck. He beat on the walls of his prison. *"Aithne!"* His face was wet with tears as he knelt down, laying his face against the wall of fire. "Please, *assai,*" he murmured. "You can't die. Not like this. We still have a lifetime planned together."

There was no movement from the bloodied figure on the ramp. She was as still as death. He cried harder, knowing his reason to greet the sun was dying just out of his reach.

"Please, Yahweh," he wept aloud. "Help us. I am your loyal servant. I have not mocked you or cursed your name. She doesn't deserve to die. Help her. Please, my Lord. Help her."

Far away, Aithne floated, caught between the choice of life or death. Her body had not yet given up entirely, but she knew it was only a matter of time, so she waited, praying that somehow, in the middle of all this, Milcham would be all right.

"Go to him, child."

The deep voice brought her out of her lethargy and she frowned.

"Go to him. He loves you. Go to him, now...before it is too late."

Her eyes opened blearily. She could see Milcham, his face pressed against the wall of flame. She tried to move, but her tired body rebelled.

"One inch at a time, my daughter. Go to him and all will be well."

Taking as deep a breath as she could through her ruined and bleeding throat, she obeyed.

Milcham's fists were bloody when he finally stopped slamming his fists against the wall. Anger and pain filled his soul. "I love you, *assai*," he whispered as he touched the palm of his hand to the flame. "Forever." He felt the sun finally touch his back and he shuddered. Though he wanted to die without her, he would not toss Aithne's gift back in her face. For her...he would live.

Just as he was turning to greet the sun, he caught a movement out of the corner of his eye. Jerking his head around, he watched in amazement as Aithne dragged her bleeding body nearer to the pillar of protective flame.

"That's it!" he shouted excitedly as he beat on the wall again. "Just a little bit farther. All I need is your hand. If I can bring you inside, I can heal you!"

His whole body strained along with hers as she inched her way closer and closer. When her hand touched the side of the nest, he gave a glad shout of joy. Her fingertips shakily touched the blue flame and her eyes once again met his.

"Come on, *assai*," he urged her. "Almost there!"

A moment later, a scream filled the air. Milcham jerked his head up to see Satan racing towards them. If Aithne didn't hurry, it would be too late. He bent and put his face level with hers. "I love you," he mouthed. "Come to me."

Her green eyes filled with more tears and with her one last bit of strength, she plunged her hand through the flame and into his. Grasping her with all his remaining strength, he pulled her to him.

Suddenly, her forward movement stopped and looking up, Milcham saw the Ancient One holding onto Aithne's ankles. "I will not let you have her," he hissed. "She belongs to me."

"*Never*!" Milcham shouted. "In Yahweh's name, she will be mine."

A tug-of-war ensued over the now unconscious woman, Milcham refusing to let her go. He'd rather miss the dawn than release her now.

Then, with a sound like a thousand angels singing, there was a loud roar. Satan screamed as his body was hurled across the meadow to land solidly against the side of a large tree. Aithne, freed from his grasp, shot through the wall of fire to go tumbling into Milcham's arms. Without a pause, he bent over her ruined neck, weeping his magical tears to knit her flesh and bring her back to him.

As he smoothed the wetness over her flesh, he heard another scream. There was a clap of thunder, and glancing up, he saw Satan bow low to the ground. The wind whipped and the thunder crashed, and then suddenly, the Ancient One was no more.

A noise brought him back to the woman in his arms. Aithne's eyes flickered open and she coughed. Her hand went to her throat, and she swallowed, hard. "I...I was dead."

Clasping her to him, he wept again, this time tears of joy. "Not quite, *assai*. You had enough strength to push through the barrier."

"It was the voice." She sat up slowly. "It told me to come to you."

Milcham's heart expanded. "The Lord heard our prayers. The evil one is defeated."

"Where...are we?"

"In my nest." Carefully, he helped her to her feet and held her as she swayed tiredly. "The dawn is here."

Aithne's eyes widened. "We...we didn't miss it?"

"No." He bent and bussed her lips as he thought of how uncommonly slow the dawn was. Yahweh had been with him all along. "Do you still wish to try the fire, *assai*? It is not too late to change your mind."

She buried her head in his chest. "I haven't gone through everything to stop now. I crawled into this nest knowing full well what might happen here. I'm willing to risk it to be with you forever."

His chest tightened. "Whatever happens, Aithne, know you are the most important person in my world. I love you more than I could ever imagine loving anyone."

"I love you, too." She bit him gently on the chin, smiling as his tired eyes glowed. "Tell me what to do now."

He shook his head and his hair took on a brighter hue. "You have done enough, my adored one. Now...it is up to me."

Turning her so she looked at him as he faced the now rising sun, he bent and kissed her one more time. Then, he lifted his arms to the sun in welcome and began to sing. His beautiful voice, roughened only slightly by age, poured forth, and all the heavens held their breath to listen.

He sang of love and hope, of perseverance and faith. He sang and sang, the splendor of the song soaring to the skies. The tattoo of the phoenix on his chest glowed with an unearthly light. It glowed brighter and brighter with every note he sang, until it almost hurt to look at him. His human body shifted away and before her tear-filled eyes, he became the Phoenix. Aged and shaky with weariness, he kept his gaze on her as he continued singing.

She gasped as the heat build around them, even though she was protected by his cocoon of fire. The inferno around them was drawing insidiously closer, and she wrapped her arms around his flaming form, holding him even tighter.

Milcham could tell she was afraid. Even though she tried to be brave, the horror of the flames showed in her eyes. He prayed she would be strong and not let it overwhelm her. He sang louder, hoping she would draw strength from the beauty of his song.

As the fire flicked at them, he continued to sing, but instead of holding his arms up to the sun as usual, he wrapped them around Aithne, not to hold her but to protect her. She was his gift, his joy and his love. As he sang his last notes of hope and adoration, her face was the last thing he saw before they were both enveloped in the scarlet-gold of the refiner's fire.

After a long, long while, the flames died down. The tree and the nest of spices were undamaged. But as for the Phoenix and Aithne...there was no sign. All that was left of them were two piles of ash. One silver and the other gold.

Then, the golden ash moved. It trembled and slowly began to heave upwards. From under the ash, there rose up a young Phoenix. Featherless and bald, it was small and scrawny, but it stretched out its naked neck and searched the nest for its companion. It refused to give up, calling in its tiny voice until it was hoarse. When it could barely make any sound at all, it bowed its stubbled head in defeat and again lifted its miniature plucked wings to the sun.

In a voice that could barely be heard, it sang. This time it sang sadly of love lost and memories that would never be forgotten. As it sang, it grew, growing stronger and stronger with every melancholy note. Beautiful feathers of gold and red, purple and yellow, sprouted and covered his nakedness. Eyes that were blind opened to reveal orbs of glowing gold. The Phoenix had risen from the ashes and been reborn.

But he was, once more...alone.

There were no songs of joy this time. Milcham knelt in the nest, huge tears rolling down his beak. He'd loved and lost. He'd gambled her love was stronger than her fear, but it wasn't. He didn't care anymore if she was his soulmate or not. She was dead, he would never see her again, and he was dying inside.

Yahweh appeared, and without a word, the Phoenix bowed before him. "You have a question, my Phoenix?"

Milcham nodded. "Is she really dead, Lord?"

The Lord nodded. "She is."

His throat tightened with grief and loss. "I...I can't believe this is happening. She almost died for me. I thought she was the one."

Yahweh smiled. "Did you not offer to die for her as well?"

Milcham's heart ached. "Yes...and I would again, if it would mean bringing her back to me. Soulmate or not, I am in love with her."

"Then what are you waiting for?"

Milcham froze and stared up at his Lord. "What do you mean?"

"Do you not remember the scripture, Phoenix?" Yahweh prompted. "'And now abideth faith, hope and love, and of these three, the greatest of them is...'"

"'Love'," Milcham supplied. "This I know. I love her. With all my soul."

"I know. You had the faith to search for her. And when you did, you hoped she would love you enough to step into the fire."

"But—"

"And when it came down to it, you loved her enough to give up everything to be with her."

"I would do it again if we could be together."

The Lord chuckled. "Oh ye of little faith. My beloved Phoenix, do you really think I would allow you to go through eight centuries of searching only to lose her at the end?"

Milcham's heart stopped. "Lord?"

"I am the Alpha and the Omega. The beginning and the end. I knew what the Ancient One would do even before he came to convince me to allow your temptation. As I knew what you would do."

"You...knew?"

Yahweh's warm hand touched his feathered cheek. "I knew. And I suffered with you when you made mistakes. But I also knew you would succeed in the end, so I allowed those mistakes to help you grow."

"But I didn't succeed," Milcham cried. "I failed. I failed and now she's dead."

"Yes, she is dead. Just as you were."

Milcham's head snapped up. "What?"

"Do not lose your faith and hope now, my Phoenix. Sift through the ash and find your love. Or do you not remember that humans develop much more slowly than a Phoenix does?"

His heart pounding in renewed hope, Milcham turned quickly and bent to the bottom of the nest. His ashes were knocked about, but the pile of ash that had been Aithne sat in a neat pile. As he watched, the ash at the center of the silver pile twitched. He blinked, wondering if his need for her was conjuring up visions, but as he reached down to touch the pile, it moved again. He pulled back and stared; more tears streaming down his face as the ash fell away.

Waving in circles was a tiny human fist.

Milcham cried out in joy and happiness. Using the tip of one wing, he carefully brushed away the silvery ash. First an arm, then her body, then with a sneeze and a loud hiccupping cry her head appeared. Soon the naked body of a human female infant was kicking and squalling in the bottom of the nest.

"Sing for her," Yahweh ordered as he faded from sight. "Sing her into being just as you do for yourself."

Wonderingly, Milcham bent and lifted the tiny infant in his wings. A human baby is much cuter than a baby bird, and he could already see Aithne in the child. Cradling his love in his feathery wings, he turned and again faced the sun. Closing his eyes, he let the knowledge she was alive and in his arms fill him. His soul expanded until all his love for her burst from inside. Opening his beak, this time he sang of rebirth and life, of love found and Yahweh's truth. He sang of his future and of hers. Of eternity, together.

And as he sang, she grew. More rapidly now, she went from toddler, to adorable youth, to gawky teenager. His heart almost burst with joy as she joined in his song when she reached adulthood.

As she grew into the woman he'd fallen in love with, his song slowed, and he shifted back into the form of a man, barely acknowledging his ability to still do so. His hand cradled her cheek as he bent and kissed her for the first time. Her lips clung to his and her arms wrapped tightly around his waist.

"Mil...cham?"

"*Assai*," he murmured hoarsely. "My precious one."

"I'm...alive?"

"Very much so. You were reborn in the fire. Although, for a while there, I thought I'd lost you."

She opened her eyes and he took a deep breath. Her green eyes glowed with the light of immortality. "I...remember now. I was so frightened, but I love you, Milcham. I could never leave you." She traced the line of his lips with her finger. "No matter what was thrown at me. Not even a fire can keep us apart. I am a part of you, as you are a part of me. As long as we love each other, we will never see death."

"Then we will live forever," he said roughly. "For I will never stop loving you."

Aithne smiled. "And you will always have my love. You have brought me to the other side of eternity."

Suddenly, he gave a shout of sheer happiness. "We did it! Together we defeated the enemy!"

She laughed happily. "Nothing can defeat the power of true love."

He pulled her into his arms. "You are my mate, my twin-flame. Forever."

She threaded her fingers into his dirty blond hair. "My husband, my mate, my love. You are my world."

As their lips met in a fiery kiss, they heard a soft chuckle. *"It will be good to see children in the garden again."* Yahweh's voice echoed in their heads. *"Come and visit often, my beloved Phoenix. My sweet Aithne. Teach your offspring the lessons you have learned so they too can greet the sun with the purity of love's song."*

"We will, my Lord," Milcham promised hoarsely as he fit his hungry frame against his new mate's. "And we will never forget what you've done for us here."

"No," Aithne whispered as she ran her hand down his newly strong body. "These memories we will keep for a lifetime. And we will make sure our children know how to fight temptation and when to give in...to love."

Milcham smiled at her choice of words. "Shall we get started on those kids right now?"

She laughed and snuggled her naked body against his. "We can definitely practice."

Her mate rolled her beneath him. "And as we know, practice makes perfect."

Epilogue

A spray of water caught her directly in the mouth, and Aithne gasped aloud. Wiping her face, she glared into the wicked, laughing eyes of her mate.

"That," she muttered, her eyes twinkling, "was unnecessary."

Milcham chuckled. "Since when do we do only what is necessary?"

She leaned back on the flat rock that sat about a foot underwater in the special swimming pool. She lifted her foot out of the water and wiggled her toes at him. "Well..."

He swam closer and kissed the arch of her foot. "Was it *necessary* for you to dive-bomb the workers that were repairing the turrets, yesterday?" He kissed her calf. "Or was it *necessary* for you to make me chase you to over five thousand feet high this morning, just so we could *properly* join the Mile High Club?" He moved higher and kissed the top of her thigh.

She grinned at him. "I thought so," she answered regally. No way she was going to admit she'd only dive-bombed the worker on the wall because she'd lost control of her fancy new wings. And as for the whole sex in the sky thing? That was simple.

Why not?

Milcham eased himself up on the rock and crawled up over her prone body. "I must admit, I do enjoy seeing you in your new form."

Aithne smiled. After they had staggered from the nest where the fire had renewed and refreshed them, they had been excited to discover Aithne had been given the body of a Phoenix as well. Milcham had shown her how to discover her flame, and before his admiring eyes, she had shifted for the first time.

Whereas he was a creature of the sun, with colors of gold, scarlet and orange, Aithne's hues were the opposite of the spectrum. Blues, greens and shades of violet, with burning eyes that glowed like emeralds. Her song was softer, more muted, better suited to moonlit glades and forest treetops.

Together, they had leaped into the air so Aithne could try out her new wings. To her surprise, it wasn't as easy as it looked, and Milcham had to save her from spinning down to the earth several times before she got the hang of it. But afterwards, they spent the morning enjoying themselves. Two immortal Phoenix, their beautiful feathers flashing in the sunlight, gliding on the breezes over their new home.

When her muscles cramped from overuse, Milcham led them to his special bathing pool. Tucked away in a mountain glade, its water was warmed by minerals in the earth. Morphing back into their human forms, they slid into the large pond. One feel of the hot water on her tired body, Aithne swore she would never leave it again.

Now, she reached up and kissed her mate's bristly chin. "I am so glad Yahweh allowed us to have two forms. I love being able to fly."

He grinned down at her, sliding his warm, naked body alongside hers on the reclining rock. "And I am pleased as well. I love being able to make love with you. In either form."

She blushed and then gasped as his lips covered one partly submerged nipple. "Oh, Milcham. I never thought I could be so happy."

"It has been a long time coming."

"Yes...it has." Aithne thought of the past and all that had been done to them. "What about the Ancient One? Will we always have to worry about him?"

He heard the fear in her voice and pulled her into his arms. "No, *assai*. He has had his chance and he failed. He will not be allowed to attack us any further. The Lord will protect us for the rest of eternity." Milcham shook his head. "Satan overstepped at the end. When he drugged us, he broke his own rules. That's when the Lord stepped in."

Aithne turned to face him. "What I don't understand was the pillar of blue flame. How could it keep me out and you in?"

"Ahhh...the flame refused you entrance when you were unconscious because you had to be allowed to make the choice to walk into the fire on your own. You also needed to be able to choose to stay, once you were there. You could have left at any time. Allowing a person's free will is the cornerstone of all that Yahweh is."

"So why couldn't you get out?"

He held her tighter. "Simply put...it was because Yahweh knew I would immediately come back to you, and he didn't want your sacrifice to be in vain. You had given up a life with me, because you knew without my immortality, I would slowly perish. You loved me that much."

She pulled away from him. "You knew what Satan had intended?"

Milcham looked at her with steady eyes. "Yes."

Hers widened. "You knew if you weren't the Phoenix, you would waste away, and you still chose to stay with me?"

He brushed his lips over hers. "I am in love with you, Aithne. I could make no other choice."

Her eyes filled with tears. "And that is why I chose to stay in the fire. No matter how frightened I was. Life without you is no life at all."

"*Assai...*" His voice broke and he had to clear his throat. "Every day, I thank Yahweh that he has given me a woman like you. Loving, loyal, brave and true...I cannot even imagine my life without you in it."

She looped her arms up around his neck. "It is pretty amazing to know he knew me even before I was born. He picked me for you, didn't he?"

He nodded and pulled her beneath him, the warm water cushioning their bodies. "He chose you out of all the souls as the one who would love me and be loved by me. He knew you wouldn't say no."

"Say no to you?" she teased as she moved her body slowly against his. "I don't think so."

"An eternity is a very long time to keep saying yes, *assai.* I hope you are sure."

"Of you? Of us?" She laughed and slid a leg up his muscular thigh, opening herself to him. "I never did tell you. I did a tarot reading after you left me that first night back at the carnival. All we would be to each other was in the cards."

"It was, huh?" Milcham smiled as with a groan, he slid with into her welcoming heat. As a Phoenix, now she was even warmer. "And what," he said hoarsely, "did the cards say we were?"

Aithne pulled his head down to hers and nipped his lower lip as he throbbed with life within her. "They knew before we even touched each other. They knew we would be... Lovers."

"I always said you had a gift," he growled as he moved inside her.

And as their bodies joined together in the immortal dance of love, the heavens rejoiced and the angels sang. Two hearts, so long separated, now beat forever as one.

And it was very, very good.

About the Author

CJ England credits her passion for writing to her second-grade sweetheart, Steven, a blond-haired cutie with dimples, who dumped her for a girl who could swing on the monkey bars. She wrote her first story about love and loss after that tragic episode.

In her life she has modeled, competed in rodeos as a barrel racer and trick rider, taught preschool, performed as an actress and singer, served cocktails at Disney World, specialized in production work and got carried away by Spiderman when she worked with him at Universal Studios.

She is a gypsy, due to her curiosity and "itchy feet", spending time in twenty-three countries and visiting all fifty states in her own. Even raising three kids didn't slow her down. Married to her own personal hottie, Jonathon, who is her inspiration, lover and bestest friend, she plans to travel the world, writing about all the places they visit.

She is known on the internet as a bestselling, award-winning author who can bring sensuality and romance together in ways that require you to keep a fire extinguisher and a box of Kleenex handy. Described as "having innovative story lines", "a whiz at character development" and "quite simply a genius!", CJ wants her books to spark the imaginations of her readers. So then they will begin to believe anything can happen if you...

Follow Your Dreams.

For more information on CJ and her other work, visit her website at www.cjengland.com. And she loves to hear from her readers! Send an email to CJ at womanofthewind1@yahoo.com or join her Yahoo! group to join in the fun with other readers as well as CJ.

http://groups.yahoo.com/group/CJsaysFollowYourDreams/